PRAISE FOR *POWERLESS*

"Childs's and Deebs's first collaboration starts out with a BANG, literally. This action-packed novel…is patently just the beginning of Kenna and gang's journey, and teens will be chomping at the bit for the next installment."

—Ingram's Youth Librarian newsletter

"Romance buffs who like star-crossed lovers will find more than one satisfying pairing to swoon over amidst the good guy/bad guy entanglements, and they'll happily return to see what Kenna does next."

—*The Bulletin of the Center for Children's Books*

"No shortage of action."

—*School Library Journal*

"This book has all the power, romance, chocolate, and plot you crave."

—Sam G., *School Library Journal* teen reviewer

ALSO BY TERA LYNN CHILDS
AND TRACY DEEBS

POWERLESS

RELENTLESS

TERA LYNN CHILDS
AND TRACY DEEBS

Published by Sourcebooks Fire, an imprint of Sourcebooks, Inc.

P.O. Box 4410, Naperville, Illinois 60567-4410

(630) 961-3900

Fax: (630) 961-2168

www.sourcebooks.com

Library of Congress Cataloging-in-Publication data is on file with the publisher.

Printed and bound in the United States of America.

WOZ 10 9 8 7 6 5 4 3 2 1

For our dads,
who are no longer with us
but remain relentlessly at our sides
every step of the way.
And also for Edward Snowden,
who showed us the dangers
of unchecked power and secrecy
and that privacy is freedom.

CHAPTER 1

T his is Jeremy Abernathy, reporting for Superhero News live from the SHN Power Chopper high above the super-villain trial of the century. Today, Rex Yes-I'm-a-Sadistic-Tool Malone and the entire Yeah-We're-Even-Bigger-Tools Collective are opening the trial of obvious-threat-to-humanity Draven Can't-Operate-a-Computer-to-Save-His-Life Cole—"

"Jeremy…"

"Ah, and there's our intrepid on-the-ground reporter now," he continues, his voice coming loud and clear through my earbud. "The situation is probably pretty tense down there in the courtroom. Let's check in with Draven's lady-love, the incomparable Kenna Who's-the-Ordinary-Now Swift. Kenna?"

Someone else on our system snickers. Probably Nitro.

I clench my teeth and fight the urge to respond.

"Radio silence," Riley reminds the group. "Before a big event like this, my dad always scans radio frequencies for chatter in case—"

Riley's feed cuts out abruptly.

Nobody says anything else, not even Jeremy, and I have to admit I kind of miss his annoying banter. Especially since I know he's just trying to keep me from freaking out. Not that it's working—but that's more me than him.

I've never been more freaked out in my life. And after growing up as an ordinary in a world of people with super-powers, that's saying a lot.

Of course, that was back when I still thought the heroes were the good guys. Back when my life still made some kind of sense.

Back before my mother went missing, my best friend gave herself up to the heroes, and my boyfriend got captured and put on trial for crimes he would never commit.

All of which have led me here to League Headquarters.

Into the lion's den.

My fake SHN credentials got me into the courtroom where Draven is to be tried, a courtroom currently filled with superheroes who are loyal to the League. Which means I'm surrounded by them, fenced in on all sides as I sit here waiting for the trial to start, terrified with each moment that passes that one of them will recognize me beneath my disguise.

I'm channeling my inner Rebel, taking a page out of my best friend's book with a platinum-blond wig, hot-pink lipstick, and a blouse unbuttoned just enough to keep secu-rity from looking too closely at my face. A face that's been plastered on wanted posters throughout the superhero and ordinary worlds in the twelve days since we destroyed the secret superhero bunker—which means if anyone recognizes me, I'll be on trial right next to Draven.

Mr. Malone doesn't think too highly of villain sympathiz-ers, as he calls us.

And if that isn't bad enough, me getting caught would be

the least of our problems. Because we all know that Draven isn't about to get a fair trial. No villain would, but especially not Draven. He's about to become an example. He's Mr. Malone's greatest capture to date, and he knows secrets Rex would kill to keep quiet. He *is* a secret Rex would kill to keep quiet. Which means once this farce of a trial is over, Draven's a dead man.

Unless we break him out of hero custody today. Now. Before this mockery of a trial can even begin.

Which is exactly what we plan to do—as long as I don't get identified before they bring him into the courtroom.

Just the thought has me slouching in my seat as Rex walks through the door in full superhero regalia—a crisp white jacket with red epaulets, decorated by an array of red, blue, and yellow ribbons over his left pec and a big, gold League badge over his right. As president of the League, he also wears a waist-length royal-blue cape.

It's the first time I've seen him dressed like this in years, and if things weren't so serious right now, I'd probably laugh. Riley's Superman pajamas make so much more sense now. Is it any wonder he grew up with a serious hero complex? Or that Rebel has an antihero one?

Shoulders back and head held high, Rex climbs the steps to the raised stage at the front of the room, walking between the long, curved table and the wall of floor-to-ceiling windows. He knows everyone in the room is looking at him, and he is totally eating it all up.

The rest of the Collective follows behind him, all ten of them walking single file, wearing matching white uniforms and smug expressions. I can almost smell the arrogance rolling off them.

Anger wells within me when I think that these are the men and women who've been holding Draven and Rebel for a dozen days, probably the same men and women who've been holding my mother for even longer. When I think about what happened to Draven's cousin Deacon in their hands, when I think about how he still wakes up at night screaming even though he's safe and free and has begun to heal, it both terrifies me and makes my blood boil with rage.

I'm going to make every single one of them pay. For what they've done to my friends. For what I'm afraid they've done to my mother. For what they've done to too many people. I'm going to make them suffer like they've made so many villains suffer in the decades since the Collective came to power.

That's not something I ever thought I'd say, but I'm not the same Kenna Swift I was three weeks ago. I'm done playing their game, done following the rules that the supposed good guys wrote.

If I have anything to say about it, Rex Malone is *never* going to hurt anyone I care about ever again. And he sure as hell isn't going to kill Draven. Not today.

Not ever.

Suddenly, the lights in the courtroom flicker.

"Hey, something's interfering with my feed," the SHN camera guy next to me complains. He fiddles with his wires like there might be a loose connection.

"Steady," Jeremy warns softly, and I force myself to take a calming breath to tamp down my power and keep it from leaking out before we need it. Wouldn't want the superhero world to miss a single second of the coming spectacle.

It took a few days to get past the brain-freezing shock at

the very idea of having a power. After a lifetime of feeling powerless, that was hard enough to process. But the realization that followed was even worse. The mark on my neck declares me not only a super, but a *villain*. Mom is an ordinary. Which means my dad, one of the most famous and revered heroes of his time, was actually a villain.

I have so many questions and no one to ask.

Rex stops at the middle of the stage, behind the long, curved table, and pulls out the centermost chair. After he sits, his minions do the same, filling in the seats on either side of him.

I slouch deeper as he braces his hands on the table in front of him and surveys the courtroom. I'm sitting in the very back row, with dozens of spectators between us, so he would need supervision to be able to identify me in this crowd, but I'm not taking any chances. The self-satisfied smirk on his face—an expression that says he is king of this domain and that he likes it that way—sends chills down my spine.

When he's done looking over all of the reporters, security guards, and special guests, he nods to the back of the courtroom and makes a come-forward gesture.

For a second I think he's seen me. *Recognized* me.

My heart stutters and I can't breathe. I feel the walls closing in. My mind starts racing, desperate to figure out how I might get out of this alive, how we can still make the plan work.

Then I sense movement at my side.

Everyone in the courtroom turns to look as Rebel Malone, my best friend and Rex's black sheep daughter, walks slowly, timidly, toward the front. And if I'm channeling Rebel today, then she's channeling Lilly Pulitzer. Dressed in a pale-pink floral dress that skims her knees and a white cardigan, with her usually spiky bleached hair dyed brown and swept back from her face by a matching pink headband, she's as far from the girl I know as Rex is from the hero I once thought he was.

She walks right by me without noticing me. Not that I'm surprised, considering she'd have to look around to see me. And she isn't. At all. She's staring straight ahead, almost like she's hypnotized, following her father's every direction as she finally makes it to the front of the courtroom and sits down in the empty, reserved first row.

Rex nods in satisfaction, then clears his throat before leaning down to the microphone that sits on the table in front of him.

"First of all, I would like to thank the members of the press corps for being here today," he says, nodding toward my section.

I pretend to scratch my forehead.

"The Collective and I have always prided ourselves on our openness and transparency, which is why you have all been invited here to report on this very important trial."

It takes all my self-control not to laugh out loud—or to scream my outrage. Because a month ago I would have been just like everyone else in this courtroom. I would have believed him without a second thought.

But now I know better. Despite Mr. Malone's insistence that secrets are for villains and that everything he and the hero squad do is aboveboard, the truth is that the superheroes keep deeper, darker secrets than I ever imagined possible.

Their supposed openness and transparency is a joke. Or, more accurately, a travesty.

I wait for him to give his usual song and dance about how

evil villains are. But he must be as anxious for this trial to start as I am—though for totally different reasons—because he doesn't say anything else. Instead, he gestures to the door on the opposite side from where he and the Collective entered.

I turn to look just as two massive hero guards enter, then turn back and level nasty-looking weapons at the doorway. From this distance I can't tell if they're ordinary guns or special weapons from the hero armory. Freeze rays, maybe, or even disintegration guns.

I wouldn't put it past them, wouldn't put *anything* past Mr. Malone.

Then Draven appears and I huff out a relieved sob-laugh. I can't help myself.

He looks exactly like the last time I saw him, streaming live on an SHN broadcast. He'd already been captured by Mr. Malone, was already a prisoner of the war we'd just begun to fight. He was standing with Rex and this new and unimproved version of Rebel that I don't recognize, the three of them in front of the mountain Draven's pal Quake had turned to rubble at his behest while Draven was still inside. All part of a plan the villain boys had cooked up to make sure that Jeremy and I got out safely with the rescued prisoners.

Draven's wrists and ankles are cuffed and connected by shackles that only a super with laser vision could cut through. He's wearing a baggy prisoner's jumpsuit—only instead of bright orange it's solid black, with the word *VILLAIN* painted in white across the chest. And on his head sits the powers-neutralizing helmet.

The helmet isn't one of my mom's inventions, but her research helped them develop the technology that can block a super's powers by creating some kind of Faraday cage for the brain. It may look like a giant fishbowl with a metal collar, but that's no ordinary glass. Tempered, shatterproof, bulletproof, and laced with invisible wires that carry a high-frequency signal that inhibits all powers, it's the perfect villain containment unit.

Draven won't be messing with anyone's memories or manipulating anyone at a genetic level—not that anyone in this room knows about his second power—as long as that helmet sits on his head.

But other than that, he looks surprisingly okay. The heroes had Deacon for only a few days, and they nearly destroyed him. In the twelve days since I last saw Draven, my imagination has drummed up all kinds of worst-case scenarios for the state he would be in when he finally got to stand trial.

I let out a tiny sigh of relief that he appears to be unharmed. We're not any closer to home free, but just seeing him looking...like *him* makes me feel better. Then again, just seeing him makes me feel better. Knowing that it's only a matter of minutes before I get to hold him, talk to him, make sure he really is all right.

Two more guards trail him into the courtroom and prod him across the room as the first two keep their guns aimed at him. I can't tear my eyes away. I need to see every move he makes, need to count every breath he takes to reassure myself that he's really okay.

"Though Draven Cole is only eighteen years old, he is a grave danger to superheroes everywhere," Mr. Malone proclaims to the rapt audience. "He is the nephew of the notorious Anton Cole, the most dangerous supervillain of our times, whose very existence is a threat to our way of life."

Ugh. Cue the fear-mongering propaganda. Everyone gasps appropriately.

"And more than that," Rex continues, "he is responsible for massive destruction at two top secret hero facilities, as well as assaulting numerous SHPD officers and security guards and kidnapping both Rachel and Riley Malone." Another gasp fills the courtroom at this revelation. "Today he must answer for his crimes."

I want to stand up and shout that Draven's only crimes are being born a villain—and having the misfortune of being Rex Malone's bastard son. Something I'm sure the head of the Superhero Collective doesn't want the rest of the hero world to know. But doing so would ruin everything, so I force myself to stay silent.

The quartet of guards push Draven up the steps to the raised box at one end of the table. As he climbs the stairs, he looks out over the crowd. He might be Rex's son, but instead of having the smug look his father wore when he surveyed the room, Draven looks defiant. Scornful. Like he's daring them to judge him.

His gaze skims over me, past me, and then darts back, the mask he wears faltering for just a moment.

I bite my hot-pink lips to keep from grinning. I want him to know that we have a plan, that we're getting him out of here, but I can't risk drawing any attention.

Even from this distance, I can see Draven's icy blue eyes narrow behind the glass helmet. He shakes his head, a small, barely perceptible movement that only someone who was desperate for any kind of communication would even notice. Still, I get his meaning, loud and clear.

Don't. Try. Anything.

Too bad. We're getting him out whether he likes it or not.

I give him a solid nod.

He's scowling when he looks away, but he does nothing else that might alert the heroes to my presence. Exactly as I expected. He may not approve of the fact that I'm here to rescue him, but he won't risk doing anything that might get me hurt.

"Today we make history," Mr. Malone drones on as the four armed guards take up offensive positions behind and next to Draven. "Today we bring to justice not one but *two* supervillains. Draven Cole and—"

He points again at the still-open side door, and like viewers at a tennis match, we all turn to see who will walk through next.

"A supervillain even more treacherous, even more duplicitous." He makes another gesture, and two more guards enter, repeating the turn-and-aim procedure we just saw used on Draven. "A supervillain who lived among us as one of our own, even as she worked to destroy us."

The second villain walks through the door.

"No!" I whisper-shout. Then slap my hands over my mouth to keep from blowing my cover. Not that I should worry. Every hero in the room had a similar reaction to seeing a familiar face wearing villain blacks.

"Kenna, who is it?" Jeremy asks in my earbud.

I shake my head, unable to speak. Unable to process what I'm seeing.

Two more guards follow, prodding the second villain to another raised stand at the near end of the table. I watch, in shock as my mind struggles to make sense of this. I might be having a stroke.

"A woman we all believed to be fighting for the right, a woman in whose hands we placed the lives of every superhero, recently revealed as a filthy villain mole." Mr. Malone gestures at the second villain as she defiantly refuses to sit. "Dr. Jeanine Swift."

My earbud explodes with shocked protests from every member of my team.

"Dr. Swift?" Riley whispers.

"Your mom?" Jeremy asks. "No way."

No way. My thoughts exactly. No freaking way my *mom* is a *villain*. Not when she's the most respected—and decorated—scientist the heroes have ever had.

This has to be a setup. They must have found out about her ultrasecret projects—like the immunity serum she made me take for years—or that I used her ID to find the secret sublevel at ESH Labs where they were torturing villains. Mr. Malone is setting her up as a villain so he can get rid of her. That's the only explanation that even remotely makes sense.

Mom is an ordinary like me. Well, like I used to be. Or like I thought I was before I found out the truth.

But there she stands, hands and feet shackled, head encased in a helmet identical to the one Draven is wearing. A helmet she helped design.

The villain label stamped across her chest stands out like a neon sign.

When Mr. Malone orders her to sit, she turns to spear him with the most venomous glare I've ever seen her give. And when she turns back around, I see the mark beneath her ear. A *villain* mark.

A mark I know never used to be there.

Oh God, I've been so stupid.

The truth overwhelms me—as does the betrayal.

All those years she was dosing me with immunity serum, supposedly to protect little, helpless me from superpowers, when in reality she was trying to hide my villain power from everyone, including myself. I thought she was protecting my dad, hiding the power that would reveal his villainous truth. But she wasn't hiding only my powers. She was hiding hers too.

Mom is a villain. Which means…what? That I got my villain mark from her? Was Dad really a hero, or was he hiding his villain identity too?

My hands shake with the enormity of the revelation. And the enormity of the hurt welling inside me. How could she do this? Why would she do it when it meant crippling both of us for so long?

"Our plan is screwed," Nitro says.

"Not necessarily," Jeremy argues. "We just have to adjust."

"How do you expect us to get Draven *and* the doctor?" Nitro asks. "Riley isn't actually Superman, you know. And neither are you."

"We're getting my sister too," Riley adds.

"Yes," Dante says, for once agreeing with Riley. "There's no way we're leaving here without Rebel."

"Did you miss the part where there is an entire *room full of heroes* who are going to try to stop us?" Jeremy scoffs. "It will be hard to grab two people, but three is practically impossible."

"You better figure out how to make it possible," Dante tells him.

"We don't even know if robot girl wants to be rescued," Nitro argues.

"Don't call her that," Dante growls.

"Forget getting out of the courtroom. I calculated our escape plan based on a six-person payload," Jeremy continues. "I can't guarantee it'll work with eight."

"Well, it has to," Dante replies. "We're not leaving any of them in hero hands."

Jeremy doesn't let it go. "But once Kenna does her thing, I won't even be able to—"

"Enough," I snarl through clenched teeth. "We're getting them all, and we're going to do it as planned."

"Are you sure?" Riley asks. "What if we—"

His voice gets muffled, like someone clamped a hand over his mouth. That's my team.

"Ready when you are, Kenna," Dante says.

I allow myself one more minute to think. To breathe. To convince myself that things are about to get very, very awesome. I ignore the voice in the back of my head that tells me the other option is that things could get very, very bad. But it doesn't matter. We have to try. Like Dante said, we're not leaving them behind. None of them.

"In one of the most extensive investigations in League history," Mr. Malone explains to the rapt courtroom audience, "we discovered that all recent security leaks can be traced back to the efforts of the woman who was, for so many years, our most trusted scientist."

That's total bullshit. At least some of the leaks are thanks to his own daughter, and he knows it.

But as I look at Rebel, I see her smiling blandly and applauding this revelation. Who *is* this girl? What have they done to my best friend?

"In fact, Jeanine Swift has been working with Draven Cole for months now, giving him access to the Elite Superhero Lab—access that led to extensive damage to property and personnel. Because this case is so unusual," Mr. Malone continues, "I will be presiding over the trial. We will first present the case against the villains and then will open the floor to opposing testimony from sympathizers."

Right. As if anyone under Rex's command would be willing to risk his wrath by testifying on behalf of my mom, let alone Draven. No one speaks out against Mr. Malone. Ever. Probably because when they do, they end up here. In the middle of a farce of a trial. Nothing else makes sense. How else could otherwise decent people let him get away with what he does?

And despite a lot of evidence to the contrary, I have to believe that some heroes are good. Jeremy is a hero. So is Rebel. And maybe my dad too—one of the best, or so they say. I can't believe they're the only ones.

"I will begin," he continues, "by reading the full charges against the defendants."

"On my count," I whisper.

I give myself an extra couple of seconds to commit the layout of the courtroom and location of our targets to memory. Rebel is a dozen rows in front of me, across the aisle. Draven is at the right end of the judicial table. Mom is at the left end.

Mr. Malone is dead center.

There are ten members of the Collective.

Sixteen armed hero guards.

More than fifty heroes who are either here to present in the case or to witness the trial of the century firsthand.

Plus the real SHN camera crew that is capturing the entire spectacle for the rest of the hero world to see.

Our goal is to get our people out with as little collateral damage as possible. I mean, if Rex and the rest of the Collective get caught in the crossfire, none of us are going to shed a tear. Well, Riley might. But the rest of us think they can all go to hell. The spectators and the camera crew are mostly innocent bystanders, and the last thing we want is for them to get hurt.

Mr. Malone begins reading the trumped-up charges. "Draven Cole, you are hereby charged with the following offenses—"

"Five," I whisper.

"—conspiring against the Superhero League—"

"Four."

"—destroying the manipulation lab at the original ESH Lab facility—"

"Three."

"—destroying the underground facility at the Lima Whiskey location—"

"Two."

"—using your psy powers to turn Rachel Malone to your side—"

"One."

"—and participating in the genocidal plans of your uncle, Anton Cole."

"Go," I whisper as I flick the switch in my earbud that Jeremy says will keep it functional through what's about to happen.

I stare straight at Rex as I concentrate my power with my mind. In the days since I discovered I have the power to affect electromagnetic forces, I've been working hard to learn how to control it. And the first thing I learned is that emotion makes it stronger.

So I keep my gaze trained on Rex and let all of my anger and rage toward him build. It isn't hard when I think of everything he's done. I let it build, bottling up inside me like a bubble ready to burst.

Then, in one breath, I release it all.

My very own electromagnetic pulse, an EMP strong enough to fry every electrical circuit in the building.

The lights in the courtroom flicker and then go out.

"Hey, my camera just died," the SHN camera guy next to me says.

"So did my phone," responds the reporter he's with.

At the front of the courtroom, Rex scowls and rubs at his ear, like he's trying to make it pop.

I place my hands over my own ears to protect them from the coming pressure change. Rex pushes to his feet, like he knows something is up, but it's too late.

The windows behind the judicial table explode into a million tiny shards.

And the courtroom erupts in chaos.

CHAPTER 2

Two figures swing in through the obliterated windows, landing with a sickening crunch of combat boots on shattered glass. A third flies in behind them.

There's no time to hesitate. No time to think. Our entire plan rests on grabbing Draven—and now Rebel and my mom—and getting out before the heroes have a chance to coordinate a response. The faster we act, the better. Superspeed would be really useful right now. Or the power to manipulate time.

But powers-beggars can't be choosers, I guess. I'll just be happy with the one I've got.

I sprint down the aisle while everyone else is still babbling in confusion, launching myself at Rebel to knock her out of the way. We hit the ground just as a hurricane-force blast of wind whips over us. The audience and half of the security guards fly back under its power, crashing into the back and side walls. Dante keeps them pinned there—struggling to breathe, struggling to remain conscious—as he uses his power to cause an ultra-low air pressure system.

I push to my feet, dragging a now-screaming Rebel up with me.

"What are you doing?" She whales on me with her fists. "Let me go!"

Now I *really* know something is wrong with her. No way my best friend ever hits me. No *way* she'd fight to keep me from rescuing her.

"Kenna, here," Dante shouts, holding out his right arm for Rebel while he uses his left to focus his power and keep the back half of the room out of commission.

I wrap both arms around Rebel and frog-march her over to Dante. He clamps an arm around her shoulders and pulls her to him.

She freaks out at his touch, looking around wildly. The next thing I know, a chair is flying from behind the judicial table and straight at Dante's head.

"Look out!" I shout.

He turns just in time to spot it. He shifts his power slightly and sends the chair sailing away—into one of the guards who is trying to catch Riley's foot as he flies by.

Rebel curses and sends someone's discarded shoe flying at Dante's head. When he deflects that too, she scowls at him with such fury and revulsion that it scares me. I've never seen her look like that before, and certainly not at Dante. It's like she really, truly despises him. Which makes no sense, considering twelve days ago she was completely in love with him.

Whatever the Collective did to her, the real Rebel would be horrified by her behavior.

"I got this," Dante yells to me. "Work the plan, Kenna."

I nod and leave him to deal with Rebel.

As much as I want to free my mom first—family instinct is begging me to save her—I don't know what her power is, don't know if she can help us. At least I know what Draven's powers can do. And right now, we need all the help we can get.

Nitro is standing on top of the table, right above Rex's seat, lobbing small, white fireballs in a never-ending stream. He has the entire stage basically surrounded, with most of the Collective cowering behind a wall of white-hot flame.

Riley has a couple of the others and two more guards tied to the track lighting in the ceiling and is going after a guard who is shooting potassium bicarbonate all over Nitro's firewall.

So, in other words, all is going according to plan. Thank God.

Draven is struggling against his shackles, which are secured to a giant loop in the stage floor. I want so much to pull him close and physically assure myself that he's fine, but there isn't time for that.

Instead, I move behind him and find the latch on the powers-neutralizing helmet. An instant later, I yank it off and toss it across the room. It's useless now, thanks to my circuit-destroying EMP.

"What the hell are you doing here?" Draven demands.

Does he really have to ask?

I flash him a more-confident-than-I-feel smile. "Saving your ass. As usual."

He gives me the cocky half smile I've come to love, and that more than anything else makes me believe that things will turn out okay.

"Kenna!"

I turn at Riley's shout, just in time to see Mr. Malone break through Nitro's firewall. Right behind me.

I freeze. This is the first time I've been face-to-face

with Mr. Malone since I found out all the terrible things he's done.

Since I found out he tortures decent people for reasons I can't even begin to fathom.

Since I found out the word *hero* was a big, fat lie and they aren't the good guys after all.

Rage overtakes me, and I lunge for him, forgetting the plan, forgetting everything but the need to make him hurt as he's hurt so many of the people I care about. In a flash, Rex's hands are around my throat. I'm completely immobilized, lifted to my toes and barely able to breathe.

Draven is enraged as he turns on Rex—his father—and shouts, "You're not going to touch her!"

"Who's going to stop me?" Rex sneers. "You?"

An instant later, he releases me and drops to his knees, howling in pain as Draven uses his biomanipulation to do God knows what to Mr. Malone.

I draw in gasping breaths, relieved at the oxygen now flooding my bloodstream.

"Never go near her again," Draven snarls, ramping up his biomanipulation grip on his father.

I lay my hand on Draven's arm. We aren't here to kill Rex, and the last thing we need is anyone in this room learning that Draven has a second power.

His muscles relax beneath my palm, and so do mine. Just this brief contact with him is enough to center me even in the middle of all this chaos.

Rex collapses into a lump.

Draven snorts with disgust as he stands over his father's prone body.

The faint *thump, thump, thump* of an approaching helicopter jolts me back into action. We have to move, now, before reinforcements show up and eliminate our escape plan.

But first I need to free Draven. I bend down, trying to find some way to remove the shackles or at least disconnect them from the loop in the floor. We have bolt cutters in the chopper. Why hadn't we thought to bring them into the courtroom?

"Allow me," Nitro says, and suddenly a flash of blue whizzes past my nose. I watch as the loop melts into a pool of liquid metal.

"Nice," I tell Nitro, and his cheeks blush bright pink.

Then I race across the room to the stand at the other end of the stage where my mom is secured, like Draven, to the floor.

"Look out!" I shout as one of the female members of the Collective breaches the firewall, breathing out something that looks like toxic fog.

Mom turns her head, still trapped in the disabled powers-neutralizing helmet. In a puff, the fog is gone. The woman frowns, confused. Then she draws in a huge breath and blows it out, as if she expects another wave of toxic fumes.

She exhales nothing but normal breath.

Mom turns back to me.

"Hurry," she says, holding up her shackled hands. "The suppression won't last long."

I repeat my removal of her helmet, just like I did with Draven, but as I'm about to throw it aside, she stops me.

"Keep it," she says. "We might need it later."

I nod and tuck it awkwardly under one arm. "Hey, Nitro, can I get another one of your—"

Another bolt of blue.

"Thank you," I tell him. And then Mom is free.

This time, I can't fight the urge to give her a hug. Since the moment I first went home and found her missing, it's been torture not knowing where she was. Not knowing if she was okay. Not knowing if she was even alive.

But as I wrap my free arm around her and feel her arms squeeze me tight, I can almost forget about everything that's happened in the last few weeks.

Almost.

God knows if it wasn't for meeting Draven, I'd wish it was all just a bad dream.

"Kenna!"

I feel Mom look up at Draven's shout.

Before I can turn my head too, she spins our bodies around so we change positions. The helmet flies from my grasp. I stand there, watching, helpless and trapped by her embrace, as a burst of plasma from one of the security guards shoots straight into my mother's back.

"Mom!" I scream as she collapses in my arms.

Fear pulses through me, like a white-hot flame. I blink, and the next thing I know, the guard who shot my mom is flying across the room with a fireball to the chest.

I turn to thank Nitro again, but he's halfway across the stage, locked in a struggle with a member of the SHN news crew.

The drone of chopper thunder drowns out the noise of wind and fire in the courtroom.

"Your chariot has arrived." Jeremy's voice comes through my earbud. "Now boarding, all members of Team Get-the-Hell-out-of-Dodge."

I'm struggling under my mom's weight. Trying to keep her upright. Begging her to say something. Anything.

"Mom, we have to go," I shout, shaking her. "Mom, Mommy. Mom!"

"Come on." Draven grabs my arm and starts to take my mother from me. "The others can't hold them off much longer."

"Mom!" She's still not answering. Still limp like a rag doll in our arms. Panic is a living, breathing storm inside me. *She has to be okay. She has to be okay. She has to—*

"Riley!" Draven shouts, and in an instant, Riley is landing in front of me. He bends down and lifts my mom into his arms. I try to hold on, and though I know it's irrational, I'm terrified that she won't make it if I let her go for even a second.

"I'll get her to the chopper," Riley promises me, his voice steady and reassuring. "I'll protect her."

I trust him, I do. But still I can't let go. "Mommy."

Draven pries me away, pulling me against him and pressing his lips to my temple. Then Riley is gone, flying my mom out the window and up into the waiting helicopter. The rest of us—me and Draven, Dante and Rebel, and Nitro—converge on the center of the table. Rebel has stopped fighting, and I can't tell if she's knocked out or if she's simply given up.

It's not like her to give up. Then again, it's not like her to try to kill the boy she loves either.

Between Dante's wind and Nitro's fireballs, we're keeping the heroes at bay. Barely. Draven is trying his best to knock the guards and the bad guys out, clearly not caring anymore if they find out about his biomanipulation power, but he is shaking beneath my palm. It's clear that whatever

Mr. Malone has done to him since he was captured at the bunker, it's taken a toll. His powers are stretched to the raggedy edge.

I wish I could do something more to help, but with all the electronics in the courtroom already wiped out, there's nothing else my power can do.

Still, I'm in charge of this mission, so I shout, "Move out!" over the roar of fire, wind, and chopper blades. "We have who we came for."

Dante nods, and as one, we back toward the wall of broken windows.

As we step out onto the lawn beyond, Dante finally drops his wind, letting Nitro fill the entire opening with bright-white flames. No one who values their skin—literally—will be following us outside.

But where Dante's wind drops off, the chopper wind picks up.

My clothes whip around my body, and my poorly secured wig goes flying into the flames.

Good riddance.

I turn to look up at the helicopter Jeremy has hovering directly above us. Two thick, black ropes hang down, ready for us to climb.

"You go first," I tell Draven.

He's the weakest at the moment. And he's the one in the greatest danger.

"Not in this lifetime," he replies. He turns to his cousin. "You're up, Dante."

Dante shifts Rebel's weight against him. "I'm not sure if I can—"

"I'll take her." Riley flies down and takes his sister from Dante's arms, then zooms back up to the chopper.

Must be nice. "Go," I tell Dante. And to Draven, "You too. Nitro and I will bring up the rear."

Nitro laughs. "Always leaving me for last. Typical Yanks."

I step close to Draven and press a not-nearly-enough kiss to his lips. "Sense before chivalry."

Then I shove the dangling rope into his hands. He opens his mouth to argue, but I cut him off. "There's no time. Climb."

Reluctantly, he does as I ask.

"I'm last," Dante says. "I can hold them back the longest."

As if on cue, a swarm of guards wielding nasty weapons emerges around the corner of the building, heading into the courtyard. Dante blasts them with a gust, and they stumble backward.

Taking my own advice, I reach for the second rope and start the climb. My hands are burning by the time I feel a hand on my back, lifting me into the chopper by the neck of my blouse. As soon as I get my footing, I turn around, leaning back out the open door. Dante is halfway up the rope Draven used. Nitro has one hand on the rope, the other wielding his power back and forth between the courtroom wall and the ever-increasing number of guards storming the courtyard.

"Oh shit," Jeremy blurts out. The helicopter lurches to the side.

I scream as Dante swings wildly, barely holding on as he spins around the rope.

"We're taking fire!" Jeremy yells.

Dante manages to regain his grip and resume his climb.

"Are we clear to go?" Jeremy asks.

"No," Draven yells. "Nitro is still on the ground."

"Well, tell him to get his scrawny ass up here!"

"Nitro!" Draven and I shout at the same time.

I add, "Hurry."

Nitro begins his climb as Dante does his best to cover him from the chopper.

Something hits the chopper hard and sends me crashing to my knees.

"Time to go," Jeremy barks. "Tell him to hold on."

We're going straight up, flying high into the sky as Nitro dangles helplessly below. He can't hold on and keep his powers going, so he wraps both hands around the rope. I watch, my heart hammering into my throat, as he tries to climb. Tries, and fails.

He can't pull himself up while we're soaring through the sky. Gravity is too much to overcome.

As one, Draven and I reach for the rope. Despite the searing pain in my nearly raw palms, I pull as if my life depends on it. Because Nitro's does.

Pull by pull we get him up to the edge, through the door, and onto the chopper floor.

"A little more warning next time," Nitro complains, pushing to his feet.

The helicopter lurches one way and then another. Nitro flies toward the door. He only just catches onto the edge, saving himself from soaring out into open space.

"Oi! I think we need a bigger helicopter."

"Jeremy!" I shout, pulling Nitro back in by the lapels of his leather jacket. "This is not a video game!"

"No," he replies, and I can hear the tense smile in his voice, "this is way better. Hold on!"

"How do you expect to get away clean?" Draven asks. "There are at least a dozen hero choppers on our ass and twice as many fliers giving chase."

"Oh, ye of little faith," Jeremy says. "Kenna, engage the crybabies."

I slam my palm down on the big, red button on the box behind Jeremy's seat.

"What did that do?" Draven asks.

"We just sent two dozen red-level news alerts," Jeremy explains. "In about thirty seconds, every SHN chopper in the region will be in the air and heading in different directions. They'll never track us."

"Kenna," Riley says, his voice soft.

As Jeremy explains the details of what he assures me is a completely brilliant plan, I turn my attention to Riley. And to my mother, who is lying unconscious in his arms.

CHAPTER 3

Mom." I fall to my knees beside her and take her hand in mine. "Mom, wake up."

She doesn't open her eyes, doesn't clutch my hand, doesn't as much as stir. In fact, for one terrible second, I'm not even sure she's breathing. Panic-stricken, I lay my head to her chest and am relieved by the beat of her heart beneath my ear. At least until I hear just how fast it's beating…and feel how shallowly she's breathing.

"Draven!" I scream his name, reaching behind me for the one person I know can help her. The one person who can make her whole again.

Draven is already on his knees beside me, his hand on her leg and his eyes closed as he uses his power to heal her.

Relief sweeps through me, and I settle back on my haunches, taking my first full breath since she took that plasma hit in the courtroom. Draven will save her.

"What is he doing?" Riley asks.

"Saving her," Dante replies. "Trying to, anyway."

Seconds pass like hours as I watch, waiting to see signs of improvement. When they don't come, I look back at Draven. He's pale and shaking, swaying unsteadily as he tries to repair her from the inside out.

"Are you okay?" I demand. He's looking worse by the second.

He nods, eyes still closed, hand still on my mother's calf. Beads of sweat are popping up on his forehead, and his breathing has become nearly as shallow as my mom's.

"That's enough." Dante knocks Draven's hand away and tries to pull him to his feet.

"I've got this," Draven rasps, struggling against his cousin.

"No, you don't. You're too weak and you know it. You'll kill yourself if you keep trying."

"Kenna's mom will die if I stop," he answers, elbowing Dante hard in the stomach. He takes advantage of Dante's relaxed grip to reach for my mother again.

"You don't know that!" Dante insists. "We can get her to a doctor—"

"There's no time," Draven says as his eyes drift closed again. "I have to help her now."

If possible, he looks even paler than he did a few moments ago. Panic twists my stomach as I try to absorb his words. As I weigh them against Dante's.

My mother is dying. Not just injured, not just unconscious, but dying if Draven doesn't save her. And he might die if he does?

Terror explodes inside me all over again. Terror for him, for my mother. For me. My deepest fears coming true before my eyes. What am I going to do if I lose one of them?

How is this happening? *Please God, don't let this really be happening.*

"Kenna, stop him!" Dante hisses. "You're the only one who can. He'll kill himself trying to save your mother for you."

And he says she'll die if he doesn't try. The knowledge— and the horror of it all—hangs heavy in the air around us.

My entire body shakes uncontrollably.

What do I do? WhatdoIdo? WHAT DO I DO?! The words pound a rhythm in my blood, a mantra in my head, a terrified plea to the universe that I can't hope to have answered.

"Draven." I call his name and press my hand on his shoulder. I don't have a clue what I'm going to say, don't have a clue what I *should* say.

When he turns to me, the tired smile on his face a weak imitation of his usual cocky grin, I know that if I don't make a decision soon, there won't be one to make. At the rate he's fading, Draven might very well die *before* he can heal my mother. And I'll lose both of them. For nothing.

For one evil man's crazy vendetta.

I run my hand along Draven's arm and swallow my grief. "Sto—"

"Don't." My mother's voice, faint and trembly though it is, cuts me off.

"Mom. Oh God, Mom!" I pull her hand to my chest and scoot forward until my face is inches from hers. "Mom, please. Open your eyes."

She does. They're dark and cloudy and pain-filled, so different from their normal cool green. Any relief I felt at hearing her voice shatters.

"Draven, stop," she orders, twisting her leg from his grasp.

"You'll die if I stop, Dr. Swift."

She smiles through her pain. "That's going to happen no matter what you do, sweetheart."

There's a softness in her voice when she talks to him that I don't understand, a tenderness that doesn't fit considering they've never met. Though I suppose that changed while they were both imprisoned by Mr. Malone. Still, how much bonding could they possibly have done in between interrogations?

She turns her head and meets his gaze with her own, brow furrowed in intense concentration. Several long, silent seconds pass as I look back and forth between them before Draven clutches his hands to his head, his face twisted in pain.

"What are you doing to him?" I demand, more confused than I've ever been.

"She's blocking me," he answers hoarsely.

"Blocking?" I echo. "How is that possible?"

"Suppressing," Mom whispers. "I have the ability to neutralize other powers."

Suddenly, everything that happened during the rescue makes sense.

"Is that what you did to that woman with the toxic fog? You *suppressed* her power?"

"Yes. I—"

"And the immunity serum?" So many of the questions that have been building up since I saw her walk into the courtroom with a villain mark on her neck—since I saw the villain mark on *my* neck—start to pour out of me. "Is that where you got the idea for it? Because it didn't just make me immune to powers, Mom. It neutralized mine."

"I know."

"You know?" I jerk back. "You knew the whole time? But why—"

"Kenna—"

"—would you—"

"Kenna, please—"

"—do that when—"

"Kenna, stop!" That's the most forceful her voice has been since she woke up, and it stops me midsentence. "I'm sorry, but there isn't time for all the answers you deserve. There are things you need to know, things I need to tell you."

She brings my hand to her face and squeezes it tightly against her cheek.

She looks so sad, so…wistful. My heart pushes against my lungs, and I have trouble drawing in a breath.

"I'm sorry, honey," she says. "I'm so sorry. But there's no time."

Tears pool in my eyes and roll in hot lines down my cheeks. "D-don't say that."

"You have to listen." She drops her head back against the floor of the helicopter, her eyes falling closed as if even speech is too much for her.

"Mom! Mom! I'm listening. I'm—"

"You need to find Dr. Harwood," she interrupts, her voice so faint I have to bend my ear to her mouth to hear her. "He… he can help you go after the heroes."

"How do you know about that?"

"You're my daughter. Draven is Lucinda's son. It was only a matter of time." She pauses and takes a shuddering breath. "Find Dr. Harwood."

"I will," I promise frantically.

A few beats pass with nothing more than the sound of her ragged breathing and the drone of the helicopter blades.

Then she licks her lips and swallows. She continues. "The formula for the immunity serum is on my phone. It's at the house. I left it when they—"

"I have it," I tell her. "I have your phone."

"Good." She lets out a weak sigh of relief. "I love you. I'm so proud of you and—"

"We don't have to do this now," I interrupt, and at this point, I'm full-on crying, eyes blurred, chest heaving, snot running from my nose. "We can talk later, when you're better—"

"Kenna, stop." Draven wraps his arm around my waist, his fingers stroking my side in a soothing rhythm. "Let her finish."

I don't want to let her finish. Not when I'm terrified of what will happen when she does.

But I can't fight her and Draven too. Not when my heart is breaking wide open.

"I love you," she tells me again.

"I love you too," I answer, desperate and devastated and so, so scared. "I love you so much, Mommy. I'm sorry. I'm so sorry I went back to the lab, so sorry—"

"Shhh." She tries to squeeze my hand but she's too weak. "I'm so proud of you. Of what you've done. Of what you're going to do after I'm gone."

I sob harder.

"So, so proud of you," she continues. "And your father will be too, when you free him."

Her words are faint, but they slam into me with the power of a sledgehammer. "My...father?"

"He's alive," she tells me, and each syllable comes slower and softer than the one before it. "Rex is holding him somewhere. Using him..."

"Using him? For what?"

She doesn't answer.

"Mom. Mom!"

She remains utterly silent.

"Mommy, please!" I grab her shoulders and shake her, but there's still no response. "Mom! Mom!"

Draven grabs me and pulls me to his chest. "I'm sorry, Kenna. I'm so sorry!"

"Nooooo! No! No! No!"

I beat at his chest, try to get away, but he holds me tight. Strokes my hair. Whispers, "I'm sorry, I'm sorry, I'm sorry," over and over.

I scream into his chest. No words this time, just a base primal scream that holds all the fear and rage and pain that rips through me. I scream again and again and again.

Draven doesn't let go. In fact, he holds me tighter, his arms warm and strong even as my world falls apart around me.

"I've got you, Kenna," he murmurs in my ear, his lips hot against my cheek. "I've got you, love."

I don't know how long we sit there like that—Draven grounding me as the shock and horror of my mother's death tear me apart. Long enough for Dante to call out a warning that I don't fully hear and wouldn't pay attention to anyway. Long enough for Nitro to cover my mother's body with a blanket from the emergency first aid kit. More than long enough for Jeremy to get us to the SHN station.

"Hold on!" he shouts, and he sounds almost as bad as I feel. "This might be a little rough."

He begins the descent to the helipad, and Draven's arms tighten around me, one hand stroking my back while the other combs gently through my hair.

The landing is more than a little rough, but I barely register it through everything else.

"I've got Rebel," Riley says as soon as we're on the ground and Jeremy shuts down the chopper. I expect Dante to argue, to insist that he'll be the one to carry Rebel's unconscious body, but he doesn't. In fact, it's eerily quiet as my team—my friends—my *family*—pour out of the helicopter and onto the ground.

The next thing I know, Draven is pulling away, his thumb rubbing tenderly at the tears on my cheek. "We have to go, love."

"I know." I can't bring myself to move though. Can't bring myself to leave my mother's side.

"Hand Kenna down to me."

I open my eyes to find Dante standing in front of the helicopter's open doors, face stoic and arms outstretched.

"I don't want to go—" I wail to Draven, holding on tighter.

I don't want to leave this chopper. Not ever. As soon as I do, this becomes real. Too real. And I'm not ready to face that.

"If we stay here, we all die."

He's right. I know he is. It's only a matter of time until heroes find us and swarm the helicopter. They wouldn't hesitate to blow us all to bits.

They wouldn't hesitate to take our bodies and continue their unethical villain experiments—postmortem.

If Rex knows what my mom's power is, that it helped her develop an immunity serum, he'll hand her body over to his scientists and—

I can't finish that thought. It's too awful to even imagine.

"They can't have her body." I clutch desperately at Draven's chest. "With her power, they'll try to—"

"I'll take care of it," Nitro says from next to Dante, and it's the most serious I've ever heard him. "I swear, Kenna. They won't get her."

"We have to go!" Jeremy shouts as he jumps to the ground.

"Give her a minute," Draven growls back.

"We don't have a minute." Jeremy waves a beeping gadget toward the road. "The Superhero Police are getting closer every second."

If the SHPD find us, we're done.

"Damn it, Jeremy," Draven barks. "Can't you see—"

"He's right," I say, and they might be the hardest two words I've ever spoken. "If we get caught, then this is all for nothing."

Using every ounce of willpower I have—every ounce of strength I have left—I pull away from Draven. Uncurl my hands from the front of his shirt. Try to stand.

My legs are too shaky to hold my weight. But Draven catches me, presses a tender kiss to the top of my head, and hands me safely out of the helicopter into Dante's waiting arms.

I close my eyes and try not to look in the helicopter. Try not to look at the silhouette of my mother's body lying there under that thin blanket. It hits me—really hits me—that this is the last time I'm ever going to see her.

I reach over Dante's shoulder and grab the corner of the blanket. I yank it down, and it falls away from my mother's face. Why do they say that people look peaceful in death? She looks awful. Pale and cold and so, so stiff. I want to scream, want to rage, want to fall to my knees and sob for an eternity.

But Draven takes me from Dante and carries me away from the helicopter. From my mother.

He carries me over to the unmarked van Jeremy secured for

us and parked here two days ago. Deposits me in the first bench seat and then buckles me in like I'm a child. I want to protest, to tell him I can do it, but everything feels fuzzy. Everything, that is, except the knowledge that my mother is dead.

She's dead.

"Here," Jeremy says from the front seat as he thrusts a bottle of orange soda at me. "You're in shock. The sugar will help."

"I'm fine," I try to say, but my tongue trips over itself.

Draven's beside me now, his arm tight around my shoulders, the side of his body pressed against the side of mine. "Just drink a little of it," he tells me. "Just a little."

I want to throw the stupid bottle of soda against the window, want to tell Jeremy to go to hell and take all his helpful suggestions with him. But that takes more effort than I have right now. So I take a couple sips. And try not to throw them back up.

Dante climbs into the back bench seat where Riley has Rebel propped up against the side. That leaves only Nitro.

His heartfelt promise circles around and around in my head as I wait for what's coming. For what I know needs to happen. There is only one way to make sure the heroes can't turn my mom's body into an alien autopsy.

But as Nitro shoots a huge fireball straight at the chopper's fuel tank, everything inside me revolts. Including my stomach.

I shove past Draven to lean out the open van door and throw up the sip of soda I just drank.

As I do, Nitro's blast hits the helicopter full on, engulfing it in flames.

I can't look away.

"Let's move," Nitro says as he races to the van.

He hasn't even gotten the door shut before Jeremy floors it.

Seconds later, we're barreling through the parking lot to the exit. As we speed through the gate, the chopper explodes. Taking my mother with it.

CHAPTER 4

The car ride is pretty much a blur.

I'm vaguely aware of the van speeding, rocking back and forth. Taking curves. Turning left, then right. And then climbing, climbing, climbing.

My forehead bounces against the cool glass of the window, but I barely notice. Outside, the rocky surface of canyon walls races by, a kaleidoscope of images—gray and beige rocks, jagged edges, lengthening shadows. Below the road, a rumbling river rushes toward the plains. Green trees, some dark pine, others bright aspen, grow in spots where it doesn't seem possible for a tree to grow.

But then impossible is everywhere today.

The image of my mom lying in the chopper darts through my mind. Tears stream down my cheeks.

My mom is dead. Dead.

How did this happen?

How did I *let* it happen?

This was my mission. *My* mission. I'm responsible for everything that happens on it—even this. Especially this.

I know my mom wouldn't blame me, but she doesn't need to. I blame myself…and I always will.

I keep going over it in my head, keep trying to think of what I could have done differently. Of how I could have kept her alive.

Maybe if I'd freed her first instead of Draven, then… Then what? Draven would have been the one to get hit by the plasma gun? Draven would be the one dead right now? Thinking about that nearly sends me spiraling further into full-blown meltdown.

There's no good way this could have ended, no good way for us all to have gotten out of there unscathed. Part of me knows I should be grateful for how things went—at least I had a few minutes with my mom. At least we had time to say good-bye…and to say *I love you* one more time. I got to hold her hand and hug her. That's more than a lot of people have.

And I got to hear more of her secrets. Including the one I'm trying so damn hard not to think about.

My father is alive. *Alive.*

I'm not sure which impossible news is more unbelievable. That my mother is gone, or that my father is not.

My memory says that it's a lie. That I saw my father disintegrate before my eyes. I may have only been a child, but that image is burned into my memory. I couldn't make that up.

But Mom was completely lucid and more honest with me than she's ever been.

Nothing makes sense.

"Mom," I whisper, my breath fogging the tinted glass. I want my mom.

Draven has been holding my hand since we left the news station, his thumb brushing lightly over my palm in an effort to comfort me the only way he can right now. He hasn't said a word—no one has—but he's there. I give his hand a squeeze, just a quick reassurance, as we emerge from the mouth of the canyon and into the wooded valley where our cabin hideaway is located.

As the woods surround us, I take all of those swirling emotions and push them down. Shove them deep inside where I won't have to feel them anymore. There's too much to do and too little time to do it. If I let myself think about my mom— if I let myself feel her loss—I won't be able to do any of it.

And I have to get it all done.

More than ever, the mission to bring down the heroes is paramount. No one else can die because of Rex's insanity and cruelty. Mom knew it. She even gave me some clues on how to make it happen. Make the immunity serum. Find Dr. Harwood. Find *my father*. I don't know how I'm going to do any of those things, but I have to try.

I'll have time for a complete and total breakdown later. When my work is done. When I make it impossible for Rex to ever hurt anyone again.

"Shitburgers," Jeremy mutters as we turn down the path that leads to the cabin.

"What?" Dante asks from behind me.

"We have company," Nitro says from the front seat. "Big black sedan. Official looking."

"How could Rex have gotten here so fast?" I demand as adrenaline floods through me. "We have to—"

Draven leans forward to look out the front window. "Damn it." He jams a hand through his hair. "It's Anton."

"Anton?" I echo, the adrenaline dying down a little. "Your uncle?"

A.k.a. the leader of the villains. A.k.a. the bad guy bad enough to be Rex's most wanted.

Not that it takes much to get on that list these days…

"It's okay," Draven says as he pulls me closer. "It'll be fine."

I'm not sure I agree, but the day has already been shit, so whatever.

"If it's your uncle's car, then who's the girl?" Jeremy asks as he keeps driving toward the cabin.

I shift a little, so I can see who he's pointing at through the front windshield. Whoever she is, she's standing in front of the cabin's main door, dressed in a serious military-looking outfit. Black boots that lace up to her knees, black cargo pants, and a black motocross jacket with hot-pink patches on the sleeves.

And a gun. A very big gun she pulls out and levels at Jeremy as we get closer to the cabin.

"Um, guys…?" he says, his voice half an octave higher than usual. Not that I blame him. It's a *very* big gun, and she totally looks badass enough to use it.

"Relax," Draven tells him. "That's V."

Behind me, Dante groans.

"V?" I reply.

"She's our"—Draven huffs out a breath—"bodyguard."

Nitro snorts. "More like babysitter."

"Shut up, Nitro," Dante tells him.

"I'm sorry, would you prefer the term *nanny?*"

"You have a nanny?" Riley demands.

Dante grips the back of my seat so hard his knuckles turn white. "I swear to God, Nitro, if I wasn't worried you'd set me on fire again, I'd kick your ass."

That shuts Nitro up.

"Uh, guys…" Jeremy again.

"Just park near the cabin," Draven instructs him.

"I'm not sure I'm going to be able to do that if she shoots me!"

"She won't shoot you." Draven huffs in annoyance.

Just then a shot slams into the driver-side mirror.

Jeremy yelps and starts slowing down. "Oh, yeah? I don't think she got that memo."

"It was a warning shot. No big deal. Keep going."

A second bullet blasts into the mirror, this time taking the whole thing off.

Jeremy slams on the brakes, and the van skids to a halt.

"Why'd you stop?" Draven demands.

"Are you kidding me? She's. Got. A. Gun. And she's *using it*!"

"What kind of nanny carries a gun?" Riley asks.

"The kind who can kill you seventeen ways without one," Dante answers.

Another shot rings out, and this time Jeremy squeals. Actually squeals. Then starts sliding down until he's little more than a puddle on the floor between the two front seats.

"I think she's gone crazy in the two weeks you've been gone," I comment as Draven climbs over Jeremy and into the driver's seat.

"No, she's always been crazy," Nitro tells me.

Draven starts the van moving again. Jeremy squeaks a little with each foot we traverse, but on the plus side, her first look at Draven seems to have calmed V's trigger finger.

When we finally stop, I half expect Draven and Dante

to tell us to wait in the van. But at this point, we're a single unit. The whole us-versus-them thing is over and has been for a while.

We all pile out together, Draven taking my hand tightly in his, while Dante and Riley work together to get Rebel out. Jeremy and Nitro bring up the rear.

"Why's Nitro hiding in the back?" I ask Draven as we start toward the cabin.

"V doesn't like him."

"Why not? I thought everyone liked Nitro."

"Everyone who's normal likes me," Nitro pipes up at the same time Dante answers, "Oh, I don't know. Maybe because he keeps setting me on fire?"

"It was one time, Cole. One freaking time!"

Dante chuckles to himself as he tosses Rebel's unconscious body over his shoulder in a fireman's carry.

V lowers her weapon as we approach the cabin. "Where the hell have you been?" she demands, her gaze shifting from Draven to Dante and back again.

"Long story," Dante says. "One I'd say you're not too anxious to hear since you were *shooting* at us. What if you hadn't missed?"

"I never miss. If I was aiming to shoot you, you'd be shot," V says with a glare as she crosses her arms over her chest. "And since your uncle is busy inside ripping your brother a new one, I'd say we have time for your tale of woe."

Draven's hand tenses in mine as his eyes shoot to the cabin door. He moves forward, dragging me along as he tries to push past her. He doesn't get very far because her arm shoots out, blocking his path and knocking into his chest.

"Let me by, V," he warns.

"Anton doesn't want to be disturbed," she says. "And I want to know how you two fools"—she nods at Draven and Dante—"got in a toe-to-toe pissing contest with Rex Malone."

Nitro snorts again.

V spears him with a searing glare. "Don't think I don't know you had something to do with this whole mess."

"Seriously, V, let me by," Draven repeats.

She pushes him back a step. "Not until you—"

My hand is around her throat before I even have the thought to be mad, and I'm shoving her back until she's flush against the cabin door. "Don't. You. Touch. Him."

There is a flash of fury in her gray eyes, right before she bursts out laughing. She turns her head to look at Draven. "Oh, I like this one."

"Kenna," Draven says, his hands coming to rest on my shoulders as he gently pulls me away. "It's okay. V is going to let us inside now." He gives her a meaningful look. "Right, V?"

She narrows her eyes, evaluating me, before she sighs with resignation. "Anton will want to see you." She casts her gaze over our entire group. "All of you."

I release my grip and slowly back away. Draven immediately interlaces his fingers with mine again. The message is clear. He's not going anywhere without me and vice versa.

We walk through the door, into the middle of an argument.

A tall man with broad shoulders and dark-brown hair that falls past his collar is standing next to the small dining table. He cuts an imposing image, looming over Deacon like an inquisitor. With his hip-length black leather coat and dark-gray slacks, he looks like some kind of Mafia boss. Or hit man.

This must be the infamous Anton Cole.

My first thought is that Deacon looks worse than when we left.

Deciding what to do with him during the rescue mission had been a big fight. Should we leave him alone in the cabin? With his fractured psyche and broken body, he wasn't up to defending himself from an aggressive squirrel, let alone a hero attack.

But we didn't have a choice. He couldn't come with us, obviously. And we couldn't spare the manpower to leave someone with him. We needed all hands on deck at League HQ.

Clearly, being on his own had only made the nightmares worse. The bags under his eyes are the color of the mountains at sunset, deep purple with black smudges. His eyes, the same dark brown as Dante's, are cloudy and shadowed. We had to shave his head to get rid of the lice and to treat the wounds that the heroes' torture had branded into his scalp.

He looks like someone who's been lost at sea for months.

"I'm done with the excuses," Anton says. "You're coming with me and that's final."

"No, Dad, I'm not," Deacon replies.

His voice is so weak that it seems to take all of his energy to make his defiant statement.

"Yes, you are." Anton leans down menacingly. "I've had enough of your playing around. We are getting you to safety—and to a doctor. Then I'll come back and deal with your brother and cousin."

"You can deal with us now," Dante says as he hands Rebel off to Riley.

Anton whirls around.

He shoots his piercing gaze over all of us, his eyes narrowing as he sees—and obviously recognizes—the Malones. The look on his face is a mixture of rage and relief. He stomps across the cabin. Not certain where this is going, I shrink back a little, waiting to see how Draven responds.

When Anton reaches Dante and Draven, his arms snake around their shoulders as he pulls them into what looks like the fiercest hug in history.

"I thought you were... I was afraid Rex had—" Anton squeezes his eyes shut and then abruptly pushes them away. "What the hell were you thinking?" he demands of Dante.

"Nice to see you too, Uncle Anton," Draven says in an obvious attempt to deflect his uncle's fury from his cousin onto himself.

It works.

"And you!" Anton jabs a finger in Draven's face. "That stunt at the mountain was the height of stupidity!"

"We did what needed to be done," Dante says.

Draven moves to his cousin's side. "We got Deacon back."

Anton barks out a harsh laugh. "He wouldn't have been missing in the first place if you idiots hadn't gone poking around in the hero labs. I've warned you to stay away from Rex—"

"Someone had to," Dante taunts. "We don't want to spend the rest of our lives in hiding. The rest of you may be okay with being cowards, but—"

The smack of Anton's palm hitting Dante's cheek echoes in the tiny cabin.

Father and son face off in a staring contest that would have the entire room in flames if either of them had laser vision. Then again, I don't even know what Anton's power is. He's known as the Annihilator, so it has to be pretty terrifying, but it's a carefully guarded secret. At least in the hero world.

The air begins to whirl around us. Not enough to make anything move, but enough to indicate that Dante's power is in play.

In a heartbeat, Anton steps so close to his son that they are literally nose to nose. "Do *not*," he says, his voice so calm and quiet that it's more menacing than a shout, "raise your power at me."

The veins in Dante's neck stand out as he struggles to control his anger. And his power.

Something crashes into the wall next to Anton's head. A glass pitcher shatters into a billion shards.

At first I think it was Dante, but then Nitro yells, "Shite, Draven, a little help?"

We all turn to see Nitro and Riley struggling with Rebel who is awake and apparently really pissed. She follows the pitcher with a stream of objects she sends flying telekinetically around the room. Before Draven gets to her, she has Jeremy speared to the wall with a fireplace poker through the shirt, sends Nitro flying out a window, and is pummeling Dante in the back of the head with one of Jeremy's gadgets. Repeatedly.

But the moment Draven lays a hand on her and does whatever he does with his biomanipulation power that knocks her out, all the objects she was controlling drop to the floor.

V stalks over to Jeremy and yanks the iron poker from the wall, releasing his sleeve.

"Did you kidnap Rex's kids?" Anton demands. "Do you have a death wish?"

"We didn't kidnap them," Dante replies.

"I'm here voluntarily," Riley offers with a small wave.

Anton nods at Rebel's limp body. "And her?"

"That's"—Dante winces—"complicated."

Anton shakes his head. "This is unacceptable. You"—he points at Dante—"and you"—Draven—"and you"—he spins around to point at Deacon—"are coming with me. Now."

Deacon pushes unsteadily to his feet. "I already told you. I'm not going anywhere."

"*We're* not going anywhere," Dante clarifies.

"That was not a request!" Anton roars.

Dante stands shoulder to shoulder with his brother. "Don't yell at him! He's been through enough."

"Enough?" Anton echoes with a humorless laugh. "Enough? Try believing your children are dead or—worse—in the hands of your enemy, and then talk to me about enough. We're leaving."

"We're not going anywhere," Dante repeats.

Nitro steps forward to defend his friends, a pair of almost black fireballs simmering in his palms.

V places him in a choke hold.

Jeremy applauds, then stops as soon as V shoots him a warning glare.

"Enough!" Draven shouts. His roar stills the entire cabin. "We just watched Dr. Swift die. Can we all just…stop?"

It's like the air goes out of the room. Out of my lungs.

No one moves. No one breathes.

Deacon collapses back into his chair. He looks devastated, if possible even more heartbroken than before.

I can feel my heartbeat in my ears. When the tears sting at my eyes, I blink them away.

"Jeanine is dead?" Anton finally asks, his voice barely more than a whisper. "How?"

Draven wraps an arm around my shoulder and squeezes me close. "Plasma blast."

"Damn it." His face contorts in pain. True anguish. True grief.

"Did you—" I step away from Draven and place my hand on Anton's arm. "Did you know my mom?"

"Your mom?" He scowls for an instant before his entire face softens. "You're Kenna."

Before I can answer what obviously was not a question, I find myself wrapped in a tight, warm hug. The kind of hug I always imagined my dad would give.

I have the strangest urge to slip my arms around his waist and press my cheek to his chest. But I don't know him. And I'm afraid that if I succumb to the urge, the fragile bits of motivation and willpower currently gluing me together will shatter.

"Jeanine is...was one of the finest people I know," he whispers against my hair. "She and my Evelyn were the best of friends."

"Mom?" Dante asks.

Anton leans back. "Jeanine, Evelyn, and Lucinda were inseparable as girls."

I think we are all reeling from this revelation. My mom, Draven's mom, and Deacon and Dante's mom were best friends. Some crazy twist of fate must have brought us all together.

"When Lucy died," Anton says, his words directed at me, "your mom turned her grief into determination. She decided then and there to infiltrate the League and bring the heroes down from the inside. With her power, she was the only one who could."

Anton guides me over to the dining table, and I fall into the chair next to Deacon. It makes me feel better to hear Anton talk about her. To tell me things about a part of her I never knew. To help me understand why she did what she did. Why she lied. Why she lived a lie for so long.

"We all blamed Rex for Lucy's death," Anton says, resting his hands on my shoulders. "But Jeanine was always smarter and more coolheaded than the rest of us. We wanted to blow up League HQ. She knew that would only get more of us killed."

"So she became a mole," I whisper.

Draven drops into the seat next to me, his attention just as focused on Anton as mine. Because Anton isn't just talking about my mother. Lucy—Lucinda—was Draven's mom. This is about both of us. All of us.

"Over the years," Anton continues, "she slipped us information. Warned us of impending attacks. Shared her discoveries. Kept us from being eradicated by the heroes."

I nod as the details start to make sense in my mind. "And kept the heroes from getting the weapons that might be used against you."

"As much as she could, without raising suspicion."

"What changed?" I ask. "How did they find out who—what—she was?"

"I wish I knew." Anton paces to the kitchen door and back again. "Her last message said she was close to finding out the truth about why Rex and his kind are so determined to wipe us out. Maybe she…"

His voice trails off as he shakes his head. He is just as lost as the rest of us.

I'm not sure if that makes me feel better or worse.

"What about my dad? Did you know him?" My voice is barely a whisper. "*Do* you know him?"

"No, I never had that—" Anton stops and spins back to face me. "What do you mean *Do I know him?* Is James Swift still alive?"

I nod. "My mom said so. She told me before she…"

I can't say the words. Draven scoots his chair closer to mine and is just wrapping his arm around my shoulders when the cabin echoes with a high-pitched alarm.

Anton pulls his phone from his pocket and curses when he sees the screen.

He walks to the nearest window. "Yes? How bad? Casualties?" He pounds his fist into the wall. "I'm on my way."

"Dad?" Deacon asks.

Anton turns to face the room. "I have to go."

"We can help," Dante says, stepping into his father's path.

"Yes, you can." Anton pushes past his son. "By staying out of the way."

"Five minutes ago you wanted us to come with you," Deacon argues.

"Plans changed," Anton replies. "Now I want you to stay put."

Draven follows Anton to the door. "It's our fight too."

"And ours," I say, joining Draven.

"Haven't you done enough?" Anton roars. "Haven't you nearly gotten yourself killed enough for one month?"

"That's not fair," Deacon says as he struggles back to his feet. "If you'd let us help in the first place—"

"What?" Anton throws back. "You wouldn't have been caught and tortured by our sworn enemies?" He turns to Draven. "You wouldn't have been put on the fast track to execution? You wouldn't have gotten Jeanine killed?"

I jerk back.

"I had a plan, damn it," Anton shouts.

"Yeah, well, we couldn't afford to wait around for you to decide that the timing was right."

Anton turns on Dante, and for a second, I think he's going to hit him again. But he drops his hand to his side with a heavy sigh.

"I don't have time for this." He grabs the door handle. "Stay put and don't try to *help* any more than you already have."

"Who's going to stop us?" Dante shouts as the door slams.

V steps in front of it. "Me."

After that announcement, the only sound in the cabin is the roar of Anton's engine as he goes off to deal with the fallout from the latest hero-villain skirmish.

CHAPTER 5

To say that things are tense after Anton's departure is an understatement. V doesn't move from the doorway. I'm sure she knows that there are other exits—a back door and a dozen or so windows that require only one of Nitro's fireballs or a gust of Dante's wind to open. Or, you know, unlatching the lock.

As much as the guys want to fly out the door after Anton, defying his orders just for defiance's sake, we all know that we are in no shape to help right now.

Deacon is still a shell.

Draven is still weak.

Rebel is a huge liability.

And I'm… I don't even know what I am.

I let Draven convince me to go into the bedroom and take a nap. I don't sleep. How could I?

Those last moments in the courtroom play over and over in my mind. Releasing Mom. Indulging in a hug. Her spinning us so the plasma blast hit her instead of me.

I'm not sure if it makes it better or worse knowing that she sacrificed herself to save me. It's bad either way.

I lie there on my side on the rough wool blanket, staring

straight ahead at nothing for as long as I can stand. When I can't handle the silence and the solitude any longer, I push to my feet and force them to carry me back into the main room.

"Rebel, stop," Riley is pleading as I emerge.

She spits in his face. "Traitor."

Dante and Riley are struggling to hold her down on the table, while Draven is trying to lay his hands on her temples. Normally he can use his power from a distance. The fact that he can't now is a testament to how much Rex's treatment or the attempt to save my mom, or both, drained him.

Rebel's power, on the other hand, seems to be at full force. Objects of various sizes fly across the room, crashing into people, walls, and other objects.

Jeremy is shielding his computer setup with his body.

"Rebel, what is the matter with you?" Riley sounds close to tears.

"Me?" She laughs like a wild dog. "I'm not the one who turned my back on family. On all of herokind."

Who is this reverse Rebel? She is *absolutely* the one who turned her back on her family and the heroes. Riley is a recent convert—and even he still has a lot more sympathy for the heroes than I have left.

Something heavy flies at the door and hits V in the stomach.

She reacts instantly, racing toward the table.

Nitro throws himself in her path. "Guys…"

"Put the bitch down," V snaps. "Or I will."

"You're not going to touch her," Dante growls.

"Wanna bet?"

"Hell, yeah, I do."

"Hurry up," Nitro urges Draven.

"I'm trying."

He finally manages to get a hand on her, and immediately her fighting stops.

"It's biomanipulation, isn't it?" Riley asks. "You have mixed blood, so you have a second power."

He sounds almost jealous.

Draven shrugs.

Before me, Dante was the only other person who knew about Draven's second power. The only other person who knew that Draven's dad was a hero.

But we're all long past keeping secrets from each other now.

"Well, we can't keep knocking her out," Riley says. "That can't be good for her."

"Do you have a better idea?" Nitro replies. "'Cuz if you know another way to stop a pissed-off telekinetic from sending everything in sight flying at my head, I'm all ears."

"He could be frying her brain a little more every time he does that. We don't know!"

"I'm being as careful as I can," Draven tells him.

"Nitro's right," Deacon says. "Eventually she's going to tear the entire cabin apart."

"If one of you geniuses had thought to grab one of the powers-neutralizing helmets, that might have been useful," Jeremy says.

One of us had. But she got hit by a plasma blast.

"They were fried, weren't they?" Nitro throws back.

Jeremy points at himself. "Technopath. Remember? Or is that too much for your tiny brain to keep track of?"

"Oi, I'm not the nutter who thinks aliens are poisoning his pancakes!"

"And I'm not the one who can't control his powers."

"That wasn't my fault," Nitro cries. "My powers just sparked out for a second."

"Oh yeah," Jeremy mocks. "*Just sparked out.* Right in the heat of battle when—"

"Stop."

My word is barely a whisper, but everyone in the room freezes as if I have a supersonic voice.

Draven is at my side in an instant. "Kenna, love, you should be resting."

"I couldn't," I say, shaking my head. "Couldn't be alone with my thoughts."

I let him guide me to the table, where Deacon is still sitting. I wonder if he's moved all day.

Once Riley and Dante get Rebel moved to the couch, they join us at the table. As if by unspoken agreement, everyone gravitates there. Everyone but V, who doesn't leave her position by the door.

I think we all feel at a loss, not sure what to do next. Only knowing that we have to do *something*.

Deacon is the one to voice it first.

"We can't just stay here," he says, looking at me as if I might somehow have the answer. "What do we do?"

I start to shake my head. I'm the last person to lead us right now.

But before anyone can respond, Dante says, "Rex Malone has to die."

My breath catches at the pure hatred in his voice.

"Wait a minute," Riley argues. "Let's not get too extreme."

"Extreme?" Dante parrots. "*Extreme?*" He points at me.

"Rex just killed Kenna's mom. He was prepared to kill Draven too. He's tortured the hell out of my brother and just about any villain he can get his hands on. *Extreme* is exactly what Rex deserves."

"I know he's done some bad things—"

"Open your eyes, hero boy," Draven says. "You're on the wrong side of the line. Good old Dad won't hesitate to catch you in the crossfire."

"No," Riley insists. "You're wrong. He wouldn't do that."

There's something childlike in his insistence, in his still-unwavering belief that his father isn't the monster we all know him to be. I almost wish we could protect Riley from accepting the whole truth. At this point, it's inevitable.

"Killing Rex isn't a plan," I whisper. "It might be one of our goals, but we have other priorities."

"Like what?" Nitro asks.

"Like finding the immunity serum formula."

"What good will that do?" Dante retorts. "You want to get rid of our powers?"

I've done my time as an ordinary. I'm not eager to ever feel powerless again. "No, not *our* powers."

Deacon nods. "Rebel's."

"Exactly," I say. "The immunity serum will suppress her power like it used to hide mine. We won't have to keep rendering her unconscious."

Riley nods. "It will make her harmless."

"Have you met your sister, mate?" Nitro asks with a humorless laugh. "A full body cast wouldn't make her harmless."

"No," I agree, "but it will make her manageable."

I hope.

Jeremy grabs my mom's phone from his station and hands it to me. "It's fully charged."

"Thanks," I say as I clutch it in my hands. It's still warm from charging, almost like it's holding on to my mom's body heat. "Once we have Rebel taken care of, we do what my mom said. We find Dr. Harwood. And then we find my dad."

As far as plans go, it's not much more than a direction. But it's better than nothing.

If anyone disagrees, they don't say so. Maybe they're just being nice because...well, because. Or maybe they just don't have any better ideas. Or maybe—just maybe—they agree that it's the right path.

We'll see.

First, I have to find the serum formula in Mom's phone.

That's not going to be as easy as a quick search. Since that awful night when the heroes took her and I found the phone in her bedroom, I've been through it a million times. I've read every message, every text, every note. All in the vain hope of unearthing some clue that might help me find her.

If there had been any notations about the immunity serum, I would have seen it.

Which means it's hidden.

I could let Jeremy have a whack at it with his power. But something inside me wants to try. Needs to try. As if searching for this secret will keep her close to me.

After entering her passcode, I start scanning through the apps. Deciding to be scientific about it, I go through them one by one. Methodically.

Mom didn't keep her phone organized in any pattern that I

can discern. Email, solitaire, decibel meter, videos, notes. On and on in random order.

In her text messages, I see the cryptic ones she's gotten from Dr. Harwood.

The scarlet phoenix flies at dawn.

How could I have forgotten?

When I saw him in the bunker, right before Quake leveled the place, Dr. Harwood begged me to give her that message. But in the chopper, when she mentioned his name and told me to find him, I totally forgot. Was it important enough that I should have told her, even as she lay dying? Should I have used a few of our precious seconds to pass the message along? The only way to find out now is to ask Dr. Harwood himself.

I push that question away for later.

My eyes are starting to blur by the time I get to her photos app.

When it pops up, the first picture on the screen is one I took of her last year when we were hiking in the foothills. She is standing at the edge of a rock, her back to the plains below. She looks so happy and free, like she is literally on top of the world.

I don't realize I'm crying until Draven reaches over to wipe my cheek.

"She's beautiful," he whispers.

I smile through my tears. "Yes."

I start swiping through her album. I've looked through these pictures countless times. But this time I have a mission.

Draven drops his hand to the table and lets his fingers trace a pattern on my forearm. "I don't remember my mom. I've never even seen a picture of her."

"Really?" I can't imagine what that must be like.

Something Anton said tickles at my memories. About my mom and Draven's and Deacon and Dante's being best friends. An inseparable trio.

"Wait," I say, swishing quickly through the pictures. "I think there's a picture of her in here."

The picture had stood out when I was looking through Mom's photos before because it was obviously a scan. Not a digital picture, like the rest of the images in my mother's phone. It predates camera phones and yet it's on hers, which makes me think it's important to her. The fact that I'd never seen it before only makes me more certain of who is in the photo with her.

"Here," I say, pulling up the full image from the beginning of her camera roll.

I hold the phone out to Draven. It displays a picture of three women—three girls, really. They can't be more than fifteen or sixteen. They're standing in a line, arms looped over each other's shoulders and legs lifted like they're doing a Rockettes kick line. All three are smiling like they don't have a care in the world.

It's heartbreaking to think that two of them are gone now.

"This is my mom," I say, pointing to the girl on the left.

While two of the girls have medium-brown hair, I recognize Mom's smile. She didn't smile enough in the last few years, but when she did, it lit up a room.

"That's my mom," Deacon says, leaning over from the other side to point at the girl on the right.

Dante is immediately at my back, leaning over so he can see.

From the wistful longing in Deacon's voice, I'm almost afraid to ask. "Is she…?"

Deacon nods.

"Car accident," Dante says. "We were, what, seven?"

"Six," Deacon answers.

My heart breaks again. All three of these girls—captured in this photo so full of life and energy—are dead. It seems like more than coincidence. More than just bad luck.

"So that's my—" Draven's voice breaks as he gets his first look at his mother.

The woman in the middle has dark hair, like Draven. They have the same full lips and the same spark in their eyes, although Draven clearly got his icy blues from Rex. More than the others, his mother—Lucinda—is looking directly into the camera. As if she's daring it to capture her likeness. As if she's daring the whole world to take her on.

It's easy to see where Draven got his defiance.

"She's so…"

"Beautiful," I finish. "You have her chin."

"You think so?" he asks, sounding more like a little boy lost than the tough guy image he usually projects.

"Absolutely," I say, my smile growing. "Here, look."

I touch the screen to zoom in on Lucy's face, to show Draven their similarities. But as soon as I start to move the image, the picture disappears.

"What the—"

The screen flickers, and all of a sudden a stream of text scrolls up the screen. After a second, the phone reboots. When it does, almost all of the apps are gone. All that remains are the photos and notes apps.

Finger shaking, I tap open the notes app.

There is only one note: **Kenna's Protection.**

"I've got it," I say as I skim the procedure. "This is the formula for the immunity serum."

Relief sweeps through me. This might not be the key to saving the whole villain world, but at least we'll be able to stop Rebel from trying to kill us all. That's one in the win column for today. At this point, I'll take what I can get.

CHAPTER 6

I need to get to the lab."

I make the announcement when we're all gathered around the table eating the dinner of tomato soup and grilled cheese sandwiches that Riley and Nitro put together for us.

Deacon's head shoots up first. "You're not seriously thinking of going back to ESH, are you?" he demands. "Because that's suicide."

"Even if it's temporarily closed," Riley says, "you know my dad will have half a squadron of guards stationed there on the off chance we decide to come back."

"Which we won't," Deacon says. "Ever."

He glances across the table at Dante, who nods. "We can't go back there, Kenna. We just made Rex look like a fool in front of all the superheroes. If he gets his hands on one of us…"

His words hang ominously in the air between us.

I know he's right, but how else am I going to make the immunity serum? Some of the ingredients are common enough that I can buy them at the grocery store, but most of them are found only in a lab. As is the equipment needed to safely contain the reaction.

And we need that immunity serum. Rebel woke up a while ago and nearly burned the cabin to the ground—this time *without* Nitro's help. Draven put her under again, but I'm with Riley. We can't keep doing that to her. I trust Draven completely. He would never hurt her on purpose. But he's putting added stress on her brain, messing with her synapses and other stuff. Who knows how long he can do that without causing permanent damage?

Besides he's so drained from the hell Rex put him through that I can see the toll it takes on him every time he uses his power.

"Does it have to be the superhero lab?" Jeremy asks, reaching for his computer. "Or will any ordinary lab do?"

My eyes widen as I get what he's suggesting. "Not just any lab, no. But a well-supplied one should have everything I need. You're a genius, Jeremy!"

"I really am," he agrees as he pulls up Google. "Tell me what to look for."

"Search for universities," I say. "Ones with graduate programs in biology, chemistry, and physics."

Jeremy's fingers fly over his keyboard.

"Won't security be tight?" Riley asks.

"Not like private labs would have," I tell him. "At night they probably only have a few campus guards who make regular rounds."

"I can knock them out without much trouble, and we'll be good to go," Draven adds.

"You're getting awfully comfortable knocking people out," Deacon tells him, raising his brow. "Not that I'm not grateful for the rescue. But still…"

"You have a better idea?" Draven demands. "If we want to get in and out without anyone getting hurt or captured, then I have to—"

"Actually," I interrupt, "I think you should stay here."

The table falls silent as everyone gapes at me. Guess I'm not the only one who has come to think of the two of us as a unit lately. But that doesn't mean we can't have different opinions. That doesn't mean we are literally inseparable. That doesn't mean I'll put our relationship before safety, common sense, and the big picture.

"What do you mean?" Draven asks, as if he really doesn't understand what I said.

The shadows under his eyes and the slump of his shoulders after knocking Rebel out this last time confirm that I'm making the right choice. "I don't think you should come with us."

"You don't want me there?" Draven does a good job of disguising the hurt in his voice, but I know him well enough to hear it.

Just like I can see the hurt in the sapphire depths of his eyes.

"Of course I want you there," I reassure him. "But you just spent twelve days with the heroes."

He shrugs as if to say, *So what?*

"You're hurt, you're exhausted, and your powers aren't what they could be right now." I don't miss how he flinches at my words. "I don't want to risk you getting hurt because you can't defend yourself."

He studies me for a second. Then something in his eyes changes, shifting from hurt to anger.

"I can defend myself just fine." His eyes narrow. "Or

is that not the real problem? Are you afraid that I can't defend *you*?"

"I know you can," I say, rolling my eyes in exasperation. "I saw what you did to Rex."

"Hey, what'd he do to my dad?" Riley asks.

I don't bother to answer Riley, keeping my focus on Draven instead. "You also know I'm no damsel in distress. I'm more than capable of defending myself."

"That's not the point."

Then what is the point? From where I'm standing, it's all about keeping as many of us as safe and healthy as possible. The fewer risks we take, the better.

"I just think you should sit this one out, okay?" I tell him. "Stay here, keep Rebel under control. Jeremy and I can handle—"

"Jeremy?" He recoils like I hit him.

"I'll need him. The labs will have high-tech locks and security systems."

"Your power can blow them," Draven argues.

"Not without leaving neon bread crumbs for Rex. Jeremy can get me inside without leaving a trace. I can take it from there. We're a good team—"

"A good team, huh? You and Jeremy?" Draven shoves back from the table so hard that his chair falls over. "By all means, why don't you and *Jeremy* go save the world while the rest of us sit here on our asses? It's not like you need us, right?"

He storms out before I can say anything else or even figure out why he's so mad. I don't understand what just happened. My plan makes sense. The fewer of us who go into the lab, the less our chance of getting caught. And Draven is weaker than usual, which makes it even more dangerous for him.

I would do anything to keep him from Rex's grasp again. Even cut him out of the plan if it will keep him safe. Can't he see that?

I turn to the rest of the table in confusion, but every one of them is determinedly looking somewhere else. Even Jeremy and Riley.

"I'm only trying to protect him," I insist, because even though they aren't saying anything, I can tell they think I'm responsible for Draven's outburst. "He's the one who got mad for no reason."

"No reason?" Dante asks incredulously. "You belittled his powers in front of all of us."

"I did not—"

"You kind of did," Jeremy says.

I glare at him. Isn't he supposed to be on my side?

"And then you said you trusted your *ex* to protect you over him," Nitro adds.

"I don't need *anyone* to protect me," I argue.

Riley tsks. "Add in that villain temperament of his—"

"Hey!" Nitro objects. "No villain discrimination at this table. My temperament is just fine."

"It absolutely is." Riley reaches over and pats him on the head. "As long as no one minds you setting stuff on fire every fifteen seconds."

"Seriously?" Nitro puts a hand to his heart and pretends to fall back. "*Et tu, Brute?*"

I ignore them, turning to Deacon who knows his cousin

better than anyone at the table. Or at least better than anyone whose judgment I actually trust…

"He's not really upset about Jeremy? He has no reason to be—" I break off before saying the word. It just seems so… presumptuous on my part. Not to mention ridiculous.

"Jealous? Is that the word you're looking for?" Dante supplies helpfully.

"No!" My cheeks heat. "Of course not."

"Well, it should be," Deacon tells me. "Why wouldn't he be jealous?"

"Because the idea that there's anything between me and Jeremy is completely absurd—"

"Really?" Jeremy squawks. "Because I thought we were pretty good when we were together—"

He breaks off as something shatters against the wall in the next room.

"You might want to keep those memories to yourself," Deacon recommends hastily. "If you want to hold on to them, I mean."

Jeremy pales. I know Draven would never try to use his memory powers on any of us, but apparently Jeremy doesn't have the same confidence in him.

"See?" Riley tells Nitro. "That's the villain temperament I was talking about—"

"Keep saying that, and you're going to see my temperament!" Nitro answers as he starts building a small fireball between his hands.

"Don't worry, Nitro. We've all seen your temperament," Jeremy says.

"Oi! Nothing but grief I get from the lot of you!" Nitro

pushes back from the table. "Maybe I should go hang out with Draven. We could break some shite together."

"Don't do that!" Riley grabs his hand and pulls him back down.

Nitro beams. "You'd miss me, huh?"

"More like he'd miss the cabin," Dante says. "We can't afford to have you blow it up quite yet."

Nitro crosses his arms over his chest and leans back in his chair. "This borders on abuse, you know."

For the first time since I've met Nitro, he actually sounds like the teasing is getting to him.

I start to say something to him about how much I appreciate his help, but Riley beats me to it. "I think your power is cool," he says softly. "I wish I could do something like that."

"Yeah, right."

"I'm serious." Riley puts a hand on Nitro's arm. "We wouldn't be able to do half of what we do without you."

Dante snorts and starts to interrupt, but I kick him under the table. We rag on Nitro all the time—let him have a minute of appreciation. Especially since Riley is totally telling the truth here. Nitro has helped us. A lot.

I glance behind me at the bedroom Draven stormed into. It's deathly quiet in there, no sounds of shattering glass or fists hitting the wall. But somehow the quiet only makes me more nervous.

"Do you want me to talk to him?" Deacon asks.

"No. I'll go." I'm the one who upset him after all. I glance at Jeremy. "Find a list of campus labs within driving distance. Then the rest of you figure out who else needs to go. As few of us as possible," I stress. "With Rebel down and Deacon still recovering, we're doing a quick in-and-out, smash-and-grab routine."

"On it," Jeremy says.

"Yeah," Dante agrees. "We'll figure it out. Go do…whatever you have to do."

Whatever I have to do. That's one way of putting it, I suppose. Too bad I have no idea what that is.

The one thing I do know is that sitting here isn't going to solve any of our problems. So, with my friends watching—all with varying degrees of trepidation that do nothing to set my mind at ease—I push back from the table.

Cross the living room.

Knock on the half-open bedroom door.

There's no answer, but then I don't really expect there to be. Not when he's this angry.

Figuring no guts, no glory, I push open the door and step gingerly inside.

Draven is on the other side of the room, staring out the window. His shoulders are hunched, his hands are in his pockets, and he's all but vibrating with a combination of rage and sorrow.

The rage I can handle. It's the sorrow that has my hands shaking and sickness blooming in my belly. The last thing I ever wanted was to make Draven sad. He's had enough sadness in his life, and the idea that I'm contributing to it, that I'm just one more thing that makes him feel bad about himself, makes me burn with regret.

It's that regret—that fear that I've hurt him—that pulls me to his side.

That has me wrapping my arms around his waist and resting my chin on his shoulder.

That has me whispering, "I'm sorry," into his ear.

He shakes his head and shifts just enough that I fear he's going to pull away. He doesn't though. Instead he shrugs. "Nothing for you to be sorry about."

"There is," I argue, tightening my arms around him. "I upset you, and I never meant to do that. It's not that I don't trust you to take care of me, Draven. It's not that I don't think you're strong enough or don't have kickass powers or won't do whatever it takes to make sure we're all safe, because I know that you are, you have, and you will."

"Then what?" he demands, whirling to face me. "We haven't seen each other in nearly two weeks, and the first chance you get, you want to run off with your hero ex-boyfriend? You want his help instead of mine? I get it. You've known him longer. You trust him more than you trust me. But—"

"Is that what you think? That I trust him more?"

He raises a brow in obvious challenge. "Don't you?"

"There's nobody I trust more than you to have my back. Don't you see? That's why I want you to stay here, why I want to keep you out of danger until you've recovered from Rex's treatment, until your powers are back at full. It's because—"

I break off, unsure if I should say the words that are racing to the tip of my tongue. Things between Draven and me have happened so fast, and while it feels good and real and like it matters, I don't know if it's like that for both of us. Don't know if he feels the same way, if saying the words out loud might ruin everything.

"Because *what*, Kenna?" He looks frustrated as he shoves a hand through his hair, face pale and eyes tortured.

That's what does it for me, what has me saying the words that have been inside me for days. For weeks. I can't stand the idea that he's hurting—and that I'm causing any of it. "It's because I've fallen for you, Draven." I blink back the tears that are suddenly blurring my vision. "I love you."

For long seconds, I've fallen into an abyss. Like all the air has been sucked out of the room, and with it, the ability for my words to make any sound.

Or maybe that's just me gasping for breath, feeling as if there's no oxygen left in the world as I wait and wait and wait for him to respond.

"I'm sorry," I finally say. "You don't have to… I shouldn't have… I didn't mean…"

My humiliation seems to spur him to action because suddenly he's wrapping his arms around me. Pulling me to his chest. Pressing soft kisses to my forehead, my cheeks, my mouth.

"Don't," he tells me between kisses. "Don't take it back, please. Don't—"

"I'm not taking it back," I tell him, turning my face up to his so he can kiss me properly.

And he does. Oh God, he does, his lips hot and sweet and desperate against my own.

I whimper a little when he pulls away and try to follow his mouth because I don't want the kiss to end. Not yet. Not when there's still so much heat and fear and jealousy between us.

It's his turn to groan as he shoves his hands through my hair and pulls me in for another kiss, this one even deeper than the last.

I press myself to him and slide my hands around his waist and under his shirt to stroke over the smooth, hot skin of his back. Deep inside I know that this isn't the time or the place, know that it's too soon, that neither of us is ready for this. And yet I can't force myself to stop, can't let go when I went so long without him. There was a part of me that was terrified I'd never see him, never hold him, never kiss him again.

Draven doesn't pull away until we're both gasping for air, until our hands are shaking and our lips are swollen. And even then, he doesn't go far. He rests his forehead against mine and just breathes. In, out. In, out.

"I'm in love with you too," he says when we can both finally speak again. "I love you so much that those days I spent in Rex's prison, not knowing where you were or if you were okay… It was bad. It was so bad. All I wanted was to find you. To make sure you were okay. To never let you out of my sight. And now you're asking me to let you go again and for me to stay here, waiting, wondering if you'll make it back alive. I can't do that. I won't—"

"You're right," I say, cutting him off with more soft kisses. "I won't ask you to stay. I won't let the fear of something bad happening to you keep us apart."

"Because that's not how this works," he says gently. "We both want to keep each other safe, but there's no such thing as safety anymore. The whole world is upside down and getting more screwed up every day. There's no way to guarantee that all of us—that *any* of us—will make it out of this alive. For as long as we have, I don't want to be separated from you again. Not if I don't have to be."

He's right. I know he's right. And still I'm terrified that

something's going to happen to him if he comes with me to the lab. Still I'm terrified that Rex will find him again, and again I won't be able to protect him. Like I couldn't protect my mom.

But at the same time, do I want to go to the lab without him? Do I want to do any of this without him? I've spent the last twelve days like that, and even though I've done what needed to be done, I would have traded almost anything to have him at my side.

"I'm scared," I tell him. It's not easy to confess, but it's true. I've lost my mother. I don't want to lose him too. I can't. Especially not when I just got him back.

"I'm scared too," he admits. "The more control Rex loses, the more dangerous he gets. We'd be idiots if we weren't afraid of him. But the only way to overcome that fear is to take action. To make a plan and follow through. Step by step, we do what needs to get done."

He says it so matter-of-factly that I have to believe him. I have to believe *in* him.

Rebel screams, and we hear things breaking in the other room.

"The first of which," I say with a weary smile, "is to get that immunity serum cooking."

He steps back and holds a hand out to me. "Ready?"

"Not even a little bit," I answer as I take his hand. "But let's do it anyway."

CHAPTER 7

I'm leaving you in charge, HB1," V says to Riley as we're getting ready to head out the door. "Do not let any of these idiots step one foot out of this cabin."

"HB1?" he asks.

"Hero Boy 1," Nitro whispers to him.

"Why does he get to be Hero Boy 1?" Jeremy asks with a whine.

"Because you ask questions like that."

Jeremy pouts out his lower lip. "I was on the team first."

V ignores him. "I'm holding you personally responsible," she says, jabbing a finger into Riley's chest. "Don't make me regret trusting you."

"I won't," he says, that naïve look on his face turning sober. "I promise."

Apparently satisfied, V nods and walks away. She must already understand what I've known my whole life: Riley thrives on responsibility. Give him a job to do and he will get it done. It's just who he is.

If anyone will take babysitting the cabin and its occupants seriously while we're gone, it's him.

Outside, Jeremy starts for the driver's door of the car, but V stops him with an arm across the chest.

"What are you doing?"

"Driving?" Jeremy replies.

V laughs. "I don't think so, HB2."

"B-but, I always drive." There's that pouty lip again.

"Leave it, geek boy," Draven says. "V is a control freak."

"Bite me, Cole." V grabs the keys from Jeremy's hand. "Unless someone else here is trained in tactical driving, I'm taking the wheel."

She leaves a stunned Jeremy, his mouth hanging open, standing in front of the car.

"If it makes you feel any better," Draven says, "Deacon and I gave up on arguing with her years ago."

"What about Dante?" I ask.

Draven grins. "Let's just say he likes testing her limits."

I shake my head and follow him into the backseat of the nondescript sedan that Jeremy secured for missions like this. Missions where we want to get in and out of the ordinary world without being noticed.

We thought the heat was bad after the bunker, but the full-court press Rex and the Collective have put on the media—both superhero and ordinary—is ridiculous. Jeremy had to write some crazy program to log all of the headlines, news alerts, and APBs just so he can keep track of them all. Everyone in a five-hundred-mile radius will be on the lookout for us, so keeping a low profile is a necessity.

V starts the car as Jeremy climbs into the passenger seat.

"Does that boy have a death wish?" V asks.

I follow the direction of her gaze to see Riley standing outside the cabin, waving like a fool.

As if V's instructions hadn't been crystal clear. Don't. Leave. The cabin.

Then again, Riley has always been on the denser side of the spectrum.

"Can I shoot him?" Jeremy asks. "Pretty please?"

He sounds way too excited by the prospect.

V growls but doesn't say a word. She puts the car in gear and floors the accelerator.

As we speed past, I see Nitro step out of the cabin and drag Riley back inside.

Between them and the twins, they should be able to keep the cabin standing for the few short hours that we'll be gone. Right?

"Are you doing okay?" Draven asks as we pull away.

It's the first time we've left the cabin since my mom was killed. I know it's barely been half a day, but it feels like a lifetime. I guess time gets a bit skewed when your entire world is pulled out from under you.

He wraps an arm around my shoulders. "Kenna?"

I nod. I mean, obviously I'm not okay. I might never be okay again. But we don't have time for me to freak out right now, so...

"Yeah," I answer, my voice cracking on the single syllable.

Jeremy reaches back between the seats. I take his hand and give it a squeeze. We may not have made a great couple, but as friends we're pretty much perfect.

"So, V," Jeremy says as she takes the curves at ridiculously fast speeds, "how long have you been Draven's nanny?"

I crack a half smile at the not-so-subtle attempt to distract me.

Draven punches the back of Jeremy's seat.

"I mean, did you change his diapers?"

When Draven lunges for my ex, I grab him by the arm and pull him back to my side. "Leave it. V can take care of him."

Draven settles back in, and I lean into him. Just feeling his solid presence against me keeps the overwhelming sense of devastation at bay. Someday when this is all over, when Rex is dethroned and our world is safe again, I'll have the luxury of giving in to the bleakness.

For now, I squeeze tighter into Draven's side and push everything else away. Being near him, feeling him against me, makes it easier somehow.

V doesn't even glance Jeremy's way. She just reaches into the inside pocket of her leather jacket and hands him a lollipop.

"Sweet!" Jeremy says, unwrapping it and popping it his mouth.

"He gets candy?" Draven asks incredulously.

"It's the closest thing I've got to a pacifier," she answers with a smirk.

Draven and I burst out laughing as Jeremy says, "Heeeeey!"

I notice he doesn't get rid of the lollipop though.

"So, V," Jeremy tries after a few more hair-raising turns, "what do you like to do for fun?"

"I'm a villain. I don't have fun."

Draven snickers beside me, and I can't blame him. Seriously? Is this the best Jeremy's got? I'm beginning to feel a little embarrassed...for both of us.

"But if you did have fun," Jeremy persists, "what would you do?"

"I don't know. Take candy from a baby?" She reaches for his lollipop, but he jerks his head away before she can grab the stick.

"Okay, so fun is out. Got it." He stares out the car window into the foggy night, still sucking on the lollipop. Silence reigns for a few minutes—until inspiration seems to strike yet again.

Jeremy turns to V with a big grin. "So, are you seeing anyone?"

That's all it takes to send Draven and me into hysterics. I know it's not fair, but the idea that Jeremy would ever in any possible universe have a chance with someone like V is just funny. Besides the fact that she looks like she could crack his skull with her pinkie finger, she is at least a couple of years older than us and, if I can say so objectively, smoking hot.

I love Jeremy, I do, but smoking-hot older woman isn't exactly his normal catch. Reasonably cute science girl his own age is more his dating pool.

Before I can shoot him some snarky comment, V replies, "You applying for the job?"

Draven and I exchange a look. My wide-eyed stare gets a shrug in return. He's right. Who are we to judge?

"Maybe," Jeremy says, drawing out the word into several syllables. "If the position's open."

"It's not. I don't date second-rate hero boys."

Jeremy leans toward her. "Nothing second-rate about me."

She shoves him so hard his seat belt can't keep him from hitting the passenger door with a thud. "You're going to be seeing my fist if you don't knock this crap off."

"Hey, you could have just said no." Jeremy rubs at the spot on his chest where she hit him.

"V has personal space issues," Draven explains.

"What I have," V says, "is stupidity issues. Do lines like that ever actually work for you?"

Jeremy grins. "There's always a first time."

V shakes her head. "Sometimes there really isn't."

"You gotta give him credit," Draven whispers in my ear. "The guy's persistent."

"You have no idea. How do you think we ended up together?"

"Hey! What are you saying about me?" Jeremy demands, twisting around to glare at us over his seat.

"All good things," I reassure him.

He frowns but faces the front.

"Speaking of stupidity…" V glances in the rearview mirror. "Time for answers, D3."

"D3?" I ask.

"I'm the youngest," he explains. "Deacon is oldest, so he's—"

"D1," I finish. "I get it."

"Answers, Dray." V's voice is laced with warning. "I'm serious. Anton might not have had time for details, but I do."

Draven gives her a quick rundown of everything that has happened since Deacon went missing. There are some things I didn't know. Like that Deacon got captured while looking for his missing girlfriend. I never even wondered why or how he got captured.

The other guys were supposed to go with him, but he left without them.

From what I've learned about Deacon in the last two weeks, that doesn't surprise me. He takes his role as oldest brother—and oldest cousin—dead seriously. I can see him not wanting to put the others in danger.

Reminds me a bit of myself actually.

"Explain again the part where you blew up Rex's secret bunker," V says, "and then decided to *hand* yourself over to him."

"It was the only option at the time," Draven says.

"If you hadn't ditched me in the first place," V warns, "then maybe none of this would have happened."

"Enough," I say. Partly because I'm defending Draven. And partly because I can't stand the thought of rehashing everything that's happened.

Of going back over every moment since I first saw Deacon through that crack in the blinds and my entire world somersaulted into chaos. Into a world in which my mom is gone. In which my dad might not be.

I can't. I won't.

Much to my surprise, V takes the hint.

She steers the car around the last curve of the canyon road before we emerge from the foothills. We pull into Fort Collins, and the town is strangely quiet. It's hugely a college town, so summer is definitely low season. And it's practically the middle of the night on a Monday, so I guess most people are home in bed.

Still, it's strange to see the streets so empty. And eerie. But maybe that's just the dark storm clouds hanging over us, turning the sky from midnight blue to a weirdly ominous violet.

I chose a lab in Fort Collins for purely practical reasons. It's not much farther from the cabin than either the abandoned ESH Lab or the University of Colorado campus in Boulder, but it's a lot farther from League HQ, and since none of us have any ties to either Fort Collins or FCU, it's less likely that the heroes will be looking for us here. I'm done counting on our luck to get us through. My only comfort now is statistical probability. Our odds are better in Fort Collins than anywhere else in the state. Or at least anywhere within a ninety-minute driving distance.

Plus, Mom took me to a bioengineering conference here once, so I feel like I can find my way around the science buildings.

"Hey, that's the campus," I say as V zooms past the main gate.

"Too much human security." She nods at the manned guardhouse that is stationed at the entrance.

Jeremy leans toward the dashboard. "And the digital security is even worse." He closes his eyes, like he's reaching out with his mind. "There are closed-circuit cameras everywhere. Connected to—oh shit, facial recognition."

He spins around in his seat.

"That is some next-level tech for a college campus."

"I told you," I reply. "They have a lot of government research grants."

"Can you take care of it?" Draven asks.

Jeremy smirks. "Are you kidding? It's already done."

"We're still parking off-site. The campus is a tactical nightmare. Too few escape routes. Too many obstacles."

How does she know that? Did she research the campus when I said that's where we'd be going? I didn't think there was time.

I lean close to Draven's ear and whisper, "What's V's power?"

"Echolocation," he replies in a normal voice. "No point whispering. She can hear everything."

"So you're, like, literally bat girl?" Jeremy asks.

V cuts the wheel sharply left, squealing across the street into an almost-empty parking lot. Jeremy slams up against the door.

"How does that work?" I ask.

I've heard of echolocation power, but I've never actually

met anyone with that ability. I don't know of any heroes who have it.

Maybe it's only a villain power. There aren't many powers exclusive to one side or the other, but this could be one.

"I send out an ultrahigh-frequency signal," she explains. "And when it bounces back, I see an image of what it hit."

"Like a 3D map in your mind?" Jeremy sounds truly impressed.

It takes a lot to impress him. He's practically the most jaded guy on the planet after all those years spent hunting conspiracies.

"Something like that."

V turns into a parking spot and slams on the brakes hard enough to make Jeremy jerk forward in his seat. He's lucky he's wearing his seat belt—without it, his head would have hit the dashboard.

"Let's go," she says, climbing out of the car without a backward glance. "The longer we're out in the open, the more vulnerable you are."

You are. I don't miss the way she phrases it. She considers herself separate from our group.

Not that I blame her. Why should she get involved with us when half the hero world is out for blood and the other half wants us to fry? Makes it hard to trust her though, no matter what Draven and the other Cole boys say.

Draven doesn't release my hand as we pile out of the car and start for the campus.

V takes the lead—of course—and Jeremy rushes to catch up with her.

To pretty much everyone's surprise, she takes his hand.

"Is this your way of telling me you want a date?" Jeremy

teases. "Because I'll have to check my social schedule. I have a lot of girlfriends, and they might be—"

"Holding hands," V interrupts with a voice that could cut through steel, "makes us look less suspicious."

I stifle a snicker.

Draven laughs so loud that Jeremy shoots him an angry glare.

We turn a corner, and as we do, we pass the front window of a pizza shop that's closed for the night.

"Oh my God." I freeze in my tracks, yanking Draven to a stop.

"Wha—?"

He doesn't have to finish his question. There, taped up in the front window, is a poster that makes my stomach lurch.

COLORADO'S MOST WANTED

Below it are really awful-looking pictures of us all. The one of me is from my ESH security badge, but they've photoshopped it, giving me dark circles under my eyes and a really menacing expression.

The rest of the team's pictures are just as bad. I have to admit, if I was an average person seeing these images, I'd think Draven, Dante, Deacon, Nitro, Jeremy, and Riley—yes, even Riley—were the most dangerous criminals on the planet.

Riley's transformation is the worst. It takes a lot to make the guy with curly blond hair, shining blue eyes, and a perpetual smile on his face look like a cutthroat drug dealer, but somehow they managed it.

"That's a Colorado Bureau of Investigation poster," Jeremy says.

"No shit," Draven retorts. "We knew Rex was using ordinary police to hunt us down."

"I know," Jeremy replies, "but…"

He trails off and shakes his head as he pulls out his phone. A few clicks and keystrokes later, his jaw drops.

"We are wanted for, and I quote, murder, domestic terrorism, and high treason. They have us listed as armed and dangerous. STK."

"What does that mean?" I ask.

V huffs. "Shoot to kill. Keep moving."

We do, but each step feels a little more ominous than the last.

When we finally make it to campus, I lead us to the lawn around which the various science buildings stand. We need items from several labs, so I quickly divvy up the list. Reading chemical labels doesn't require any real scientific knowledge, so I don't need to be there for that.

"Jeremy, you and V go to chemistry and get everything on this list." I hand V a slip of paper while pointing at the building in question. "There should be a chemical storage vault on the ground floor."

And Jeremy's techno-powers will be able to get them in.

"Okay," Jeremy says. "What about you?"

"Draven and I will get what I need from biology. Then meet us in physics." I point to the building. "We'll need help with the heavy stuff."

Everyone agrees to the plan, and we split up.

I try not to consider how slight the odds are that we'll get across campus, carrying a bunch of stolen equipment and a vacuum chamber, without getting caught. One step at a time.

First, we have to get the stuff. Then we'll worry about how to get it to the car.

CHAPTER 8

Draven and I are only in the physics lab for a minute when, suddenly, the room is bathed in light.

"Freeze!"

We both turn toward the door, where a man in uniform is leveling a weapon at us. It might be a Taser, or it might be a real gun. Neither of us are willing to take the chance.

"What are you doing in here?" he demands.

Draven moves forward like he's going to take the lead. But I stop him. I'm not sure if his powers are recharged enough yet, and I don't want him to drain them even more by trying.

"It's my fault," I explain. "I have a huge quantum physics report due tomorrow, and I left some of my research at my station."

The guard narrows his eyes. "So you thought that made it okay to break and enter?"

"We didn't break. We just entered," Draven argues. "The door was unlocked."

But the guard isn't buying it. "Nice try. You aren't the first kids I've caught trying to steal equipment for a meth lab."

Meth lab? Seriously? Photoshopped poster aside, do we actually look like tweakers? Sure, Draven and I may be a little wrung out. But I like to think it would take a lot more than a few days of missed sleep to make us look like aspiring meth heads.

Secondly, you don't need a vacuum chamber to make meth. As Walter White taught us, you only need the right chemicals, a steady heat source, and a way to extract the precipitate. And, oh yeah, a well-ventilated space. Pretty much the opposite of a vacuum chamber.

"Look, I'm sorry, okay?" I say as Draven inches a little closer to the guard. "I'm on scholarship, and if I blow my GPA, I'll be on academic probation and then—"

"Hold it right there!" the guard shouts as Draven gets a little too close for comfort.

Draven stops. I stop with him.

"I'm not strong enough," Draven says, not bothering to try to keep the guard from hearing. "I can't use my powers from this distance."

"It's okay," I tell him at the same time the guard asks, "Powers?"

Then he shakes his head and backs away, clearly trying to put distance between us and him. "Oh shit," he says. "I know you. You're on that APB the CBI sent around. Don't. Move."

He reaches for the small black microphone attached to the shoulder of his uniform.

"This is Officer Pulaski," the guard says, keeping his eyes and his gun on us, which means he doesn't see or sense the movement behind him. "I'm in Physics 127 with two intruders from the CBI alert. Repeat, I have two of the wanted criminals cornered in the—"

The guard slumps to the ground. I guess a chop to the neck from V will do that to a guy.

"You're out of my sight for ten minutes," she says, pushing the guard out of the way so she and Jeremy can get in the room, "and you're caught by a freaking campus security guard." She shakes her head. "It's embarrassing."

The radio on the guard's hip crackles. "Pulaski? Pulaski! Are you there?" When there's no answer, the voice on the radio says, "I've called in your report."

"Damn it," V mutters. "We need to put space between us and here. Right now."

"Just give me a sec," I tell her.

"You get your gear. I'll take care of this guy." She squats down next to the unconscious guard and grabs him under the arms.

While she drags him out into the hall, I hurry to the end of the counter where the vacuum chamber I need is sitting out in plain sight. When I try to lift it, my arms strain against the weight. It barely budges.

"I can't—"

Draven steps in. "Here, let me—damn! How much does this thing weigh?"

"And more importantly, how the hell are we supposed to carry it out of here?" Jeremy asks.

I spin in a circle, looking for something—anything—that can help. I spot our salvation by the storage room door.

I race across the room, grab the lab cart, and wheel it back to the vacuum pump.

"Help me slide it on," I tell Draven.

Jeremy hurries over to help, but I think we both know that I have more upper body strength than he does. He ends up moving to the back of the cart and holding it in place as

Draven and I struggle to pull the equipment off the counter. It takes more effort than I'd like to admit, but we get it on.

Draven quickly shoves all the chemicals onto the bottom shelf, and Jeremy does the same with his haul from the biology lab.

By the time we're wheeling it to the door, V is back.

"All taken care of," she says.

"What does that mean?" I ask. "Did you...?"

"What? Kill him?" She laughs as if that's the most ridiculous thing she's ever heard.

As if it's such a stretch for me to think that the villain girl who shot up our van might not think twice about taking out a human guard. Especially one who is an actual threat.

"Tell your conscience to take a break, good girl," she says. "I locked him in a closet."

I nod in relief, not even caring about her "good girl" comment.

"Let's move," she says, "before the—"

She twists her head to one side, like she's listening for some far-off noise.

"Now!" She puts a hand behind my back and propels me into the hall. "We need to be gone *now*."

We run down the hall to the accessible exit at the far end, the one with a ramp instead of stairs. No way can we get this cart outside otherwise.

As soon as we're at the base of the ramp, I start to turn in the direction of the parking lot. V stops me with a hand clamped to the cart.

"There are a dozen cop and government cars converging on the campus right now." She closes her eyes for a second, listening. "Head north. There's a circle drive behind the theater building. I'll get the car and meet you there."

My heart is pounding as we race across campus—Draven and I pushing the cart, and Jeremy pulling out his smartphone. Head down, he starts punching at the screen with his thumbs. I'm amazed he doesn't run into a tree. Coordination isn't exactly his strong suit at the best of times.

A few seconds later, there's a loud squelch and then a voice coming from his phone.

"*Repeat, we have two suspects from the CBI alert confirmed on the campus of FCU. Last seen leaving the physics building.*"

Jeremy holds down a button. "Copy that," he says in a voice that sounds way more like a cop than a hacker. "They were just seen heading southwest. Must be making for the main entrance."

"*Copy that,*" the voice says. "*Units seventeen and eighty-one, head to the entrance gate.*"

I smile. Leave it to Jeremy to find a way to hack police-band radio.

The people looking for us might be heading in the opposite direction for the moment, but they won't be for long. We run faster, push harder. We steer around the theater building and, just as V said, find a circle drive out back that leads to a loading dock.

We're just reaching the base of the driveway when our car squeals around the corner, skidding to a stop right in front of us.

No one wastes time talking. V pops out of the car. She and Draven heft the vacuum chamber into the trunk—I know better than to think I have any upper body strength on her—while

Jeremy and I pack in the supplies from the bottom shelf. When the cart is empty, I send it rolling toward the loading dock.

Within seconds, we're all in the car and speeding away. Just as a small army of cars with flashing lights round the corner in front of us.

"Hold on!" V shouts.

She cuts the wheel sharply to the right, sending the car into a fishtail and me crashing into Draven's side. He puts his arm around my shoulder and holds me tight as V spins us back the other way.

Everything is a blur. I can't really see what happens or how she does it, but soon we're speeding down a street with the flashing lights in the rearview mirror.

"That was close," I say.

For an instant, a strange image fills my mind. A gray map showing the buildings around us and a convoy of cars that is hot on our tail. Then, just as quickly, it's gone.

That was weird.

"We're not out of the woods yet," V replies.

Jeremy groans as he looks up from his phone. "Not by a long shot. They just called in the FBI."

"The *FBI*?" I choke out.

Jeremy twists around to show us his phone screen. "It seems we've made it onto the national Most Wanted list."

How is this possible? "Rex hates asking for help almost as much as he hates villains," I say.

Draven shakes his head. "He hates us more than he loves his pride."

"Rex must really want you all dead." V's eyes don't leave the road.

"This can't be right," Jeremy says, staring at his phone.

"What?" we all ask.

"They're tracking us." He types furiously on his phone. "They know exactly where we are."

"How is that possible?" I ask. "Are they tracking your phone?"

"No way." Jeremy sounds insulted. "This is a ShadowPhone. Completely untraceable. It hijacks private cell signals, clones nearby phone profiles, reconfigures its mobile ID number every five seconds—"

"Okay, okay," Draven interrupts. "We get it, geek boy. Not your phone."

"Did anyone else bring a phone?" Jeremy asks. "I told you to leave them at the cabin."

We all quickly confirm that we didn't bring our phones.

Jeremy presses a few more buttons, his phone emits a series of sonar-like pings, and then a computerized voice says, "No surveillance devices detected."

He leans forward over the dashboard, looking around outside as if he might find a drone following us or a cop sitting on our roof. As if one could have held on with V's crazy driving.

Jeremy curses and punches the dashboard. "Traffic cameras. I should have thought of that."

"They're tracking us on video?" V asks.

Jeremy nods. "Following us from one camera to the next. Normally that would require algorithm-heavy software or manual scan-and-click. But if Rex has a technopath involved..."

If he has a technopath involved, then we are totally screwed. Panic slides down my spine. Not for me so much, but for my friends. For Draven.

"How do we beat it, Jeremy?" I demand, my voice going shrill.

Even if they can only trace us to the edge of town, it'll narrow their search window. They'll find us at the cabin that much faster.

"I'm going to lead them off the scent," V says, taking a sharp left. "Let me know when they're off our tail."

Jeremy turns around in the passenger seat. "We're moving too fast for me to locate, access, and disable the cameras before they spot us on them. Not to mention, that will give them another kind of trail to follow."

"Then what?" Draven squeezes me tighter. "There has to be a way to lose them."

"Kenna," Jeremy says. "You have to do it. Use your power to cut the cameras before we're on screen. And if you can, blow them all at once."

"Is that all?" I ask a little sarcastically as I start to focus my energy.

"Actually, no." Jeremy stops me with a hand on my arm. "You have to restrict it to *outside* the car. If you blow the circuits in the car's electronics systems, we'll stall out."

Which means we'll be sitting ducks waiting for the cops, the feds, and the heroes to descend on us. Not to mention that we all might get electrocuted in the process.

No pressure or anything. I haven't had to be this precise before. I'm not sure I can be.

Draven takes my hand. "You can do this."

"I guess we're about to find out."

"Don't screw up," V advises. She certainly knows how to coddle a girl.

Shoving the fear of everything that could go wrong out

of my mind, I close my eyes and try to focus, using some of the techniques the others have been teaching me since I learned about my power. But they've had whole lifetimes to learn control. I've only had a couple weeks.

That doesn't matter, I tell myself. I've totally got this. And if I don't, well… No, I've totally got this. It all comes down to visualization.

I picture the car in a bubble. A big, shiny sphere of protection, like Glinda's in *The Wizard of Oz*. It's a shield nothing can get through.

Then I start to manipulate the energy, to pull the electricity from the air. Within seconds, sparks tingle around the bubble, crackling at the surface. Pushing at it a little, trying to find a way in.

I push them back and build up the bubble a little more. Make it a little stronger. Then, when I feel like the sphere is as secure as I can make it, I take a deep breath and release the energy.

With my eyes closed, I can't see it. But the bright sparks of electricity, the flash of streetlights blowing out, the sizzling streams of lightning cutting through the air, glow through my eyelids.

And—on another positive note—the car keeps moving.

"You're doing it," Draven whispers.

Jeremy whoops at my success.

"Are we good?" V asks.

"Oh yeah," Jeremy answers. "We are so good. It'll be a long time before they ever track anyone again."

I smile, but keep my eyes closed. I don't want to lose control now.

After what feels like an eternity of sharp turns, fishtails, and the distant echo of sirens, the tension in the car finally releases.

"You can stop," Jeremy tells me. "We're in the canyon."

"Are you sure?" I ask.

"Positive," Draven says.

With a huge sigh of relief, I relax my power. Release the bubble. Open my eyes.

We're back on the narrow canyon road, city and government surveillance disappearing behind us.

"Stellar driving, V," Draven says, patting her on the shoulder.

"I've driven the getaway car tons of times. No one ever tells *me* 'good job,'" Jeremy complains. "I could have done that."

"Sure you could have," Draven agrees with a laugh.

I want to laugh too, but I am suddenly so exhausted I can't keep my eyes open. Using my power so intensely for that long has really drained me, and for a moment I can't help wondering if this is how Draven feels. Wondering how much hell Rex must have put him through—and for how long—for his powers to still be so exhausted that he can barely use them.

It's too awful to think about.

I'm so tired I can't keep my brain focused. Instead, soothed by the gentle swirl of the car on the winding canyon road, I let my head fall against Draven's shoulder. I let myself forget, just for a little while, that nothing is ever going to be the same again.

CHAPTER 9

What the hell happened here?"

V stops walking so abruptly that Jeremy crashes into her back—although I can't be entirely certain he wouldn't have done that no matter how slowly she stopped. He was a little too preoccupied with looking at her butt to pay attention to anything else.

Not so the rest of us. We're staring, openmouthed, at the mess that the cabin has become in our absence.

Nitro, Dante, and Riley all speak at once.

"Nothing!"

"What are you talking about? Everything's fine."

"Rebel got loose."

V steps into the cabin, and I get my first full look at the disaster area.

"Whoa," Jeremy says, echoing my thoughts exactly.

Nothing in the cabin's main room has remained untouched. The couch is upside down against the wall, with the dining table crushed beneath it. Half of the windows are broken. The kitchen chairs have been smashed into splinters.

As for the floor, it's littered with the remains of everything that wasn't nailed down—including what looks like most of my Froot Loops.

Dante and Deacon are kneeling over Rebel's unconscious body, one winding rope around her wrists, the other around her ankles.

"How did you let this happen?" V demands. She turns to Riley. "I left you in charge."

He holds up his hands defensively. "We didn't even know she was awake until we heard the crash." He inches back, pointing at the table full of Jeremy's electronics.

Correction, at the table that *used* to be full of Jeremy's electronics. Now it's flipped over backward like a barricade, with its former residents scattered around it like shrapnel.

Jeremy makes a strangled sound that's somewhere between an angry bear and a drowning cat. He shoves the box of chemicals he's carrying into Riley's arms and then rushes to the aid of his fallen gadgets, hurtling debris as he goes.

"On the bright side," Riley says with a nervous grin. "At least she didn't get away."

"You are all completely incompetent." V drops her own load on top of Jeremy's with a little extra oomph, and Riley almost buckles under the weight. "It has to be sheer dumb luck that's kept any of you alive."

"It's not like you lot coulda done any better." Nitro takes V's box from Riley's load. "It ain't easy keeping a crazy bird with telekinesis and a serious rage issue under control."

"Don't be too sure about that. When I put people out, they stay out." She gives him, hands down, the scariest smile I've ever seen. "Next time I'll show you how it's done."

It hits me the wrong way, pissing me off more than one

snarky comment should. But she's been like that all night, telling us over and over how incompetent we are and it's getting really freaking old.

What's also getting old is people talking about my best friend like she's our enemy, like she's some kind of rampaging animal that has to be controlled. Whatever is going on with her, whatever Rex and the heroes did to her, she's still Rebel. Somewhere inside, she's still the girl I grew up with. I have to believe that. A quick glance at Dante's face tells me he feels exactly the same way.

"Hopefully," I say, pushing past V hard enough to get her attention as I head toward the kitchen, "there won't be a next time."

"There is always a next time," she counters.

I ignore her, focusing on the job to be done instead.

"Get Rebel into the bedroom," I order Deacon. "Put her on the bed and make sure she's comfortable. If we're lucky, she'll sleep until the serum is ready."

To my shock, and pretty much everyone else's shock, V moves to Deacon's side and says, "I'll help."

I turn to Nitro and Dante. "I need space to work, and since the table's a lost cause, get the mess cleared off the kitchen counter. As for you"—I point at Draven and Riley—"get the rest of the equipment from the car and bring it into the kitchen. We'll leave Jeremy alone with his electronics. Hopefully he'll be able to salvage something."

Although, I have to admit, that doesn't look likely. My ex-boyfriend is currently in the middle of the living room, sorting through his broken electronics and emitting a low, mourning cry that I'm certain will have every wild animal in a fifty-mile radius trying to break down the door.

It takes about half an hour for us to get all the equipment in place and powered up. When I tell them I won't need any more help, Riley and Nitro take over the other half of the kitchen, preparing what Riley is calling the Breakfast of Hillains. V supervises, stating that she doesn't want to give Nitro the chance to set anything else on fire, and the twins head out the front door to do God only knows what.

Draven stays by my side.

"Do you think it will work?" he asks as I get ready to start making the serum.

I want to reassure him and tell him that it will. That my mom was a genius and that the instructions look easy enough to follow. But the little flop in my stomach reminds me that nothing is guaranteed. One misstep. One timing error. One drop too much or too little, and Mom's perfect formula could turn into a placebo. Or, worse, a poison.

But I'm not going to think about that right now. I'm going to focus on positive thoughts. I have to succeed so we can stop knocking Rebel out every time she so much as blinks.

"It has to work." I pull out the bag of safety gear from the chemistry lab. "It just has to."

None of the materials I'm working with are dangerous, but just in case, I put on goggles and latex gloves. Then I hand a set to Draven and he does the same.

"What?" he asks when I flash him a half smile.

"You look like a science geek."

He flashes me a cocky half smile of his own. "You know you love it."

I do. I really do.

When this is all over—when we fix Rebel, when we stop Rex, when we find my dad, when I've mourned my mom—I can take time to indulge in my fantasies about Draven in a science lab. But for now, I have work to do. Work that requires my complete focus and attention to detail.

I pull the formula up on Mom's phone and prepare the first step.

"What's wrong?" Draven asks.

"Nothing." I line up the chemicals I need for the first phase of the process. "Why?"

"You're frowning." He presses a latex-gloved fingertip to the spot between my eyebrows.

I force my forehead to relax.

"It's nothing," I insist. "It's just…"

He doesn't push me to finish, to explain, which is probably why I do.

"I've read over the formula at least twenty times since I found it. And one thing keeps standing out as really weird."

I fill a flask with 300 milliliters of distilled water.

"Yeah?" he asks.

"I don't know why it's supposed to take so long."

"What do you mean?"

"It always took Mom three days to make a new batch. But see, here." I point to the spot in step seven where she adds the orichalcum chromate to the serum and puts it all in the vacuum chamber for two days. "This compound is a retardant. It slows down the chemical reaction."

"And that means…?"

"If she added a catalyst instead, it would get done in a fraction of the time."

"Maybe it needs that time to, I don't know, cook or something."

I shake my head. "This isn't like putting cookie dough in the oven. More like putting it in the freezer instead of letting it thaw."

"Maybe your mom didn't know she could do that."

I give him a you've-got-to-be-kidding look. When it comes to powers-related chemistry, my mom is—was—unrivaled. If any of her hero-sponsored work could have been made public, she would have won a Nobel Prize for sure. There's no way she didn't know a catalyst would cut the production time by eighty percent.

So the question is…why? Why do it this way when there is a better, faster way available.

"She must have had a reason," I say, staring to measure out the chemicals I need. "I just can't figure out what it is."

And right now, I don't have time to wonder. Rex could find us at any moment. Or Rebel could wake up again and bring the whole cabin crashing down around us. Someone could get hurt, and I won't let that happen.

For now, I'll try it both ways. I'll make one batch per Mom's exact recipe and another using my shortcut.

One of them has to work.

✦ ✦ ✦

While the first batch is cooking, Draven and I join Dante and Deacon on the porch. The twins are sitting on the thick pine railing, eyes unfocused as they stare out into the woods. They seem to be content with the silence.

Good for them. Personally, I'm not so sure I want to be alone with my thoughts. But I don't want to break them away from theirs either, so I leave them be. Instead, Draven and I cross to the pair of Adirondack chairs on the other side of the porch and each sink into one. Which means, of course, that we also fall into our own pensive silence.

Without a task to occupy my mind, my thoughts drift. A series of images. Mom behind ushered into the courtroom. The look in her eyes when I set her free. The look in her eyes when the plasma blast hit her in the back. The helicopter.

Draven rubs his thumb in soft circles against my palm.

Somehow it makes everything a little more bearable.

The front door swings open with a bang. V storms out, car keys in hand, and a look of such utter rage on her face that it sends chills straight through me.

Riley and Nitro are right behind her, seemingly oblivious to her fury as they talk French toast recipes.

"What's up?" Draven asks, straightening from where he's slumped in the chair.

"These two idiots," she replies, gesturing over her shoulder, "insist that the world will end if we don't go get maple syrup and chocolate chips right now."

"It won't end," Riley argues, "but breakfast will be terrible."

Nitro shrugs. "Can't have a proper pancake bar without them two. Like trying to bake an apple pie with no apples."

"Do you think that's a good idea?" I ask. "I mean, going out."

Our faces have been plastered on every billboard and TV station in the Front Range. And since the security guard on campus caught us and radioed his boss, the whole law enforcement world—and the whole hero world—knows we're around.

V rolls her eyes as she shakes her head. "It's fine. The Gas 'n' Grocery in Bear Lake doesn't have a security camera."

"I don't think *anything* in Bear Lake has a security camera," Draven amends.

"We'll just fly in and out," Riley says with a huge smile at his own pun. The rest of us groan.

The three of them tromp down the porch steps and cross to the car. As they do, Nitro leans close to Riley and whispers something only he can hear. Riley laughs so hard that V spins around and spears him with a fierce glare.

Riley stands up straight and stops laughing...at least until she turns and he starts giggling.

I can't help exchanging a half-amused, half-concerned look with Draven. If this keeps up, the two of them will be lucky to make it back alive.

As the trio climbs into the car, Dante runs a hand over his head, flattening his fauxhawk. "God, I'm going stir-crazy in there."

"You could go with them," I suggest. "The first batch of serum won't be ready for a couple hours. There's nothing to do until then."

"I can't leave her when she's like this. What if—"

"Go," Deacon says so quietly I almost don't hear him. "We've got her."

"Yeah, man." Draven pushes to his feet and crosses to his cousin's side. "We'll watch over her. We won't let anything happen to your girl."

Dante hangs his head and roughs up the rest of his hair, and I can almost see him debating with himself. V is just closing the driver's side door when he lets out a frustrated growl.

"Hang on," he calls out to her, jumping down to the ground and jogging toward the car. "I'm coming with you."

As they drive away, I watch until the dust settles back onto the road.

"Is he okay?" I ask, joining the guys at the railing.

Draven nods. "He will be. As soon as we get Rebel under control."

"He takes it personally," Deacon adds. "Blames himself for what's happened to her." There is a long pause and then, "For what happened to Draven. And to me."

I take a long look at Deacon. He looks a lot better than when we first got him back. Some of the color has returned in his cheeks, and he's regained some of the weight his unwilling hunger strike took off. As he fills out, he's starting to look more like Dante again—minus the fauxhawk, of course.

It's amazing how much damage the heroes did to him in only a few days. How much they broke him. Draven, by comparison, is already almost recovered. The dichotomy has my mind firing with questions like why and how, and is the difference power related or something else entirely.

"Can I ask…" I start, but then realize I'm about to sound like a scientist more than a friend. And though I barely know him, Deacon *is* my friend. I rephrase my thoughts. "How did they get you? The heroes—did they grab you off the street?"

Draven doesn't move, but I can tell he's listening. He wants to know the answer too, probably more than I do.

"Hardly." Deacon lets out a weak, humorless laugh. "I walked right through their front door."

That is pretty much the last thing I expect him to say.

Why would he do something like that? It's practically suicide. He had to know what the heroes were doing to villains.
He had to know he wouldn't walk away from that.

"I don't understand."

"It was all part of the plan," Draven says. "Only he went
in without us, before we were ready, and never came back."

"I couldn't wait any longer," Deacon replies, his gaze still
focused somewhere off in the forest. "I couldn't risk it."

There's something about the dark implication in his tone
that makes me afraid to ask, "Couldn't risk *what?*"

Deacon turned his haunted eyes on me. "Her life."

"They had his girlfriend," Draven tells me, steeping forward
to place a comforting hand on his cousin's shoulder. "Becca."

Neither of us misses the flinch.

"We don't know how it happened," Deacon begins. "How
they got her. When she didn't call me after work and didn't
answer when I called her, I stopped by her house. We had
plans. She wouldn't stand me up without a reason. But she
wasn't there. Her parents hadn't seen her, and neither had any
of her friends. Disappearing like that—it wasn't like Becca.
She didn't do that. That's how I knew the heroes had taken
her. And that we needed to get her back."

My heart aches for him. I saw how messed up Dante was
over Deacon's capture and then Rebel's. I know how I felt
when I knew the heroes had Draven and my mom.

"We put together a plan to get her out," Draven says.

His words seem to snap Deacon out of whatever hell he'd
gone to, because he continues. "It went like clockwork at first.
ESH Labs was having orientation for new interns, and Rebel
got me on a list so that I could get in."

"You were in the new batch of interns?" I ask, startled.

He turns to look at me, like he's the one surprised by my question.

"I just…" I give him a weak smile. "I led the facility tour for the last bunch of interns. I must have seen you."

He nods. "I remember."

I try to think back, to cull my mind for some memory of anyone who stood out in that group. If Deacon was there, in that group, right in front of me, how could I not have noticed? A villain right under my nose.

The old Kenna would have been disgusted and terrified at the very thought.

Then again, the old Kenna would have been the first to run to Rex to turn in the infiltrator. It's that knowledge, more than anything else, that tells me what happened.

"Someone caught you."

I almost phrased it as a question, but considering the outcome—a.k.a. Deacon becoming the heroes' favorite torture test subject—I know it has to be true.

But I am still surprised by his answer.

"Yeah. Your mom."

My breath catches in my throat. "My mom turned you in?"

"No," he says. "She recognized me. She tried to help me, told me to get out of there. But I wouldn't listen. I wouldn't leave without Becca."

That makes way more sense. Mom had been friends with Deacon and Dante's mom, just like she was friends with Draven's mom. She'd recognized Draven immediately when she saw him, which means she must have kept up with the Coles over the years. So of course she would recognize

Deacon when she saw him in the lab. Of course she would try to get him out safely.

Deacon half smiles, mostly to himself. "I might have caused a bit of a scuffle."

"Might have?" Draven asks with a laugh.

"Next thing I knew, alarms were blaring and I was surrounded by pissed-off heroes."

I can definitely picture that. Three weeks ago, when Deacon got taken, I would have counted myself among them. And so would Riley.

The golden boy is very much on our team now, but I can tell he still harbors sympathies for the heroes. For his dad and the Collective. He might be working against them, but that doesn't mean he considers them the enemy yet.

It's only a matter of time before he finds out the truth. Before he realizes just how awful they are.

"They had powers like I couldn't believe." Deacon runs his palms over the knees of his jeans. "Not much my ability to manipulate water could do in a situation like that, unless I wanted to drown every last one of us."

I find the courage to ask the question that is hanging heavy in the air. "Did you...find her?"

The agony on Deacon's face is all the answer we need. He suffered more than just physical torture at Rex's hands. The psychological torture had to have been as bad or worse.

No wonder he is still such a wreck.

I glance at Draven. The anguish in his clear-blue eyes may only be a fraction of what Deacon is feeling, but I know the pain is the same. The source is the same.

Draven could make it all go away. With just one deep stare,

one gentle twist of the memories that haunt Deacon's dreams, he could pull them right out of his mind.

But he won't. He wouldn't mess with his friends' memories without their permission. And Deacon has made it clear that he isn't going to ask.

Some pain you have to hold on to. Some pain makes you stronger. I know I'm going to remember watching that chopper blow up with my mom's body in it for the rest of my life. And I'll fight anyone who tries to take away that memory, hideous though it is. Partly because it was the last moment I will ever have with my mom. But also because it fuels my determination to bring Rex and the heroes down for good.

Pain is a powerful motivator.

In my back pocket, the alarm on my mom's phone dings with the timer that I set.

"Time to add the next reagent."

I head back inside. Hopefully, when V and the other guys get back, the immunity serum will be ready to try.

And if we're really, really lucky, it will actually work.

CHAPTER 10

Three hours later and I'm sitting by the side of the bed, my hand shaking as I bring a syringe full of immunity serum toward Rebel's arm. She's out cold—she woke up just as Dante got back, but the serum wasn't ready so Draven put her back out as quickly and painlessly as he could.

And now it's go time. Now we find out if my version of the serum will work.

The knowledge that it might not makes an already stressful situation even worse.

I've had to inject my own immunity serum a few times over the years. When Mom was out of the country for a conference. When she got snowed in at some big-wig science retreat in Jackson Hole. When I went away to summer camp before eighth grade. That was bad enough.

But trying to inject someone else with it? My mind races with unrealistic possibilities of what might go wrong. I might hit a vein or, God forbid, an artery. Or I might hit bone—that would be horribly painful, not to mention make it impossible to deliver the right dose of the serum.

These thoughts are enough to have me wavering, the hand holding the syringe freezing inches from Rebel's arm. The absolute last thing I want to do is hurt my best friend. But at the same time, I want to stop her from being able to hurt anyone else. At least until we can figure out what the hell her dad did to her.

"What's the hold-up?" Dante asks from his spot on the other side of the bed.

He told everyone but me and Draven to get out of the room and is watching everything that happens with eagle eyes. V refused to go, of course, and is standing guard by the door. Just in case.

Dante kneels at Rebel's side, holding her hand and petting it like she's a sick child. All he wants is his girlfriend back. And I'm the only one who can give her to him. It's that thought that finally gets me moving.

"Nothing," I say, leaning forward to jab the needle into her arm before I have any more second or third or fourth thoughts.

I squeeze, letting the serum flow into her bloodstream as I say a little prayer to the chemistry gods that it works like it's supposed to. Like I think it will.

"How long does it take?" Draven asks.

"I don't know," I answer honestly. "Once Mom started me on it, I was never off. So I don't know how long it takes for the initial dose to kick in."

V raises a sardonic brow. "Care to hazard a guess, science girl?"

"Considering how much I used," I say, ignoring the nickname as I try to calculate the answer to her question. "I would think only a matter of minutes."

"We'll give it ten," she says.

I don't ask what she's planning on doing at eleven.

And then we're waiting, watching, hoping that when Rebel wakes up, she'll do so without her powers. Since Draven's power knocked her out, it's possible that when the immunity kicks in she'll regain consciousness. But it's also possible that his power caused a physical reaction that wouldn't be retroactively affected by her immunity.

Sometimes ten minutes passes in the blink of an eye. Sometimes it feels like an eternity, like your whole life is passing by in those six hundred seconds.

Waiting to find out if I've fixed Rebel is definitely the latter.

To pass the time, and because I'm terrified I somehow did something wrong, I trace back through all the steps of the formula, double-checking that I hadn't missed anything.

But no matter how many times I run through it, it all seems to add up. Even taking the shortcut that Mom apparently didn't want to take, the end result should be the same.

So what's taking so long then? Why won't she wake up and show us whether it worked or not? With each minute that passes, I get more and more nervous. I try to hide it—nobody needs a leader who freaks out—but Draven notices. Of course he does. He doesn't make a big deal of it, but suddenly he's right there, his chest pressed against my back, his hand stroking the side of my neck. That's all it takes for me to steady myself, to refocus. Then I start working the problem.

If this doesn't work, then does that mean the other batch won't work either? What will we do then?

A powers-neutralizing helmet would be the first choice. Of course that's a carefully guarded hero secret, so getting our hands on one would be no easy task. Then again, we haven't shied away from a challenge yet. Whatever it takes, we won't stop until Rebel is Rebel again. Or at least not trying to kill us.

"I'm done waiting," Dante says. "Wake her up."

We exchange a round of nervous glances. We're all afraid that it won't work and we'll have to go back to the drawing board. But better to find out whether or not the serum worked instead of sitting around worrying. At least that's what the scientist in me says, and I'm putting her in control, not the scared little girl who is desperately afraid that she's only made things worse.

Dante scoots to the side so Draven can reach Rebel's head. I watch as my guy reaches for my best friend's forehead, ready to use his biomanipulation power to undo whatever he did to render her unconscious in the first place.

Before he can touch her, her eyes flutter open. I suck in an anxious breath. Wait for the hatred, the alarm, the power that runs through her like a geyser.

Her eyes grow wide, her skin pale, but nothing flies across the room. It worked!

Then she screams and everything goes to hell.

The whole room seems to start flying at once.

Dante goes sailing into the nearest wall.

The door slams in V's face.

The lamp next to the bed crashes to the floor.

Shit. It didn't work. She still has her power. And obviously isn't afraid to use it.

Maybe we didn't give the immunity serum enough time to sink all the way in. Maybe if we give it a few more minutes…

"Draven!" Dante yells as he scrambles back to her side, pinning her hands back to the bed. "Put her back out!"

114

He goes flying back across the room.

"I'm trying," Draven answers.

His hands are on Rebel's shoulder, and he's focusing his power on her. But nothing is happening.

V pounds on the door. "Let me in, assholes!"

"I can't." Draven looks at me, his eyes full of panic. "My power isn't working on her."

My stomach plummets. My immunity serum doesn't need time to kick it. It's working already. It hasn't taken Rebel's power from her as planned, but it apparently has made her immune to the powers of others.

I've just made things about a thousand times worse.

Between V's fists on the door, Dante's shouting, and every object in the room whirlpooling through the air, I'm on the verge of hyperventilating.

I have no idea what to do.

Then, in an instant, every object falls to the ground. A strange combination of terror and relief works its way through me.

Dante stops yelling, and only the echoes of V's pounding fill the silent room.

At least until Rebel speaks. "Why the hell am I tied to a bed?"

"To make it harder for you to kill us," Draven answers.

Her forehead crunches into a frown.

"Kill you?" She sounds utterly confused. "Why would I do that? You're my best friends."

The rage that had burned in her tone since she woke up in our custody seems to have vanished as quickly as it had come. The constant tension in her body is gone, replaced by a sense of panic.

Her cloudy eyes scan the room. She sees Dante pushing to his feet against the far wall. "Baby," she cries out, "what's going on?"

Tears spring to my eyes. "Rebel?"

"Kenna! I don't—" She shakes her head sharply. "Where am I?"

Dante is by the bed in an instant. But before he can kneel at Rebel's side, Draven throws an arm across his chest to keep him back.

"Dude!" Dante snarls at Draven and shoves at his arm. "Let me by!"

"What's wrong?" I ask.

Draven shakes his head, his eyes fastened on Rebel's face. "It could be a trap."

"A trap?" Rebel sounds horrified. "Guys, come on. It's me."

Dante elbows Draven in the ribs and shoves him out of the way. Then he's diving for the rope knotted around Rebel's wrists while his cousin doubles over, gasping for breath.

Part of me wants to agree with Dante. The part of me that wants to believe that my best friend is back and my immunity serum snapped her out of whatever the hell Rex did to her. I want so badly for those things to be true that I would do almost anything to believe it.

But another part of me, the scientist part, knows that even the slightest bias can alter the observed results of an experiment. And I am more than slightly biased in my desire to fix Rebel.

I can't rely on personal observation. I have to leave the scientist in charge.

Jumping into action, I yank Dante away from the bed.

"Draven's right," I tell him. "We have to make sure."

"No way," he barks, struggling against my grip.

"It's better to be safe than sorry," I tell him. "Think about how much worse it will be for Rebel if we have to try to wrestle her into submission again. She could get hurt, really hurt, and I know you don't want that to happen."

He stares at me, like he's trying to come up with a valid argument.

In the end, he doesn't have to.

"Listen to Kenna, babe," Rebel tells him. "I have no clue what's going on here, but she's usually right."

"Usually?" I affect a fake-insulted tone.

She smiles at me, equal parts terrified and relieved. "*Almost* always. Except when it comes to fashion."

I smile back, relieved because she's sounding more and more like my Rebel with every second that passes. "That's better."

"So, how do we test her?" Dante asks, clearly impatient to set Rebel free.

That is the question. How do you figure out what's going on in someone's mind? If we had a thought reader in the group, it would be easy.

Then again, if she really is immune to other powers, a thought reader wouldn't be able to penetrate her mind anyway.

Same with Draven's ability to mess with memory.

"What's the last thing you remember?" Draven asks her.

She closes her eyes. "I remember…leaving Riley's apartment."

"Yes, we split up in the alley," I say, trying to prompt her memory. "The heroes were closing in."

"I…led the zeroes away," she says slowly. Her eyes flash open. "Kenna! You have a power!"

I grin at her. "I do."

"If I weren't tied to a bed right now, I would hug the shit out of you."

Nothing gets more Rebel than that. I exchange a look with Draven. He nods.

"I never pass up a chance for a suffocating Rebel hug."

In a flash, Dante has her untied and on her feet. Then the three of us are wrapped in an epic hug that is long overdue.

I slip out of the hug, and Dante kisses Rebel like he thought he would never get to kiss her again. My arms slip around Draven's waist, and I bury my face in his chest. Rebel is back, and we have the immunity serum formula. Tears of relief stream down my cheeks—things are finally going right for a change—and my emotions flood out of me.

"Come on," Dante says, an arm slung over Rebel's shoulders. "Let's tell everyone the good news."

We walk into the main room of the cabin, which is mostly still a disaster from when Rebel got loose earlier.

"What happened in here?" she asks.

Jeremy looks up from his workstation, his eyes dark with accusation. "You did." He doesn't look like he's going to forgive her anytime soon.

"Me?" Rebel scans the cabin, mouth slightly slack with shock. "I did this? I… Wait…" She walks over to the crushed dining room table. "I remember this. I remember—"

She freezes. Her breath catches, and her eyes are wider than the time I told her I was actually going out with Jeremy.

"I remember," she says again, her voice faint. Then she whirls toward me. "Oh shit. I called my dad."

"What? When?"

"Earlier," she says. "When I got loose. Shit, shit, shit. I told him where we are. Or at least as much as I know about where we are. Enough for him to figure it out."

We all stand there frozen with shock before the reality of the situations sinks in. It's been hours since Rebel got free. Hours that Rex has had to put the pieces together. It's only a matter of time before his goons show up and try to take us into custody. Or worse. There's always a worse.

"We need to get out of here!" Draven shouts to the entire cabin, already reaching for my hand and racing for the kitchen. He shoves open the door and shouts at Riley and Nitro, "Now!"

Dante sprints down the hall for the bedroom where Deacon is resting.

V drags Jeremy away from his electronics, which he is desperately trying to shove into his backpack.

"No time, HB2," V tells him. "Don't make me throw you over my shoulder."

Everyone bursts into the living room at the same time. I let go of Draven and grab onto Rebel's hand as I lead the race out the front door.

"What's that sound?" Riley asks, an instant before the van explodes.

The *whomp, whomp, whomp* of chopper blades pulses through the air. Multiple chopper blades.

"Damn it," V shouts above the roar of the burning vehicle. "It's too late. We go on foot."

As one unit, we beeline for the forest's edge. The trees and undergrowth should provide cover from the heroes above. Unless they have infrared.

Who am I kidding? Of course they have infrared.

"Wait!" I stop.

"No waiting," V yells. "Keep moving."

Ignoring her, I turn to Nitro. "Can you fireball the cabin from here?"

He looks at me like I'm insane. "You want me to blow it up?"

"No," I say. "I want you to make them think we're still in there."

Nitro nods with a wicked grin. "I feel you."

With more precision than I've ever seen him possess, he lobs several pale-pink fireballs through a broken window. The cabin fills with a faint glow. Hopefully, if anyone is scanning for heat signatures, they'll see a bunch of warm bodies inside.

That should buy us some time. We need all the head start we can get.

We're about to turn away, to continue deeper into the forest, when the sound of the choppers becomes clearer. I watch in horror as a pair of white helicopters painted with the insignia of the Denver PD fly into the clearing around the cabin.

I can't move, can't look away. Either Rex really does have everyone involved in the manhunt for us, or he is camouflaging his forces as ordinary cops.

Suddenly there's a whistling sound as something flies out of the lead chopper.

A heartbeat later, the cabin disintegrates in a burst of light and flame.

CHAPTER 11

Ican't breathe. I can't breathe. IcantbreatheIcantbreathe
Icantbreathe.

Something heavy is on my back, pressing me into the ground,
and I can't move. I try to push it off, try to pull some air into my
tortured lungs, but whatever's on top of me is so not budging.

"Just a little longer, Kenna," Draven whispers in my ear, and
that's when I realize *he's* what's on top of me. "It's almost over."

I try to answer him, but I don't have enough air to form
words. I stop struggling as it all comes back to me. The sound
of helicopters. The firebombed cabin. Draven throwing himself over me and knocking me to the ground as the world
exploded around us.

With that understanding comes a calmness, and I push
against him a little, to get enough space to let my lungs reinflate.

"Rex…bombed the cabin?" I grate out as the roar of a
helicopter's rotors comes close again.

"He's doing more than that," Draven answers grimly. "He's
burning the forest all around it."

Sure enough, there's another high-pitched whining noise followed closely by a second explosion. Draven covers me again
as I hear the crackle of wood catching on fire all around us.

"We have to get out of here!" I yell, terrified more of burning alive at this point than of being blown up. But that explosion—and the ensuing smoke—must have been what Draven was waiting for, because he's up and pulling me to my feet before I even manage to finish the sentence.

"Run!" he shouts, like I have a choice or something. But I don't. His hand is around my wrist and he's running full out, dragging me toward the trees in front of us as I struggle to keep up.

The others are scrambling along with us. I can see the vague shadows of them through the smoke, can hear them coughing as they run.

All around us, the trees and undergrowth are catching on fire. It's been a long, dry summer. It makes me wonder— even as we run—how Rex plans to explain this. I know we're isolated, but if he doesn't get the fire out quickly, half this mountain is going to burn.

And if we don't escape, we'll burn right along with it.

Draven must have the same thought, because he yells, "Faster, Kenna! Faster! We've got to move."

I don't bother trying to answer him. I save my breath for the run. At this pace, I need every ounce of oxygen I can get.

As we tear through the forest, I can hear the helicopter above us, trying to keep pace though the trees that are giving us decent cover. I can also hear the shouts of the hero troops as they get boots on the ground and start tracking us. It ter-rifies me.

We've been through hell the last few weeks, have seen the most awful things imaginable. My mother *died*. And still, I think this is the most scared I've ever been. Rex is completely out of control, and I can't imagine what he's going to do when he realizes we weren't in that cabin. Can't imagine what he'll do if he actually gets his hands on one of us *alive*.

That spurs me to run just a little faster, though I didn't think that was possible even a few minutes ago. I'm using every ounce of strength I have to keep up with Draven—to lead the others out of danger—but I know I don't have long before I collapse. I'm in good shape, but there's a difference between running and sprinting. What we're doing is long-distance sprinting, and it's absolutely exhausting. Adrenaline will get us only so far.

"Over here," Draven yells to the others, before we zig around a rock formation and then down into a small ravine.

The others follow without question. "Are you sure this is a good idea?" I gasp out, looking around while we run. If they catch us down here, we'll have nowhere to go. Suddenly I know exactly what that old expression *shooting fish in a barrel* means. And I have no desire to play fish for Rex Malone.

"I'm hoping the rocks will block their heat signature sensors," he yells back as he pulls me along. The ravine is narrow, so we're running one in front of the other, single file, but Draven still refuses to let go of my hand.

Not that I'm complaining. Right now, his palm is my lifeline.

"What if it doesn't?" I ask.

"If it doesn't, then we're screwed."

There isn't much to say after that. And not just because I don't have the breath for it.

The ravine is long, thank God. Probably a couple of miles,

and we work our way through it like we're going for a gold medal at the Olympics. We don't stop until we get to the rock wall that signifies the end. By that time, Draven and Dante are the only two who can breathe at all. The rest of us are seconds away from collapsing in one big dog pile on the ground. Even V is bent over, her hands braced on her knees as she sucks in huge gasps of air.

"Stay here," Draven orders as he starts to climb the wall, grabbing hold wherever he can find purchase.

"Where...are you...going?" I manage to gasp out.

"I want to look around, see what's up there."

The sound of helicopters is fainter here, more distant. As if Rex is concentrating his search closer to the cabin. Good.

But I'm not arguing with Draven's caution. We can't afford to get careless or underestimate Rex.

"I'm going with you," Dante says, beginning to climb right next to him.

Rebel whimpers and clutches at him. I grab on to her and pull her back. We need to know what's up there sooner rather than later, and right now the two of them are the only ones physically capable of climbing. The rest of us need a few minutes to recover.

"Oi! Be careful," Nitro tells them between hacking coughs. "Rex wants us all dead."

Draven nods but doesn't say anything. Neither does Dante. Then again, what is there to say? Nitro's only stating the obvious.

"My dad tried to kill me," Riley whines between pants.

Oh, yeah. I guess there's still that...

Deacon, who has gotten his breath back faster than the

rest of us who *weren't* recently tortured by Rex, snorts. "You didn't actually think he *wouldn't* try to kill us?"

"Well, you guys, yeah." Riley gestures vaguely at our group. "But Rebel? *Me?*"

He looks so bewildered that I almost feel sorry for him. No, wait, I actually do. He's had the rug pulled out from under him as much if not more than the rest of us.

"I'm his favorite." His voice sounds like it's about to crack. "I was supposed to be his successor. I'm—"

"A traitor," V says bluntly.

"What?"

V pushes upright. "He probably wants you dead as much as he wants Kenna's head on a spike. Maybe even more."

"Thanks for the visual," I mutter.

"Hey!" Nitro glares at V as he moves a little closer to Riley and wraps a comforting arm around his shoulders. "Don't say that shite to him."

"What? You want me to sugarcoat it? Men like Rex don't take betrayal lightly. As far as he's concerned, Riley is acceptable collateral damage."

The thought makes my stomach roll. I know it's true, have known it was true since I watched that newscast with Rebel dressed up like a clone of Mrs. Malone. Rex will do anything to anyone if it means getting one step closer to his goal. But still, I feel bad that Riley has just figured out how disposable he is to his own father.

I can't imagine what that must feel like.

Whatever problems Mom and I had over the years, I always knew—deep down in my core—that everything she did was meant to protect me. She put me first. Always.

Just like she did in the courtroom. She sacrificed herself to save me. Something Rex would never do.

"It's not like it's a surprise," Rebel tells him when she can finally breathe enough to string words together. "Dad's a narcissistic douche nozzle. He'll crush anyone who gets in his way. Even blood."

"I get that," Riley says, leaning in to Nitro for comfort. "I do. But still, he tried to kill me."

"He tried to kill *all* of us," V reminds him.

"Well, yeah, but you're *villains*. I'm...*me*."

"Sorry to break the news to you," Jeremy tells him. "But it looks like being you isn't all that special."

Deacon chuckles.

Nitro shoots Jeremy a murderous glare, then turns his attention back to Riley. "Your father is a bloody idiot," he says, stroking Riley's back soothingly.

"But he's not," Riley argues. "That's the point. My father is really smart and really disciplined. He doesn't act on impulse. He thinks before acting. When he firebombed that cabin expecting Rebel and I were inside—knowing we were inside—when he did that, he wasn't acting on emotion. He knew what would happen to us, and he..." He shakes his head. "He did it anyway."

For the first time, the shock in Riley's voice gives way to anger.

I'm glad, because sad, heartbroken Riley was killing me. As much as I always thought he was a bit of a tool, he really is just a little boy on the inside.

Sometimes on the outside too.

It sucks that Rex has blasted away his son's innocence, but it's about time Riley grew up.

Before any of us can respond, Draven shouts down, "I'm at the rim, but I can't see anything. I'm going to climb out and take a look around."

"Right behind you, Cousin," Dante calls out.

"Be careful," I whisper, not loud enough for anyone else to hear.

While my emotions want him back on the ravine floor with the rest of us, I know that none of us are safe right now. We're basically sitting ducks, and he's trying to find us a way out. He's only doing what he has to in order to get us out of here alive.

That doesn't mean I like being separated by even this small distance. If I had the upper body strength, I would be at his side, looking out for him while he's looking out for all of us.

Rebel loops an elbow through mine as she watches Dante finish the climb to the top next to Draven. She's as tense as I am, her arm around mine more a vise than a comfort. But I don't mind. I can barely feel it, if I'm being honest. I'm too wrapped up in my concern for Draven.

I suck in a breath as he peeks his head above the ravine and looks around. Then pulls himself out. Dante starts to do the same, but Draven gestures for him to stay put. Dante glances down at us—at me—and he doesn't look happy. He doesn't want Draven shouldering all the risk any more than I do. But he stays where he is.

The next five minutes are some of the tensest of my life. I barely breathe, listening, jumping at the slightest rustle of pine boughs, the clatter of tumbling pebbles. Every little sound feels like a blaring alarm.

I try to tell myself that no one is up there, that Rex's

soldiers haven't made it this far this fast, that Draven's just being cautious. But neither my head nor my heart are buying it. Not when we've been discussing what a psychopath Rex Malonc is. And not when Draven is out there alone.

Rex has proven he isn't above killing his legitimate son. He certainly wouldn't hesitate to gun down his illegitimate one.

Suddenly, we hear a shout followed by a crash.

"Dray?" Dante calls out.

"What was that?" I yell up, but Dante's too busy scrambling out of the ravine to answer me.

My heart explodes. Something's wrong. Like Rex wrong.

I glance at the others, all of whom look as terrified as I feel.

"Get Nitro up there, now!" I tell Riley, who looks like he's recovered enough to be able to fly. I want to be the one to go up, to see what's going on. But in a fight, Nitro's power is way more helpful than mine.

Riley doesn't argue. Instead, he picks Nitro up and pretty much tosses him onto his back before shooting straight up to the top of the ravine. They sail over the edge and then I can't see anything anymore.

Screw this.

I start up the rock face, suddenly wishing I'd taken my mom up on her invitations to take a climbing lesson or two. The others climb too. V and Deacon are in the lead—they're way better at this kind of thing than the rest of us—but Rebel, Jeremy, and I are holding our own. Turns out desperation and adrenaline are a good combination.

Before any of us get to the top, Draven is back. He doesn't look surprised to see us climbing and drops to the ground and reaches both hands down to pull me up. Dante does the same for Rebel, while Riley and Nitro help out Deacon and Jeremy. V climbs out unassisted.

"What happened?" I demand as soon as we're standing. There isn't much light left in the sky, but Nitro has a small fireball burning between his hands and I can see well enough to make out blood on Draven's mouth. And his knuckles.

"There were three hero special forces scouting the area." He shrugs his shoulder. "We took care of them."

He doesn't elaborate and I don't ask him to. Instead, I pull him close and concentrate on the feel of him against me—the feel of him safe in my arms. Of me safe in his. At least for now.

He holds me for a second, then pulls away to hand something to Jeremy. "Can you do something with these?"

Jeremy holds up what looks like a wired communications earpiece, the kind with the curly cords that security goons wear. "I can get into their channel. If we can listen in on their chatter, maybe we can figure out what's going on."

"What's going on," Dante says softly and furiously, "is we're being hunted."

Rebel nods. "Which means we need to get out of here before the next wave shows up."

"To where?" Riley asks. "We don't even know where we are."

V pulls out her phone and starts typing. "Working on it."

"Can't your echolocation figure that out?" Jeremy asks.

V doesn't look up from her phone. "I can draw you a perfectly to-scale map of the surrounding five acres if you'd like," she says, "right down to the fifty-seven highly trained hero SWAT operatives who are currently crunching through the woods, but I can't place the map in context." She raises a brow. "Can you do better?"

Jeremy snorts. "Of course."

V look up. "Oh really?"

"I checked my compass app when we were still in the ravine." He waggles his phone at her. "And I pulled up a map." He points over his left shoulder. "North is that way, but our best bet for getting off this mountain quickly is south."

He starts moving fast in the opposite direction from where he pointed, and for a second, we all stare at him—or rather his retreating back—in shock. Who is this new, take-charge Jeremy, and where has he been hiding? I glance around the group, waiting to see if anyone is going to follow the techno-path down the mountain.

Finally, Draven shrugs and starts walking.

The rest of us follow, a ragged, worn-out group traipsing through the woods. Between Jeremy's tech skills, V's echolocation, and everyone else's fighting abilities, we might just make it out of here alive.

Despite the danger we're in, I can't help grinning when Nitro whispers, "He did hear us when we said V knows seventeen ways to kill a man with her bare hands, right? We were really clear on that."

"You know Jeremy," I reply. "He likes to live on the edge."

Several of the others laugh, and for a moment we can forget the danger fast on our heels. Sometimes a moment is all it takes.

CHAPTER 12

Three hours later we finally make it to a campsite toward the top edge of the foothills. We're all tired and hungry and miserable, but at least we're all alive so I'm not complaining. Especially when Jeremy spots a giant SUV in the campsite's parking lot with the Forest Service emblem emblazoned on the side.

"Give me a minute to figure out the alarm code," he says, pulling his cell phone out of his pocket and doing God only knows what with it.

V brushes past him. "Like we need the code."

She reaches into her boot, pulls out a tool, and seconds later, she's in the driver's seat. The alarm blares for less than three seconds before she does something to cut it off.

"Get in," she orders as the SUV roars to life.

We don't have to be told twice. Jeremy takes shotgun—for logistical reasons, he insists—and though it's only a seven-seater, the rest of us manage to cram in the back. Jeremy's giving V navigational directions from the map on his phone before the rest of us can even fasten our seat belts.

The two of them are scarily efficient when they work together, though I'm not stupid enough to say that out loud.

V may put up with Jeremy's nonsense, but I'm pretty sure she'd cut me without a second thought. There doesn't seem to be any love lost between us.

And who am I to judge? From her perspective, I'm probably a huge part of the reason her boys are in danger. If our roles were reversed, I might feel the same way.

We don't say anything as we speed through the night for what feels like the millionth time in the last few weeks. If this is what life on the lam is like, I don't envy lifetime fugitives.

I have no clue what everyone else is doing as the dark zooms past, but I can't stop thinking about where we're supposed to go from here. What we're supposed to do. And how.

We need to stop Rex, obviously, need to keep him from doing any more damage. But right now, I don't know how we're supposed to do that. He's ahead of us at nearly every turn, and the violence is escalating with every confrontation. A part of me is terrified that not only are we going to end up dead, but that we'll die for nothing. Die without changing anything.

That scares me more than anything else.

All of this can't be in vain.

I don't know how long we drive before we end up in the parking lot of a diner. The mountains and foothills are far behind us, and we're so far into the plains that I can only see the very tips of the snowcapped peaks. The sun is coming up though, the sky in the distance a hazy orange-pink that promises daylight soon. I'm not sure if that's a good thing or a bad one at this point.

As soon as we make it into the diner, I head for the bathroom. Not because I have to pee, but because I need a few moments to myself. A few seconds where I can just breathe after the claustrophobic crunch of the backseat. As the only child of a single mom, I'm not used to being around so many people all of the time. Sometimes it wears on me.

I just need a few seconds alone in the bathroom to get my sanity back.

I've barely splashed water on my face when Rebel comes in.

She flashes a small smile at me before disappearing into one of the stalls, and I take the extra minute to try to compose myself. To try to hide the dread and the disillusionment that's pressing in on me from every side. Too many people are counting on me to figure it out—the people squished into the huge booth out there in the diner, and the countless villains that Rex is hell-bent on annihilating. I can't let them see how scared I am of letting them down.

But this is Rebel—the real Rebel, not that automaton Rex created—and all it takes is one look at my face while she's washing her hands to have her pulling me in for a hug.

"You okay?" she asks. "You look like hell."

I consider lying, but only for a heartbeat. "I feel like hell."

"I'm sorry," she says against my hair. "My father—"

"Is not your responsibility." I lean back to look her in the eye. "What he does isn't your fault, and neither is what he made you do. There's nothing for you to apologize for."

She pulls away from me, turning to look at herself in the mirror. She scrubs her hands through her newly brown hair until it's spiking up in all different directions. Then she stands there, staring blankly at herself, like she doesn't recognize her own reflection.

"I remember everything, Kenna." She tears up before blinking rapidly. "I tried to kill you. I tried to kill *everyone*. And then I called my dad and told him where we were. If I hadn't, we wouldn't be—"

"It's. Not. Your. Fault." I turn her back to face me, look her dead in the eye as I say the words. "You were brainwashed."

Her face twists in pain. "But how? How could I let him do that to me?"

"You don't *let* someone brainwash you. It just happens."

"I must have let him. He had to get close enough to talk to me." She shakes her head and looks up at the gray ceiling tiles as she fights away the tears. "How could he convince me to do those things? To believe him? You know how much I—"

Her control breaks. Rebel has always been the strong one, the tough one, the one who took on bigger and badder heroes when they wanted to mess with us. It's both weird and reassuring to finally be the one holding her up.

"We'll figure it out," I promise her. "But I promise you, we are not going to let him do that to you again."

She wipes at her tears, sniffling through a watery smile. "That's what Dante says. I'm not sure what I did to deserve the two of you."

With a twist of her fingers she has a paper towel floating out of the dispenser and into her hand. I'm not complaining about the power I've got—after a lifetime of powerlessness, I'm not dumb enough to be ungrateful—but it would be so much cooler to have a more physical power like hers. Telekinesis would be pretty awesome.

She's blowing her nose before it hits me.

"Rebel! You just used your power!"

She looks at me like I'm nuts. "Yeah. So?"

She crumples up the paper towel and shoots it at the

wastebasket near the door, sending it twirling through the air like something out of a Disney movie before letting it land in the bin.

"I gave you immunity serum. That's what brought you out of the brainwashing." Which was weird because I only thought it was going to take her powers and stop her from trying to kill us every two seconds. "So how are you still able to use your telekinesis?"

My mind is whirling at the possibilities.

All those years, Mom's immunity serum hid my power. Why isn't it hiding Rebel's? Is there something different about her? Or something different about me? Maybe I should run a small-scale experiment with some of the others. Maybe the results vary depending on the individual super. Or the specific power. Or whether one's a hero or a villain. The possible variables are almost limitless.

"That doesn't make sense," she tells me. "You used the same immunity serum your mom gave you, right? The same one that took your power away?"

"Yeah, of course. I—" I break off, because that's not necessarily the truth. I used my mother's formula with one exception. Substituting a catalyst for a retardant shouldn't have affected the results. But what if it had? What if that subtle change had actually made an exponential difference in the function of the serum?

Only one way to find out.

Focusing my power energy on my hands, I send a spray of electricity straight at Rebel.

"What the hell?" she barks, ducking to the floor to avoid the sparks.

But she didn't need to. My electricity moved faster than her, and before she hit the ground I saw it warp around her like a stream around a rock.

"You're immune," I say. "But you still have your power."

As she gets back to her feet, I see it.

"And you still have your mark."

She examines herself in the mirror, confirming my observation.

When Mom gave me the serum, it not only suppressed my power. It made my villain mark disappear too. I understand now why she did it. If anyone in the hero world had seen my mark, they would have known—or at least suspected—that maybe my mom wasn't who she said she was. And they would have been right.

So why didn't my serum erase Rebel's mark? Why didn't it suppress her power?

"Kenna? Earth to Kenna?" Rebel waves a hand in front of my face, but I'm lost in thought, following the logic trail.

I reconsider the facts. My serum left Rebel with her powers while still making her immune to other people's powers. My serum broke the brainwashing. Which can only mean...

"Oh my God." I stare at her wide-eyed as the truth occurs to me. "You weren't brainwashed!"

She looks horrified. "What? Of course I was brainwashed! I would never do any of the things I did if Rex wasn't controlling me—"

"Exactly! He was controlling you. Not brainwashing you. *Controlling* you!"

"I don't understand."

But the look on her face tells me she's beginning to.

136

"Come on." I grab her hand and pull her out the door. "We need to tell the others."

"What exactly are you saying?" she asks as we make our way over to the corner booth where the others are sitting.

I don't think the booth is designed to fit nine people, but between the curved bench seat and a pair of chairs stolen from another table, somehow we manage.

"You said yourself that you can't believe you did the things you did," I tell her as I drop into the empty spot next to Draven. His hand immediately goes to my thigh, his thumb rubbing a spot right above my knee. It's a gesture meant to soothe as well as show support, and I take a moment to shoot him a smile before racing ahead with my new theory. "Real brainwashing means you have control over your actions, that you're doing what you do because you *believe* the lies. You *believe* in the cause. Did you?"

"Of course not," she says, her face paler than I've ever seen it. "I mean, I know what I did. At the time, it felt like I believed that Rex was good and you guys were bad."

She breaks off, and Dante smoothes a hand over her shoulders.

"But I didn't *really* believe. The instant you gave me that immunity serum, that belief went away. I suddenly remembered that you were my best friend and that Dante was my boyfriend. I'm so sorry for all the terrible things I said to all of you."

Tears stream down her cheeks, and I feel awful for making her relive this, especially in front of everyone. If it weren't vitally important—literally—I would make her stop.

"As soon as the serum hit my bloodstream, I knew you were good, knew that I would *never* want to hurt you."

"Kenna's right," Draven says slowly, his thumb still rubbing small circles on my leg. "That doesn't sound like brainwashing. It sounds like outright control."

"Especially considering the immunity serum changed everything," I say. "You snapped out of whatever it was Rex was doing to you. *And* you still have your powers."

"She still has her powers?" Jeremy demands. "I thought that was impossible. The serum you took—"

"Masked my own power," I finish for him.

I think he's still more than a little miffed that I never told him about the immunity serum. Since I'm not an electronic gadget, it wasn't like he could try out his power on me anyway. It never came up. Plus, Mom would have killed me if I went around telling people about the serum. Only Rebel knew, and I made sure Mom never found out she did.

"Pardon me for being ignorant here," V says, leaning forward to brace her elbows on the table, "but what the hell are you all talking about?"

Oh right. V is a late addition to our group. She doesn't know the history.

"Dr. Swift cooked up a serum that made someone immune to other people's powers," Draven explains. "For a long time, that's why Kenna thought she was taking it. To protect her because she was powerless."

"But we recently found out," Jeremy says, way too excited to let Draven finish, "that the serum actually kept Kenna's power locked away. Even made her villain mark disappear."

Jeremy reaches across the table, pushes my hair back to show the newly revealed mark behind my left ear.

"We dated for more than a year," he says, sounding insulted, "and I had no clue."

Draven glares at him, though I'm not sure if it's because Jeremy is touching me or because he's reminding everyone that we dated for that long. A tiny part of me likes the idea of Draven caring enough to be jealous, even if he has no reason to be.

I reach under the table and take his hand.

"My mom's version did both. Made me immune *and* masked my power."

"But your version didn't mask Rebel's power?" Dante asks.

Rebel jerks her head at the collection of condiments in the center of the table. The red plastic bottle of ketchup slides easily to the other side.

"And my mark is still here." She twists her head to the right, showing everyone the spot beneath her right ear.

"Did you change the formula?" Riley asks.

"Not exactly," I reply. "We didn't have time to wait around the three days my mom took, so I took a shortcut. It must have changed something."

"I'm still immune to powers," Rebel says, like she's trying to reassure me that the formula worked.

"Are we sure?" Deacon asks.

"I couldn't use my biomanipulation on her," Draven says. "Once she had the serum, I couldn't knock her back out."

"Maybe you were still too weak," Riley suggests.

Draven shakes his head. "I wasn't."

"But maybe—"

Nitro ends the debate by lobbing a small fireball straight at Rebel's head.

"What the hell?" Dante exclaims, using his wind to bat it away at the same time as Deacon uses his water power to douse it.

"Draven, use your power on her," I say. "Try to manipulate her memories for the last ten minutes."

"Don't you dare!" Rebel says, pressing herself back in her chair. "I don't want anyone else running around in my head."

It's a strange way to put it—that Rex was running around in her head. I don't say anything though. I'm too busy waiting for Draven to confirm my hypothesis.

He looks uneasy, his gaze going from Rebel to me to Dante, who says under his breath, "Don't even think about it."

"Screw this," Nitro says, lobbing a second fireball at her, this time much faster than the first one.

Dante isn't expecting it—too busy glaring at Draven to see it coming—so he doesn't have time to react. I can see that Deacon's already onboard with what I'm trying to say, and he doesn't do anything to stop the fireball either.

Then again, he doesn't have to. Because it does exactly what I expect when it comes in contact with Rebel—exactly what used to happen when someone tried to use their powers on me. It hits a kind of invisible force field and dissipates immediately. We're all left staring at the intended point of impact, which in this case happens to be Rebel's shoulder. She's totally unharmed, and the fireball has ceased to exist.

Draven stops hesitating. From the icy swirl in his eyes, I can see that he's trying to use one of his powers on Rebel. It doesn't work.

If Dante and Deacon's wind and rain powers wouldn't be completely inexplicable inside a roadside diner—not that Nitro's isn't, but it's at least fractionally more plausible—then I have a feeling they would both be testing out the theory themselves.

"So, it half worked?" Jeremy says. "The serum made her immune to other powers, but she still has her own. That's better than what your mom gave you."

"Way better," I agree. "I mean, we were trying to block her power the way my mom hid mine. But instead, we made her immune to others…"

I trail off at the end, waiting for someone to fill in the blank. Waiting for someone else to figure it out. Because if I tell them what I'm thinking, that might bias their interpretation of the data. But if they come to the conclusion on their own… Well, then, maybe—just maybe—I'm on the right track.

"We made her immune," Deacon echoes, "and we broke the brainwashing."

I nod expectantly. *Come on, guys…*

"Oh my God!" Jeremy exclaims, the first one to put all the pieces together.

"What?" Riley asks.

"Oh my *God!*" Jeremy repeats. His eyes are wider than I've ever seen them.

Draven punches him in the shoulder. Just because, I guess.

"Making her immune," Jeremy says, laying it all out, "broke the brainwashing. Which means whatever Rex was doing to Rebel…"

"Was a power?" V says slowly, her eyes narrowed and face serious. "The brainwashing is an actual power?"

I release the breath I didn't realize I was holding. They've confirmed my thoughts. Rex was using a power to brainwash—to *control*—Rebel.

"It has to be," I tell her. "Rex or someone close to him must have the power of mind control. Nothing else makes sense. Not when you think about how Rebel was acting—and not when you realize that the immunity serum freed her."

"Hold on a minute," Dante says. "Do you even know what you're saying?"

The way my stomach plummets to the floor tells me I know *exactly* what I'm saying. "Someone out there has the power of mind control." I scan my gaze over the eight pairs of eyes focused entirely on me. "And has no problem using it to further Rex's agenda."

CHAPTER 13

For long seconds, silence hangs eerily around us as everyone tries to absorb the bombshell I just dropped.

It's kind of a big deal. Actually, more than kind of. Mind control is the most dangerous and feared power in the books. Supers with that power—with any mental power, really—are carefully watched and regulated and taught from an early age that abusing their ability is tantamount to terrorism. The idea that someone with such a power is willingly using it to bring others under Rex's complete authority, is… well, it's unthinkable.

No wonder the team is so utterly stunned by the revelation.

They seem to snap out of it all at the same time though, because suddenly the table explodes with everyone talking at the same time.

"That's impossible…"

"How would we not know…"

"They'd be using it on villains then…"

"It doesn't make sense…"

No one seems to be able to finish a sentence, as if they're only half able to process their thoughts. Their expressions are a mixture of revulsion, rage, and terror.

"Actually," Deacon says after the others quiet down, "it makes perfect sense."

He keeps his eyes focused on the table. I'm not sure if it's because he's lost in thought or if he's trying to avoid our gazes. Maybe both.

"When they were torturing me...it always felt like it was about more than just causing pain, you know. More than simply getting information from me."

"What do you mean?" V asks, very interested. "What did they do to you?"

I feel Draven's hand beneath my palm, and across the table I see Dante have the same reaction.

"At first, they asked a lot of questions," he explains, his gaze getting even more distant. "Where was villain headquarters? What kind of attacks were we planning? Did we have undercover operatives working inside the League?"

Dante pounds his fist on the table. "Typical hero paranoia bullshit."

"Then the questions stopped, but they kept doing things to hurt me. They'd burn me or waterboard me or shock me or whatever, then when they were done, they'd tell me to do something. Give me a command. An order. Over and over again." He raises his head a little. "It always felt like they expected me to comply."

I feel sick at what Deacon is saying—and the matter-of-fact way he's saying it. Like, it wasn't a big deal that he was tortured.

A quick glance around the table tells me everyone else feels the same way. Riley looks as if he might actually throw up. Nitro's eyes are glossy as if he's fighting back tears, and Draven... Draven looks like he wants to kill Rex with his bare hands. At this point though, he's going to have to get in line. I've never been one to wish bad things on anyone—even bad people—but that philosophy doesn't extend to Rex. I want that man to hurt like no one has ever hurt before. Repeatedly.

"Did it work?" V asks into the murderous silence that engulfs us all. "Did you ever do what they wanted?"

"No."

"Not even to get the pain to stop?" Jeremy asks. "No one would blame you—"

"You think I can't take *pain*?" Deacon asks with a mocking emphasis on the last word. "When you grow up a villain, *hero boy*, pain is a way of life."

I want to believe he's exaggerating because of his own recent experience, but none of the other villains contradict him. They all nod like they know exactly what he's talking about.

My body pulses with rage. That an entire group of people should be raised to expect a life full of pain? It's horrifying. Especially when I think about my mom. She grew up a villain, then spent her adult life hiding among heroes…only to end up dying at their hands anyway. If what Deacon says is true, her whole life was ruled by heroes in one way or another. She suffered her whole life because of them.

Torture is too good for Rex Malone.

"They must have been trying to control you too," V says, breaking me out of my thoughts. "Using pain to make you vulnerable, to force you to lower your defenses."

"What defenses?" Deacon lifts his hands in a helpless gesture. "I wasn't actively trying to block them. I didn't even know what they were trying to do."

"You don't have power-suppression ability anyway," I tell

him. "Only a super like my mom could have actually blocked a mind controller. And only if she knew what they were going to do before they started."

"Maybe you have a natural defense," Rebel suggests.

"That's possible," I say, turning the puzzle around in my mind. "Like V said, they were trying to break down your defenses so the mind control could take hold. That must be why they told you to do things. They wanted to see if it worked."

"It didn't. I never did anything they told me to."

Dante pats his brother on the back. "That's my boy."

He shook his head. "Usually, I did the exact opposite just to spite them."

"They must have loved that," Draven says.

"Rex's face would turn a really ugly shade of purple," Deacon says with a smile, "and then he'd mutter a bunch of garbage about Arizona."

"Arizona?" Draven and I repeat at the same time.

The waitress chooses that moment to come to take our order. I want to tell her to forget about it, that we aren't hungry. But we need to eat. After the stress of what happened at the cabin and the exertion it took to get away, our bodies will be severely depleted. We need to replenish.

Besides, we can't sit here all day talking or someone is bound to notice us. And if they notice us, that increases the odds that they'll recognize us. We need to eat and get out before more customers start piling into the diner.

We may be halfway to Kansas, but Rex is going to spread his net wide looking for us.

I wait impatiently as everyone gives their order, then panic-order an omelet when it's my turn because I haven't even bothered to open the menu. Once she walks away, which feels like it takes forever, I lean forward to grab Deacon's attention again.

"He mentioned Arizona specifically?" I look at Riley. "Is there a secret base there or something?"

He shrugs. "Not that I ever heard about."

"Arizona," I repeat, trying to think if my mom ever mentioned anything about it to me. "Arizona, Arizona. What's in Arizona...?"

"Well, they didn't say Arizona, exactly," Deacon says. "But Phoenix. He talked a lot about Phoenix, which is in Arizona."

My thoughts slam back to Dr. Harwood and his message for my mother before everything went to hell. I never got the chance to give her the message though, because she died before I could ask her anything.

"He talked about Phoenix?" Riley says suddenly. "Or the *scarlet phoenix*?"

"Is there a difference?" Rebel demands.

He gives his sister a *duh* look. "Phoenix is a city in Arizona. But the scarlet phoenix protocol is something else entirely."

"*The scarlet phoenix flies at dawn.*" The words tumble out before I even know I'm going to say them.

Everyone turns to look at me.

"How do you know about the scarlet phoenix protocol?" Riley asks, genuinely confused.

"What is it, Riley?" I demand. "What *is* the scarlet phoenix protocol?"

His cheeks flame a bright red. "Oh God."

"What?"

"I-I-I never thought about it before now." Now he really

looks like he wants to throw up. "I mean, it never occurred to me that Dad would ever use it, let alone against Rebel."

"Tell us," Draven demands. "And I swear to God, Riley, if you've been holding out on us——"

"Chill out!" Nitro tells him, slapping him on the shoulder hard enough to get everybody's attention. "He's not holding out on us. You don't need to jump down the hero's throat every time something goes wrong, you know. Give the guy a second and I'm sure he'll tell us all about it."

"Since when do you defend heroes?" V asks, incredulous.

"Since he fell for one," Dante answers her. "Obviously."

"Takes one to know one," Nitro shoots back.

Dante just grins. "Exactly."

"Whatever." Nitro tries to play it cool, but suddenly he's looking anywhere and everywhere *but* at Riley.

Riley looks a little dazed himself, but I'm not sure if that's because of the Nitro falling-for-him thing or the scarlet phoenix thing. It had better be the latter because we don't exactly have time to worry about his love life at the moment.

Apparently V and I are on the same page.

"Can we focus, please?" she demands, snapping her fingers in front of Riley's face. "Start talking, HB1, or your ass is going to get really well acquainted with my foot."

"It-it's been a goal of Dad's for a long time," Riley says. "But it was just talk. A pie-in-the-sky dream. He never said anything to make me think he actually got it off the ground. But-but, he must have."

"What exactly *is* it, Riley?" Rebel demands, sounding close to tears. "What did Dad do to me?"

Dante wraps an arm around her waist and pulls her against

him. She relaxes into his side, but her face all but screams that she's still upset. Not that I blame her. Rex is a bastard, no doubt, but still…mind-controlling his daughter? Using a weapon on her he meant to use on the villains? If I didn't know him so well—if he hadn't killed my mom and just blown up a cabin that he thought contained all of his children—it'd be unthinkable.

"A psychic weapon," Riley says softly. "Dad's been talking about it for ages. Ever since I was a little. I remember hearing the name for the first time at least ten years ago—"

"How would you know that?" V interrupts. "You were just a kid."

"It was right after James Swift was killed." Riley looks at me. "Or a least right after we *thought* he was killed."

"My dad?" I ask.

I didn't know the Malones then, but my dad was a big deal in the hero world. It's not surprising that Rex would have talked about my dad's death, that Riley would remember that.

"Even I remember that," Draven says, "and I didn't know the guy."

"Thirteen," I say. "It was thirteen years ago."

"I was in the room during a Collective meeting," Riley continues, "sitting in the corner, reading a comic book. Dad was going on and on about what a shame your father's death was, and how much he would be missed. But then he said that it didn't have to be in vain. That your dad had left behind something that could change the nature of hero-villain relations forever. Something that would make villains bow to the will of the League and bring peace to everyone. He called it scarlet phoenix, in honor of your dad, who—"

"The tattoo," I say breathlessly as a memory surfaces. "My dad had a huge red phoenix tattooed across his back."

My stomach twists, and for a second I'm convinced it's going to heave up the cup and a half of coffee I've sucked down while sitting here. Rex did this to *honor* my father? Decided to try mind control on villains because they'd killed my dad and he wanted to make sure it didn't happen again? I don't remember much about my dad, but he was a good man. A great man. I'm sure this mess—this torture and violence—isn't what he would have wanted.

Especially considering he was married to a villain and father to another.

And the fact that, according to my mom, he wasn't really killed.

"So Dad's been trying to mind-control people for years?" Rebel demands. "And he finally found the formula when he mind-controlled me?"

"I don't know." Riley shrugs. "Like I said, I thought it was all talk. A hero-world urban legend. I've heard it mentioned over the years, but never anything more that rumors."

"It doesn't seem like a very effective program," Jeremy says.

Every last one of us turns to glare at him.

"What?" he says with a defensive shrug. "I just meant that it's awfully difficult to implement, if it takes torturing a super to make it work. That's a lot of effort."

Awfully is right. What Rex and the heroes did to Deacon was one-hundred-percent awful.

"But he didn't torture me," Rebel says.

"You sure?" Nitro asks. "Maybe it was so traumatic you blocked it—"

"No! My memory was foggy at first, but now I remember everything that happened after his troops caught me in that alley and brought me to him." She shudders. "*Everything*. We talked. He told me how disappointed he was in me. I told him he could bite me, which didn't go over well. Then he put me in a powers-neutralizing helmet and locked me in my room, with guards at every possible exit.

"I remember lying on my bed all night, worrying about you guys and trying to figure out what to do. How to get away from him so I could help you. I didn't sleep a wink. Sometime in the middle of the night he knocked on my door, saying he wanted to talk more.

"He left the door unlocked, with no guards in sight, and I remember thinking that it was my best chance for escape. The moment he took off the helmet, I started to use my power on him, but he ordered me to stop. Ordered me to get the clothes out of the bag he'd brought with him, take them into the bathroom, and put them on.

"And I did. I did exactly what he wanted me to until you gave me the immunity serum."

She is shaking with rage and tears by the time she finishes.

Draven curses and so does Dante, who looks as close to murder as I've ever seen him. Deacon just looks sick, not that I blame him. If he'd been a little less resistant, a little harder to break, Rex could have mind-controlled him too. Rex could have sent him back to his family—back to Draven and Dante and *Anton*—and used Deacon to do whatever he wanted to them. He would have been the perfect weapon.

"How do we stop him?" I ask. "We can't let him use this on

anyone else. What if he finds villains who aren't as resistant as Deacon? He could cause all kinds of problems."

"What if he's already using it?" Jeremy asks. "I mean, he must be, or he wouldn't have used mind control on Rebel. He wouldn't have been so sure it would work on the first try. So who else is he mind-controlling? Who else is a walking, talking, powers-wielding Rex Malone robot?"

"You mean villains?" Nitro asks.

"Villains," Jeremy says with a nod, "and heroes."

"Heroes?" Riley chokes out.

"Yes, heroes," Jeremy repeats, as if Riley is a child. "The good guys with the white capes and the black hearts."

"No way," Riley says, shaking his head. "No way my dad is mind-controlling *heroes*."

Jeremy shakes his head. "It's a powerful weapon, dude, and Rex is nothing if not power-hungry. He used the thing on his own daughter. What makes you think he wouldn't use it on the Collective or anyone else in the League who got in his way?"

The implications are positively mind-blowing.

"You don't know that," V says, trying—and failing—to sound calm. "Maybe Rebel was the first hero—" She breaks off as the waitress brings our food.

We all wait in tense silence as she doles out the plates, then makes a trip back to the kitchen for a second round. It probably looks suspicious for us all to stop talking and just stare at her, but for the life of me I can't think of any small talk right now. Not when the whole world feels like it's collapsing.

As soon as the waitress walks away, Jeremy asks, "Do we really want to chance it? Do we really want to risk the possibility that Rebel *isn't* the only hero Rex has used the power on?

Think about all the weird and terrible things that have happened recently and then tell me again we shouldn't assume."

When none of us immediately jump in to refute him, he nods to himself in satisfaction before popping a bite of pancake in his mouth.

"The first rule of conspiracy theories," he says after swallowing, "is that the more implausible something sounds, the more likely it's true."

For the next couple of minutes, we all eat in silence as we try to absorb the idea that Rex might be controlling heroes to forward his own agenda. I have to admit, horrible as it sounds, it would be classic Rex. What he did to Rebel is a perfect example. He got her to toe the line and show the whole hero community that he has his own house in order.

I stare at my omelet, which is pretty much untouched. All I've managed to choke down is half a piece of toast. "We need to find Dr. Harwood."

"Dr. Harwood?" Draven asks. "He's the one who gave you that message for your mom?"

I nod.

"What message?" Deacon asks.

"About the scarlet phoenix protocol," I tell him.

Riley gives me a weak smile. "So that's how you knew."

"Sounds like he's involved in the project," V says. "Why would we want to find him?"

Nitro rubs his hands together gleefully—and for once, a stray fireball doesn't shoot out from his palms. "Torture him for information, of course. I'm sure I can cook up something worthy of a hero who—"

"No torture," I interrupt before he can head too far down

that road. "Besides, I don't think he's actually part of the project. My mom told me to find him. She said he could help us bring down Rex."

They were among the last words she said to me.

I don't say that part out loud. I don't have to. Not here with my team, who know how devastated I am by her loss. And most of whom know as much about loss as I do.

I reach for Draven's hand, and it's already open. Already waiting for mine as if he was doing all he could not to reach for me first. I appreciate that more than I can say. The fact that Draven respects me enough to let me handle what I can even when he wants to handle it for me.

I give his hand a squeeze to let him know I'm okay.

"So where do we find this Dr. Harwood?" V asks. "Assuming I let you go after him."

"Let us?" Dante asks. "I'd like to see you try to stop us."

She lifts a brow at him, then looks him up and down. She doesn't say anything, just lets her look—and her well-known ass-kicking skills—speak for her. None of us have any doubt she could stop anyone she set her mind to.

"We *are* going after him, V. With or without your help."

This time Deacon makes the pronouncement.

I expect her to treat him dismissively, the same way she does Dante, like he's a child, a responsibility instead of a teammate. But she just looks at him for a second before nodding her head.

Maybe it's because Deacon seems so much older, even though he's the oldest by mere minutes. Then again, surviving torture probably does a lot to mature a guy. Whatever the reason, she's not inclined to argue with him, which I'll take as a win. Because we *are* going after Dr. Harwood and I'm just as glad I don't have to fight her to do it.

"I've got his known addresses right here," Jeremy says, and I have to admit I'm impressed with what that boy can do with a smartphone.

I mean he's a genius with a computer, obviously. But I wouldn't take odds against him hacking into the NSA mainframe with just that phone. He can do everything else.

"Let me see." I take his phone, prepared to program the addresses into the maps app. But it turns out Jeremy has already done that—of course he has—and they're splayed out in front of me. There are three red pins on the map, two yellow ones, and a green one. "What are all of these?"

"The red ones," Jeremy explains, "are former addresses. The yellow ones are current."

"And the green one?" I ask.

Jeremy's eyes twinkle. "That's the one he owns through a complex series of false names and dummy corporations. The one that's listed on property documentation as a private lab."

"You found all that playing with your smartphone for five minutes?" V looks reluctantly impressed.

"It's a gift," he says, puffing out his chest.

"What do you think the odds are he's there right now?" I ask, not really expecting anyone to answer.

"Pretty good," Jeremy answers, "considering his car is parked out front."

Jeremy reaches over and punches a couple of buttons, and the map switches to a satellite view. As I zoom in on the driveway, I can see a nondescript white pickup truck parked there.

"Is this *live*?" I can't keep the awe out of my voice. "How?"

Jeremy pretends to pull a zipper across his lips. "Technopath trade secrets."

I ignore him and tilt the phone so Draven can see it.

"How far away is it?" Dante asks, trying to get a look.

"About an hour from here, in the foothills south of Castle Rock. So eat up and then let's get going." Draven slides the phone back across the table to Jeremy.

"What am I supposed to tell Anton?" V asks as she takes a bite of her gravy-soaked biscuit. "You know he won't be okay with this."

"Tell him whatever you want. Or don't tell him anything at all," Draven answers. "He's not going to change our minds, so why does he have to know?"

"Because I'm your bodyguard. I've been hired to guard your bodies."

"So guard us then," Dante says with a shrug. "Just do it at this Harwood guy's lab."

"And if I can't?" she asks. "What then?"

It's Draven's turn to shrug. "Then you've got a much bigger problem than Uncle Anton."

CHAPTER 14

Two hours later, Rebel, Riley, and I are standing outside Dr. Harwood's secret lab, ringing the doorbell and waiting for him to answer. Hopefully.

Draven and the others are not impressed at having to wait in the newly stolen van—we traded in the Forest Service SUV when Jeremy realized it had a GPS beacon—but if Dr. Harwood has knowledge of hero secrets, I'm pretty sure finding half a dozen villains on his doorstep isn't going to put him in the mood to talk. I mean, sure, I'm a villain too, but he doesn't necessarily know that. Unless he's been following news from the outside world.

I pull my hair forward, trying to make sure my mark is covered.

The longer we stand here though, the more anxious I become. We've been standing here for five minutes and have rung the doorbell several times. If he's coming to answer the door, he should be here by now. Or at least have acknowledged us via the intercom installed above the doorbell.

Four vehicles are parked in the circular driveway in front of the house. The white pickup I saw in Jeremy's satellite feed, a black Porsche, and two totally generic silver sedans. The hood on the Porsche was still warm when we walked up—Riley swears that's why he touched it, but I'm pretty sure he just wanted to pet the sports car.

The fact that Dr. Harwood hasn't opened the door tells me either he really doesn't want to talk to us or something is really wrong. Either way, standing out here isn't going to get us the information we need.

Rebel presses the doorbell one more time. No response. I start knocking on the heavy wooden door, calling, "Dr. Harwood? It's Kenna Swift. I really need to talk to you. Please, Dr. Harwood, open up. It's about my mom."

He had seemed really worried about her when he gave me that cryptic message. Has he heard about what happened to her?

There's still no answer.

"Something's not right." Rebel hugs her arms around herself.

"I don't like this," Riley says, pressing his face to the long window on the left side of the front door. "Dr. Harwood wouldn't leave you standing out here like this. He cared about your mom."

I try not to let the past tense get to me, but it's so, so hard. Every once in a while I can let everything else that's happening push the reality from my mind, can forget about how she died in my arms, how we had to leave her body in that helicopter to burn, but then something will remind me and I'm flattened by her absence all over again.

She's dead. She's really dead, and nothing I do will ever change that.

It's a terrible thought—and an infuriating one. I pound harder with my fist, determined to get his attention.

"Kenna, stop," Draven calls, and I turn to find him

striding up the front walk, the rest of our team at his heels. "I don't like this."

"That's what I said," Riley tells him. "If he wanted to answer the door, he would have done so by now—even if he was coming from the very back of the house."

"Maybe he didn't hear us," I say, grasping at straws.

Dante moves to Rebel's side. "You were pounding loud enough to wake the entire county."

"So what do you want to do?" Jeremy asks. "I can try to hack the security system and see if I can get in that way."

"Hold your horses, Neo." V scoots around me. "Has anyone tried the door?"

It's a rhetorical question because she's turning the door handle even as she asks. I expect her to be disappointed—Dr. Harwood has always been a stickler for security—but the door swings right open. An invitation if I've ever seen one... or a trap.

I raise my eyebrows at Draven, who just nods before taking a step into the house.

I brace myself for I don't know what. An explosion, maybe, considering the way the last twenty-four hours have gone. But there's nothing. No alarm, nobody coming to check on the opened door, nothing.

My sense of foreboding grows, and I step in behind Draven.

"Wait outside," he tells me, but I just roll my eyes at him.

I know he's trying to protect me, but seriously. I've never played the damsel in distress and I'm not about to start now.

"If you're in here, I'm in here," I answer, walking beside him and grabbing his hand. "Besides, Dr. Harwood is less likely to shoot you if he sees me."

"If he's likely to shoot anyone," V says, following me into the house, "then I'm taking the lead. Anton hired me to—"

"Guard our bodies," Draven says, stealing the words out of her mouth. "Yeah, we get it." He pulls me close as he gestures for V to move ahead. "Be my guest then. Do what you need to do."

"What I need to do is keep you safe," she snarls, flipping him off as she moves into the lead, a gun appearing in her hand as if from thin air. "Any thoughts as to where this lab is situated?"

"My guess is underground," I tell her. "If he's got secrets, he's going to want to keep them that way. So the lab would probably only have one way in and out."

"Two, actually," Jeremy says, pushing to the front of our team so he can glare at V. "There's an emergency exit."

"And how do you know that?" V asks.

He waggles his phone at her. "Because I downloaded the blueprints from the county assessor's website."

Suddenly V gets a lot more interested in him—or at least his phone. "Show me."

"Basement stairs off the kitchen," he says, pointing to the plans. "Like Kenna said, it's underground. And since those stairs are in the pantry, I'm pretty sure it's also secret."

"Great. Another secret hero lab," Deacon says, crossing the threshold behind us. "Never thought I'd find myself in one of those again."

"You don't have to come," Draven tells him immediately. "You can wait outside—"

"And what am I going to do out there? Practice tai chi?"

"Besides," Dante says, "if he's outside, who will put out the fire when Nitro gets scared."

"I don't get *scared*," Nitro argues. "I just get…"

"Flustered?" Riley offers helpfully.

Nitro beams. "Exactly."

"Will you idiots please shut up," V growls.

Deacon waves her forward. "Lead the way, bodyguard."

She snarls at him, but does as he suggests, cautiously making her way through the foyer and down the hall to where Jeremy says the kitchen should be.

We follow, hot on her heels.

Gun extended in front of her, she makes the turn into the kitchen. And then stops so fast that I nearly run into her. She holds a hand up, signaling for us to stay back.

"Describe Dr. Harwood," she says.

"Older guy," I say, referring to a mental picture, "balding on top with a bushy mustache."

"Kinda Mr. Clean meets Mark Twain?"

"Exactly."

"Then I have some bad news."

I push past V into the kitchen, and my heart plummets. His body is laid out on the kitchen floor, surrounded by a pool of blood.

I scream, my hand tightening instinctively on Draven's.

"Help him," I tell Draven.

"Kenna, he's—"

"Help him!" I'm desperate, even though I know there is too much blood for his wounds to be anything but fatal. When Draven doesn't move, I shout again, "Help him!"

"I'm trying. But I can't bring someone—"

"Fine," I say, shrugging out of his grip. "I'll help him."

Then I'm on my knees next to Dr. Harwood, his blood seeping into the denim of my jeans. I don't know what I can do—CPR? Electroshock? Prayer? *Something. Anything.* I try them all. And when I have no other options left, I place my hands over his chest, wishing for just a moment that I could have Draven's power, that I had the ability to heal.

Something inside me shifts, and suddenly there's a strange vibration emanating from my hands. "What the—?"

I pull my hands back and stare at them. As Draven pulls me back to my feet, he gives me the strangest look.

"It gets worse," V says, from the other side of the room. Every instinct I have is screaming for me to run the other way, but I don't. I gave up the chance to do that a long time ago. Walking away isn't an option anymore.

Instead, I move to her side. And get my first good look at what she's seeing.

Dr. Blankenship, another scientist who worked at the lab with my mom—and who carried lollipops in the pocket of her lab coat that she was always willing to share—is lying behind the kitchen's center island. Blood is still leaking from a gaping wound in her chest, but when I start to drop to my knees to try to staunch the flow of blood, V stops me.

"She's already gone," she says.

"How do you know?"

She looks at me grimly but doesn't answer. Instead, she moves on as I bend to check Dr. Blankenship's pulse. V was right. She's dead.

"There are two more over here," Draven calls from the pantry.

I join him there, looking through the doorway Jeremy told us would be there. The doorway to the secret lab.

"You don't need to see this," he tells me, catching me around the waist and trying to pull me away.

But I need to see it. I do. Dr. Harwood, Dr. Blankenship—I knew them. I liked them. They were always kind to the nerdy little girl who had too many questions and even more hypotheses, always took the time to answer my questions or check in on me and see how I was doing when my mom got wrapped up in her research. I want to know who else is here. Who else I care about is dead.

I'm pretty sure I know the answer even before I shoulder Draven aside and look down the stairs. My mom had a core group of four friends at the lab that she did almost everything with—probably because they were the only ones she could trust in Rex's viper pit. Which means that if Dr. Harwood stayed true to form, Drs. Destry and Villanueva are down there.

The thought makes me shake. Silent tears leak down my face as I look at the two bodies tangled together at the bottom of the stairs. Dr. Villanueva is lying in a pool of her own blood, and Dr. Destry is beside her, his neck obviously broken, his body sprawled at a funny angle.

"No," I gasp, stumbling down the stairs toward them. "No, no, no!"

I'm vaguely aware of Draven following after me. I drop to check their pulses. Just in case.

There's nothing there.

As if from far away, I hear Rebel scream. Hear Riley moan in distress. They both spent nearly as much time at the lab as I did through the years. They know these people almost as well as I do. I mean, just before all hell broke loose a couple weeks ago, Rebel snuck into Dr. Blankenship's lab and scattered hundreds upon hundreds of lollipops over every available surface.

She'd laughed when she saw it. Laughed and given us each a lollipop.

I laugh at the memory, a loud, hysterical sound that has Draven wrapping both arms around me and pulling me to my feet.

"It's okay, Kenna," he tells me. "It's okay."

"It's not," I sob into his chest. "Nothing is ever going to be okay again. These people were my friends."

"I know, love," he says, rocking me softly. "I know."

"We have to get out of here," V says from the top of the stairs. She's so unemotional, so blank, that a part of me wants to slap her. Four people are dead here. Four kind, wonderful people, and she doesn't care at all.

But I do. I do.

"What we need to do," Riley says as he joins me at the bottom of the stairs, and his voice sounds shakier than I've ever heard it, "is search this lab. See what they were working on that might have gotten them killed. And see if there is any information about scarlet phoenix."

He's right. I know he's right, and still I can't bring myself to skirt their bodies, to walk around them like they're nothing. They were people and now they're dead because they got in Rex's way. Just like my mother.

I scream, a loud, anguished wail that echoes through the stairwell. Draven tightens his grip on my shoulders and pulls me closer, and for the first time I realize he's shaking as badly as I am.

He didn't know these heroes—*true* heroes—but he is just as affected by their deaths as those of us who did. His empathy only makes me love him more.

I give myself a minute, one short, finite minute, to grieve. To try to wrap my head around these new and senseless acts of violence. To add them to the growing list in my mental catalog. Then I pull away from the comfort of Draven's arms and force myself to walk around the bodies of my mother's best friends and move deeper into the lab, trying to look at it with objective eyes.

It's one of the hardest things I've ever done. But then, these last couple of days have been filled with hard and terrible things. As I move to the laptop still open on the desk, I can't help wondering how many more people need to die.

"Don't touch that!" Jeremy shouts as I reach to wake up the computer. "It could be a honeypot."

"A what?" Draven demands.

"A trap."

I freeze, my finger hovering over the keyboard.

"He's right," V says. "The bodies are still warm. Whoever did this might still be—"

She breaks off as a loud crash echoes through the house above us, followed by the unmistakable sound of breaking glass and booted footsteps pounding over the hardwood floor.

CHAPTER 15

V is up the stairs before I even have a chance to react, with Draven right behind her.

I race up the stairs after them, just in time to watch seven heroes in full desert camouflage pile into the room at the same time three more come crashing through the sliding glass door on the other side of the kitchen.

"It's a trap!" Deacon growls from beside me. "Get down, Kenna!"

He tries to shove me behind him, but yeah. Like that's going to happen.

"Freeze," shouts one of the heroes who came in through the window. He's tall and blond, around my age, and looks distinctly familiar. He also looks distinctly dangerous. Which he is, I realize, as he lets loose a blast of ice straight at V and Draven.

"Bugger that!" Nitro yells, lobbing a fireball straight at the ice blast.

For the second time today his aim is right on. The ice turns to water and falls harmlessly to the floor as V and Draven turn to confront the hero.

V grabs him behind the neck and pulls his head down as

she thrusts her knee straight up into his forehead. There's a loud crack and then he hits the ground.

At the same time, Draven is focused on the other two door-crashers. With a wave of his hand, he has them on their knees, clutching their heads as blood leaks from their noses.

Deacon, Dante, and Nitro are locked in battle with four of the heroes who came in the front of the house and are doing their best to hold them off. Nitro lobs bright red and yellow fireballs at two of them, while Dante creates a mini-vortex of wind around a third and fourth. After an aborted attempt to use his water power that ended up putting out three of Nitro's fireballs prematurely, Deacon has taken to punching whatever hero he can get his hands on.

Two other heroes are headed straight for Rebel, who is telekinetically winding a power cord around the feet of a hero Riley is holding suspended in midair. I grab the first weapon I can find—a cast-iron frying pan that is sitting on the stove with scrambled eggs still in it—and hit one of them in the face with it as hard as I can. He goes down like a rock.

The other hero sends what looks like a sandstorm at Rebel's back. But her immunity sends it swirling around her harmlessly before falling to the ground. While that hero stares in shock at his failed attack, I bash him with the frying pan.

As he's falling, the huge guy V knocked down grabs her around the leg and yanks her to the floor as bolts of lightning fly all around us. Jeremy ducks between a couple of the lightning bolts and launches himself at the guy's back, and then the three of them are rolling around on the ground together.

More heroes flood in through the back door, and Rebel uses her power to lift them and throw them back out, one at a time. A few get through, and Draven turns to confront them while the other two heroes he was fighting pass out at his feet.

He can't take on all of them though—there are too many. And their powers are too strong. One is zipping around the room so fast I can barely see her, while Dante is struggling with what I can only imagine is a hero with the power of invisibility because he seems to be fighting thin air. A hero with super stretch reaches between bodies to grab Jeremy's ankle. One shifts into the shape of a mountain lion at the same time as another grows so huge his head hits the ceiling.

It's a complete zoo in the not-so-spacious kitchen.

A girl with a nasty-looking weapon turns her attention on Rebel. I narrow my power into laser focus and send a flash of electromagnetic energy right at her. The weapon explodes in her face.

Lightning continues to zing around the room from one of the heroes Nitro is fighting, and between the two of them, half the kitchen is on fire. Deacon is doing his best to put the flames out, but he's also locked in hand-to-hand combat with a hero whose power seems to be elasticity since he keeps bending and contorting himself out of Deacon's grip. Dante's wind is knocking things over and fanning the flames that Deacon can't put out, and Riley is flying above the whole scene, throwing dishes, a toaster, boxes of cereal—whatever he can get his hands on—at the heroes. At least until one of the heroes jumps straight up and grabs Riley's feet, and then the two tumble to the ground.

A hero woman in black leather slips past Draven and into the fray. I head straight for her, determined to keep her from hurting anyone. But before I reach her, she opens her mouth and lets loose a sonic scream so high-pitched that it shatters windows—and some eardrums.

Everyone on my team freezes—everyone but blissfully immune Rebel—their hands clapping over their ears to block out the sound. The heroes must be wearing earplugs, because they keep fighting. It takes only seconds for them to subdue my friends, some of whom have blood leaking out of their ears, but the woman continues to scream.

I fall to my knees, sharp agony shooting through my head. Through my whole body. I try to fight the pain, but that only makes it worse. At least until I see Draven on the ground, a hero on his back, handcuffing him, while another beats the hell out of him.

Anger wells in me, a fury that's more than fury, a hate that's more than hate, a hollowness that starts in my core and over-whelms my entire being. What I'm thinking. What I'm feeling. What I'm seeing and what I'm hearing. It overtakes me, until nothing exists for me but it.

I stagger to my feet and stumble across the room toward the screaming woman. I can feel the heroes staring at me. They start toward me as freeze blasts and lightning bolts and sandstorms fly at me.

I hold my hands out as if to block them, and as I do, some-thing strange happens.

Everything stops.

Not stops as in freezes, but stops as in disappears.

The lightning bolts poof into thin air.

The freeze blasts disintegrate.

The screaming woman warbles and chokes, her deadly shriek completely silenced.

It's just for a few moments, five seconds max, but that is all the time my team needs. Draven jumps to his feet with a roar, the handcuffs dangling from one wrist as he throws his arms out and sends biomanipulation waves straight at every hero in his sight line.

The kitchen faucets spring to life, water flooding out of them so fast the hardware breaks and water starts spurting straight into the air. Deacon gathers all the water and sends it crashing toward the heroes near the glass door in a giant wave that propels them through the broken glass. Then he maintains the wave, making it impossible for them to fight their way back in through the barricade of water.

Riley flies through the door after them—above the wall of water—and V and Jeremy leap out one of the kitchen windows to join the battle outside.

Rebel sends out a telekinetic blast so powerful that it lifts four heroes right off their feet and pins them against the wall, while Dante and Nitro create a fiery vortex that cages all the remaining heroes inside of it.

Well, all except sonic scream lady, who I take care of with another well-placed slam of my frying pan. She falls face-first to the kitchen floor, hitting her head on the corner of the granite countertop as she goes down.

I don't know if she's dead, and for the first time since this nightmare began, I can't bring myself to care. The heroes have done so much damage, have hurt and killed so many people. I would never deliberately kill anyone, but if she hit her head on the counter hard enough to crack her skull, I'm not exactly going to be crying for her. I have too many other, better people to cry for.

Draven finishes with the heroes he's fighting inside, then beelines for the clash outside. Once that happens, it's only a matter of a couple minutes before the hero force is laid out on the ground in front of us. Most of them are passed out, and the ones who aren't are in bad enough shape that they won't retaliate, which is all that matters—at least to me. V is another matter altogether though, as she and Draven go through and knock out everyone.

"What are we going to do with them?" I ask as Jeremy runs down to the lab to find something to tie them up with.

"I've got some ideas," Nitro says. There's a look on his face I've never seen before. One that's filled with rage and hate and so much fury it's a miracle he doesn't spontaneously combust where he stands.

I don't blame him. The scientists who were used to bait us were my mother's friends. Each of them was kind to me in his or her own way, and each of them feels like family. That they died because the heroes wanted a way to bring us down—to bring *me* down—hurts immensely.

But then again, that's kind of the point of their whole futile exercise, isn't it?

Jeremy comes back with a couple rolls of duct tape, and we all go to work binding hands and wrists. We use a lot, doing our best to ensure that they won't get free. Then Jeremy goes from hero to hero, taking whatever electronics they have on them and piling them high on the kitchen table.

Only then does he nod to Rebel, who uses her power to pick the heroes up, one by one, and carry them down the stairs and into the environmental chamber in the lab. I follow behind to close the door and lock them in. If there was a key,

I would throw it away. And just like that, the threat is neutralized and we're safe. At least for now.

CHAPTER 16

W hat are you doing?" Rebel asks as I walk around the
lab, gathering ingredients and equipment.

"Making more immunity serum."

If I don't keep busy, I'm going to keep thinking about
everything that's happened in the last couple of days. And if
I do that, I'm going to start crying—and I don't want to start
crying. I can't give in to the despair. Not now, when there's still
so much to do. Still so much to take care of.

Everyone else can search for clues. Only I can do this.

"The last batch I made got left at the cabin," I explain.

"Do we have time for that?" Deacon asks, peering over
my shoulder.

"We're making time," I answer. "This is the only way we
know to break Rex's mind control. Don't you think it's a
good idea to have some of it around? Maybe that craziness
upstairs would never have happened if we'd been able to
immunize them."

What we really need is one of my mom's injection guns, so
we could dose mind-controlled heroes from a distance. Too
bad Rex cleared out her secret stash when he took her from
our house.

"Wait a second," V says, her eyes narrow and her face all scrunched up as she watches me pour the first ingredient into a glass beaker. "You think the heroes we just fought were under mind control?"

I shrug. "I can't know for sure."

"But it's a possibility?" Rebel asks.

"A *strong* possibility."

V demands, "How do you know?"

I start measuring out the compounds required for the first stage of the serum recipe. When I look up, my whole team is staring at me. Waiting for me to explain the inexplicable.

"It's only a theory," I say. "But that hero with the braids and the nose ring who came in the back door? I know him."

"You know him?" Draven asks. "How?"

"His dad was a friend of my mom's. I wasn't sure at first, during the fighting, especially with how he was acting. But after, when we were tying them up…" I pour the first-stage ingredients into an Erlenmeyer flask. "It was Will."

"Just because you knew the guy doesn't mean he wouldn't follow Rex's orders to bring you in," Dante says.

"Wait, that was Will?" Jeremy says, making a kissy face. "*Your* Will?"

Draven's eyebrows practically hit his hairline. "*Your* Will?"

"We were…kinda friends for a while. I mean, it's been a few years, but I know him."

"You mean you *knew* him," Draven says. "Kenna, people can change a lot in a few years."

"Not like this. Will is not the kind of guy to use his power to hurt anyone," I say as I stir the mixture until it turns a cloudy blue. "Let alone to hurt me."

"Let alone you?" Draven repeats. His eyes are turning stormy again.

"You might want to close your mouth," V tells him, tapping his cheek. "It's not a good look for you, D3."

I turn away from the workstation, where the initial reactions are already beginning.

"He was my first kiss," I tell them. "And I was his. At science camp a long time ago. He and his dad used to have dinner at our house every week before they moved to New Mexico. We still chat online—or at least we did, before all this started. I *know* him. He wouldn't do something like this, any more than Rebel would deliberately try to kill one of us."

"But you can't know for certain," V says.

I flash back to the memory of a younger, scrawny Will with a ponytail and a tendency to hiccup when he's nervous. "He isn't a soldier—he's an artist. There's no way Will should even be here, no way he *would* be here trying to kill me unless Rex did something to his brain."

"That's just wishful thinking," V argues. "Nothing more than a guess."

Her attitude is starting to get on my nerves. "It's an *educated* guess."

V is like a dog with a bone. "I'm not betting your lives on a guess."

"Then let's test the theory," Nitro suggests. "Let Kenna cook up the immunity serum, and then we shoot him with it and see what happens. If Will snaps out of it like Rebel did, he was mind-controlled. If he doesn't, then he wasn't. Sounds pretty simple to me."

Riley gives him a thumbs-up.

"We can't sit around for a couple hours waiting for the serum to process," Dante says. "We'll be sitting ducks for the next wave of attacks."

"We'll be sitting ducks if armies of mind-controlled heroes keep coming after us," Nitro replies.

"The serum is the only weapon we have," I tell them.

Draven nods. "It's our only chance."

"Besides," Riley says, "what else are we supposed to do?"

He's right. It's not like we have any better plans. After Mom died, I had four missions: fix Rebel, find Dr. Harwood, find my dad, and stop Rex. We've done the first and, I guess technically, the second. I have zero clue where to even start looking for my dad, and as for Rex... Well, if anyone has any thoughts on how to stop his quest for world domination, I'm all ears.

The silence in the room says it all.

V throws her hands in the air. "Fine. I give up. Let me know when you know what the hell you're doing." She turns and storms up the stairs. "I'll be outside—"

"Guarding our bodies?" Riley finishes helpfully.

She doesn't even bother to flip him off.

"So we make the serum," Draven says. He nods at the chamber full of heroes. "Find out if lover boy is a Rex robot. And then what?"

"I'm working to find the code for their frequency, so we can see if Rex is trying to communicate with them." Jeremy says from the back of the lab where he's fiddling with the electronics we took from the heroes. He's got Dr. Harwood's laptop connected to one of the handhelds and is working on both simultaneously. "If we're lucky, we'll find out what else is coming our way."

"And if we're not?" Nitro asks.

No one has an answer for him. I guess we just have to be lucky.

I turn back to the workstation, even though there is nothing for me to do but watch until the contents of the flask turn orange. I pull out my phone and start making notes about the scientific process. Recording the time line of the reactions and my observations along the way might not tell me anything I don't already know, but it gives me something to do.

And right now I need something to do.

While everyone else gets lost in their thoughts, Draven moves to my side.

"We need to talk," he says, his voice so low I can barely hear.

I sigh. I should have expected this.

"Will and I are just friends now," I tell him. "Actually, we were never really more than friends."

"Not about that," Draven says with a cocky smile, "but that's good to know." He leans forward and drops a quick kiss on my lips.

I surprise him by wrapping my arms around his waist and pulling him closer. He comes willingly, his hands coming up to frame my face as he gives me another deeper kiss.

He feels good. This feels good. Normal in the very best way, even in the middle of all this chaos and destruction. I'm not sure how we got here so quickly, how I fell for him this deeply. But I did, and though I know I could do this without him if I had to, I'm so, so glad that he's here and I don't have to.

Eventually, he starts to move away, but I'm not ready to let him go yet. I slide my hands up to tangle in his hair and hold him in place as I kiss him until we're both breathless and shaking.

When we finally come up for air, he keeps me close. "You doing all right?" he asks.

I nod against his chest. "How about you? Are *you* okay?"

We haven't really talked about what happened while he was Rex's prisoner. Partly because there's been no time, but I'm guessing also partly because he doesn't want to talk about it. I can hardly blame him.

He hesitates, takes a couple deep breaths. "I'm good."

There's something in his voice that says otherwise. "Yeah?"

He sighs. "I can't stand the idea that there's anything of him inside of me. Even if it's just DNA."

I hold him tighter, try to get him to look at me. But he's very determinedly staring over my head.

"Nothing about you is like Rex Malone," I insist.

"How do you know?" His voice is quiet, like he wants to make sure no one else can overhear. "How do you know I won't lose it one day and abuse them the way he abuses what he's got? Maybe it's genetic."

"Because I know you." It's my turn to cup his cheeks, to force him to look at me. "You could be super egotistical and power hungry with what you've got right now. But you've never been like that. That's not who you are. It's insane to think that one day you'll just wake up and a switch will be flipped."

"How do you know that didn't happen to Rex? How do you know—"

"That man has been an asshole his whole life. No switch got flipped. He's been like this for at least as long as I've known him. My mom knew him even longer, and she never liked him. You're. Not. Like. Him."

He searches my eyes like he's looking for something. Whatever it is, he must find it, because his shoulders relax and he finally smiles. It's a small smile, but it's there.

"Thank you," he says softly.

"For what? All I did was tell the truth." I pull his head down, press his forehead against mine in a gesture meant to comfort both of us. "You're a good guy, Draven. One of the best. Never let Rex make you doubt that."

He nods, then glances over his shoulder to make sure no one is paying attention to us. "We still need to talk."

"Sure. About what?"

"About what happened upstairs. When every power in the room stopped."

"Oh, right." In all the craziness that followed, I'd put that bizarre moment out of my mind. It had been a turning point in the battle. We'd been on the verge of total defeat, and then…we weren't. I can't explain it—don't even know where to start.

One look at Draven's face tells me he thinks he has an explanation. A shiver goes down my spine, and suddenly I'm not so sure I want to hear what he has to say.

"And before that," he continues, "when you were trying to save Dr. Harwood."

"I don't know what you mean."

"You put your hands over his chest and tried to heal him. I saw you."

"That's…ridiculous." I shake my head. "That's your power, not mine."

"It is," he agrees. But then he holds his arm out to me. It's got a nasty cut below the elbow that has to hurt. "Try to heal me."

I draw back. "I can't."

"Just try."

I want to argue, but seeing him injured like that makes my chest tighten. Before I can think, I lift my hand and let my fingers hover right above his wound. It looks so painful.

I wish I *could* heal him.

And then, something shifts. I feel that strange vibration in my fingers again. Just like when I was kneeling over Dr. Harwood's body. Only this time, the vibrations leave through my fingertips.

Draven's wound heals before my eyes.

"What the—?"

"Shhh." He shakes his head.

My gaze darts from his unmarred skin to his icy blue eyes. "You did that!"

"No," he says, leaning close to whisper in my ear. "You did."

"How is that—?" It doesn't make sense. My power is electricity, not biomanipulation. "I don't understand."

His breath tickles my ear. "A second power, Kenna."

I gasp, shaking my head, ready to deny the suggestion. But then my mother's voice is in my head, reminding me to be logical. Be scientific.

Sure, it's rare for supers to have two powers, but it happens. Look at Draven. He's got two incredible powers. I've never stopped to wonder why, but maybe it really is genetic. He has one parent who's a villain and another who's a hero.

Just like I do.

Maybe that's the key.

"I have biomanipulation?" I say, my voice full of awe.

My mind fills with all of the possibilities. All of the people I can help, the people I can *save*. Could I have saved my mom?

"I don't think so," Draven tells me.

"Then what?"

"Absorption," he answers. "I think you can absorb the powers of other supers."

"I—what?"

I've never heard of that power. Is it even possible? Does it even exist?

"Remember in the courtroom, when Rex was trying to grab you?"

Of course I do. That's not a moment a girl forgets.

"At the end, when I was on the verge of upping his blood pressure to do more than just disable him, my power slipped." He tucks a lock of hair behind my left ear. "You put your hand on my arm, and I lost my hold on him."

"I remember," I tell him. "I wanted to stop you from killing him, from revealing your second power to everyone in that courtroom."

"At the time, I thought I was just weak. But now, after seeing—and feeling—what happened upstairs…"

I nod. Other pieces of the puzzle fall into place. The fireball that took out the guard who plasma blasted my mom, and Nitro later saying his power sparked out in the courtroom. Seeing that weird mental map of our surroundings, one that could have been a product of V's echolocation, when we were escaping in Fort Collins. The vibrations I felt over Dr. Harwood's body and over Draven's arm.

Had I really being using other people's powers?

This is almost as hard to process as finding out I had a power in the first place. In the space of a couple weeks, I've gone from being completely powerless to having *two* powers? It's seems too impossible to believe.

"Should I…?" I nod toward the others, who are mostly gathered on a couch in the corner of the room.

He shakes his head. "Don't tell anyone. At least for now. They don't need to be freaking out about losing their powers if yours kicks in. Let's wait until you have more control."

He's right. I know he's right. The last thing we need in a fight is everyone worrying that I'm going to zap away their powers.

No, that's the second-to-last thing. The last thing is me accidentally doing it. It has taken me hours and hours of focused practice to get even a semblance of control over my electromagnetic power. I don't know anything about this power. How does it work? How do I take the power? How long do I keep it? Do I have to give it back or does it return naturally? I have so many questions, and no time to answer them.

I nearly jump out of my skin when Rebel taps me on the shoulder.

"The heroes are gone."

"What?" Draven and I demand at once.

She gestures at the environmental chamber. "See for yourself."

I cross to the door and peer inside the small window. The chamber is empty.

"Damn it," Draven mutters when he confirms it for himself.

The door is still locked, and Draven I have been in the room the whole time. There is no way they snuck out past us, let alone V, who is steadfastly guarding the top of the stairs.

"One of them must have had the ability to teleport," Rebel suggests.

Of course. I've never actually seen anyone use it myself, but that power is legend. Supers who can disappear in a flash, along with anyone who is touching them at the time.

The one with that power must have woken up and poofed the whole lot of them out of the chamber.

"Great, now what?" My shoulders slump. "How are we going to test my theory?"

"We have a suggestion," Riley says, appearing at Rebel's side.

She nods. "We want to use the serum on Mom."

I ask, "What?"

"Our dad may be a monster," Riley says, "but what about our mom?"

Rebel's eyes have a haunted look. "What if she's under his control? Like, literally under his control?"

"Oh, Rebel." I reach out and press a sympathetic hand on her shoulder. "Your mom has always gone along with Rex."

"What if it's not her fault?" she says.

Riley nods. "What if Dad's been controlling her all along?"

"Admit it," Rebel says. "It makes sense."

"It's at least possible," Riley adds.

"We have to try," Rebel pleads. "If she's being controlled, we have to save her."

"Babe, come on," Dante interrupts. "We have bigger problems at the moment. We should be steering clear of your parents as long as Rex is trying to kill us. We need to focus on stopping him."

"Mom can help with that!" Riley exclaims. "She knows him better than anyone, knows how he thinks, what he's capable of—"

"What his secrets are," Rebel chimes in. "If we can cure her, she can tell us where he's hiding. Then we could go after him instead of waiting around for him to try to kill us."

I have to admit, the idea of getting the upper hand on Rex, of being on the offensive and not the defensive, is pretty appealing.

"It's a huge risk," I tell them.

"It's more than risky," V calls down the stairs. "No way I'm letting you idiots march up to Rex Malone's house to shoot his wife full of immunity serum. It's suicide."

"It's not suicide!" Rebel shouts up at her. "Once we break the mind control, she will protect us. I guarantee."

"Fine, you heroes can go," V says, descending back into view. "But the Cole boys aren't going."

"The hell we aren't," Dante says.

"No offense, but I'm not about to put my charges' lives in the hands of the girl who was trying to kill them less than twenty-four hours ago!"

"Unfair, V, and you know it," Dante snarls.

I slip my hand in Rebel's, letting her know without words that we all understand that wasn't really her. "I'm in."

She gives me a watery smile.

Dante moves to her other side. "I'm not letting her go home without me."

"And I'm not letting Dante go anywhere without me," Deacon chimes in.

"Where the twins go—" Draven starts.

"Yeah, yeah. I get it," V snaps. "You're going and there's nothing I can do about it." She reaches for her phone. "Except call Anton and see what he has to say about all of this."

She clearly expects the guys to back down at the threat, except apparently she doesn't know the Cole boys as well as she thinks she does. Draven just looks at her, one brow raised challengingly. "You can do that, but I'm not sure what you think it's going to accomplish. By the time he gets here, we'll be long gone."

"And you'll either be with us," Dante says, "or locked up with the heroes."

Deacon stands shoulder to shoulder with them, arms crossed over his chest. "Your choice."

I bite back the biggest grin I've felt like smiling in weeks. It takes all my restraint not to applaud their stand.

V pulls herself up to her fairly intimidating height of almost six feet and looks Draven straight in the eye. "It's cute that you think you can take me."

"We both know I can. But I don't want to. Rebel thinks Mrs. Malone can help us, and at this point it's the only lead we have. My girl is going with her, which means so am I. Dante is going with Rebel too. And Deacon's with us."

"Me too," Riley adds, joining the line of us standing up to V.

Draven nods at him. "I don't know what the rest of you are doing, but the six of us are going to the Malone house, and there's nothing you or Anton or anyone else can do to stop us."

Silence reigns for long seconds as Draven and V square off in the middle of the room. Nobody moves; nobody blinks. I'm not sure any of us even breathe. At least not until Nitro says, "Oi. You set one guy's hair on fire, and suddenly you're not an honorary member of the pack anymore? I see how it is."

It's the tension release we need, and everyone cracks up—even V and Draven. They break eye contact and step out of their pissing match.

"Right?" Jeremy says. "You guys wouldn't last two minutes without me."

"That just leaves you, V," Draven says.

We all turn to look at her expectantly. She glares at each of us in turn, clearly trying to decide if she needs to save face or just throw in the towel. In the end, she rolls her eyes. "Fine. But when Anton kills me, I expect you to mourn."

Deacon laughs. "Forget Anton. If you hang around us much longer, we'll get you killed way before you have to worry about Anton."

CHAPTER 17

It's getting dark by the time the immunity serum is ready and we make the long, tense drive to Rebel's parents' house. After everything that's happened, it feels weird calling it *her* house, so I don't. I find it telling that neither does she.

Then again, it never really felt like a home to her. More like a place she lived in until she could get away.

And now she's away.

The closer we get to the Malones', the quieter the van gets. Riley is in the far back, resting his head on Nitro's shoulder. Rebel is next to me in the middle seat, nervously tugging at the hem of her T-shirt while Dante massages her shoulders from behind. She's spent so long pretending she doesn't need or want her parents' approval that I almost forgot what a crock that was. Until now.

She may despise her dad and everything he stands for, but at her core he's still her dad. It's not in Rebel's nature to write someone off completely.

I just hope we're doing the right thing.

Jeremy volunteered to be a test subject for the new batch of serum, arguing that he should be on prophylactic immunity to make sure the heroes don't start controlling him. As crazy as it sounded, it also made sense.

We gave Riley a dose too. If heroes really are more susceptible to the mind control, then they should all be protected.

The serum started working on both of them right away. Which makes me think it only took so long to work on Rebel because she was unconscious. In a conscious subject, the effects are almost instantaneous.

So we know the serum works—and works quickly. Now we just have to wait and see if it works on Mrs. Malone.

I glance at Draven, hoping he can reassure me. But the moment our eyes meet, I realize he's as uncertain about this as I am. My confidence level plummets. It must be written on my face, because he wraps his arm around my shoulders and pulls me against him.

I go gratefully, so tired and confused and sad that all I really want to do is bury my head in his chest and stay there forever. When this is over, I promise myself as we make the turn into Rebel's old neighborhood, I'm going to spend hours—days—blocking out the world with the help of Draven's arms.

"You doing okay?" he murmurs softly into my ear as he strokes my shoulder and tangles his fingers in my hair.

"Yeah." It's a lie and both of us know it, but he doesn't call me on it. He just nods and pulls me a little bit closer, his lips ghosting over my temple.

It feels good, really good, and I'm so glad to have him back at my side.

I haven't had time to truly appreciate it since we rescued him, what with being constantly on the run and all, but it's a huge relief to know he's just…here. I don't have to do any of this alone anymore.

I've had my team through everything that happened—even when Draven was a prisoner and Rebel was under mind control—and they were invaluable. They kept me sane. Even Nitro, with his fireballs and weird sense of humor, somehow managed to keep me from falling apart.

But having Draven here now, absently playing with my hair, checking in on me, knowing what I'm thinking almost before I do—it's different than only being surrounded by our friends. It's… I don't know how to describe this feeling except *better*.

"This will all be over soon," he says, his lips moving from my temple to my cheek to my jaw. I turn my head and press my mouth to his. And for a few seconds let myself pretend that this kiss, this moment, this *boy*, is all that matters.

He kisses me back, his mouth sweet and hard against my own. I burrow closer, wanting to lose myself in him. He pulls away, his breathing a little harder and his hand a little shakier than it was moments ago.

I want to protest, to press my mouth to his again and kiss him until all the doubt and fear and pain go away. Until everything we've done, everything we still have to do, no longer exists.

But the van slams to a stop—V wants to make sure we all know she is driving under protest—at the curb in front of Rex's house. Nerves flutter down my spine, and I grab hold of Draven's free hand as he uses his other to push open the door.

He climbs out and then helps me out, all without letting go of my hand. I take Rebel's hand as soon as she's on the sidewalk. With her other hand, she checks her pocket, where the syringe of immunity serum is tucked away.

Dante wraps her close to his side, but I don't let go of her hand. She's nearly vibrating out of her skin with nerves or excitement or, most likely, a combination of both.

The four of us take the lead, walking up the driveway as a united front. The rest of the team follows close behind. V hesitates, like she's thinking about staying in the van out of spite. But then she falls into step, bringing up the rear. I remind myself that, together, we are unstoppable.

"I'll talk us in the door," Rebel says, going over the plan one more time before we reach the entrance. "If I can't get close enough to shoot her full of immunity serum, Riley will get her with his syringe."

I give her hand a squeeze. "It should only take a few seconds to start working."

"When it does," Rebel continues, as if it's a foregone conclusion that her mom is being controlled, "we'll explain everything my fa—everything Rex has done. Once she knows the truth, she'll have to help us."

I nod encouragingly, but I know it's not enough. I know she's waiting for me to say something about how perfectly our plan will go. How I'm sure she's right about her mom and how this is going to help us take down her dad and the whole evil hero organization.

But I can't force out the words—not now, when I'm feeling so shattered. I'm waiting for the next blow, and I'd be lying if I said I'm not afraid that that blow is going to come at the hands of Morgan Malone.

Rebel waits a few more seconds for me—for someone—to chime in, but when we all just look at her solemnly, she huffs out a sigh. Then turns and presses the perfectly polished doorbell.

The door is answered moments later by Celia, the Malones' housekeeper. She gasps when she sees Rebel, her eyes growing huge at the entourage her boss's only daughter has brought with her.

"Hi, Celia," Rebel says, stepping over the threshold and into the foyer without waiting to be invited in. "These are Riley's and my new friends. We were just stopping by because we want to see Mom. Is she around?" She doesn't give Celia a chance to answer before ushering everyone inside and then launching into a rapid-fire speech about how much she likes Celia's dress. Her shoes. Her new hair color.

By the time Rebel's nervous babble winds down, we're all a little shell-shocked. Including Celia, who lets out a little squeak that, along with erratic hand gestures, I take to mean *have a seat in the parlor*. Then she dashes down the hall toward the wing of the house that Mrs. Malone uses for her office and personal space.

"Should I follow her?" Rebel asks. "I mean, this *is* still my house, right? I don't need to wait for my mom like I'm some stranger."

"It's okay, babe," Dante tells her, ushering her toward the parlor. "Let's just sit down."

His eyes meet mine above her head, and that's when I know that he has the same sense of foreboding I do. The same sense we're going to have to pick up the Rebel-shaped pieces when this goes very, very wrong.

We all follow Rebel into the parlor and take seats on the various pieces of fussy furniture. It feels more like a museum than a home. And then we wait.

More than once I glance at Draven. I'm uncomfortable

and afraid that we're going to have to fight our way out of this place too. But what if Rex has security that even Jeremy and I can't disable? What if we don't have what it takes to get out of *this* house?

After what feels like forever but is probably only a couple of minutes, Mrs. Malone comes striding across the foyer and into the parlor.

"Rachel," she says, eyebrows raised and mouth tight with disapproval. "What are you doing with these people? And why are you dressed like that? Go to your room and put on something more appropriate."

Out of all the possible reactions I'd imagined from Morgan Malone, from shock to rage to instant ice storm, that one didn't even make the top hundred. I exchange another look with Dante. Maybe Rebel and Riley are right. Maybe their mom *is* under mind control.

She turns to her son. "And, Riley. What have you been thinking? Consorting with criminals. Bringing them into my house. It's a miracle they haven't killed all of us in our sleep!"

Yep. Mind control is looking more and more like a real possibility.

"Look, Mom." Rebel stands up, her hand in her left pocket. "Things have been crazy lately, and I want it all to be over. I just want to come home. Riley wants to come home too."

Mrs. Malone sniffs. "Yes, well, you can explain that to your father when he gets home. I left a message for him to come and deal with this situation once and for all."

Her words send a ripple of fear through the whole room. She's already called Rex and told him that we're here *in his home*! Why didn't any of us think about that? Why did we let Celia go get Mrs. Malone? We should have snuck in and ambushed her.

Before any of us can react, Rebel throws herself into her mother's arms with a sob. "I'm sorry, Mom. I'm so sorry. I got confused and I made a terrible mistake. But I'm going to make it better."

"You certainly will. And while your—" Mrs. Malone screams as Rebel slams the needle hard into the flesh where her neck meets her shoulder and pushes in the plunger.

"Rachel! What are you doing?" She struggles to push her daughter away.

"It's okay, Mom. Everything will make sense in just a few seconds."

"Have you poisoned me?" Mrs. Malone shrieks, grabbing at her neck.

"Of course not! I'm trying to help you."

"Mom, it's okay," Riley says. "We just want you to hear the truth from us—"

"I know the truth!" Her eyes are wild as she stares at Riley. "How did you break your sister free from the mind control?"

"What?" Rebel sounds like someone punched her in the stomach.

Mrs. Malone ignores her, focused on Riley. "Your father said yours would fade in time—they didn't have all the kinks worked out until a few years ago—but Rebel's should have been permanent. Foolproof."

"You know about this?" Rebel asks, her voice stretched thin with tears. Her hands fall limp at her sides, and she backs away from her mom. "You know about the mind control?"

"Of course I know about it," Mrs. Malone says indignantly,

shifting her attention back to her daughter. "Your father and I don't keep secrets from each other."

"And you let him do it? You let him control you too?"

Now she looks at Rebel like *she's* insane. "I'm not being controlled. I support his mission."

"It's not working." Rebel looks at me frantically. "Did you make it wrong?"

"I don't think it's the—"

"You made it wrong," she insists. "Make a new batch."

Dante reaches for her. "Babe, you saw it work on—"

"No," she says, wrenching out of his reach. "No! She's not immune."

Nitro lobs a fireball straight at Mrs. Malone. She squawks, tries to duck, but it slams straight into her. It doesn't do any damage when it hits though. Instead, the fireball disintegrates on impact.

"The serum is working just fine," Nitro says in disgust. "It's her brain that ain't."

"That can't be right," Riley whispers.

Dante sends a gale of wind straight at Mrs. Malone. It knocks the china off the shelves behind her but doesn't touch a hair on her head.

"Traitors!" Mrs. Malone yells. "You are traitors to your family, traitors to your people."

V snarls. "She's as crazy as her husband."

"Villain bitch," Mrs. Malone says, spitting in V's direction.

It all happens in a flash. V lunges for her, but freezes midstep—literally—when Mrs. Malone fires back with a wave of ice.

"Draven?" Dante says, with a hint of desperation as Mrs. Malone turns on Rebel.

"I'm trying," Draven says. "But she's immune."

Then, before anyone else can act, Deacon grabs Mrs. Malone in a headlock and applies a sharp pressure to the side of her neck, just behind her hero mark. And we all watch in silence as Rebel and Riley's mother falls to the ground, out cold.

CHAPTER 18

"What did you do that for?" Riley demands. He crosses to his mother's body and picks her up, then tenderly lays her on the fainting couch at the end of the room.

Deacon looks just as appalled by his actions as Riley does.

"What was the alternative?" V answers. "She can't be trusted. She's totally drinking your dad's Kool-Aid. And she's immune to powers. So until we figure out what to do with her, knocking her out was pretty much our only option. Unless you wanted me to kill her."

"No, I didn't want you to kill her! That's my mother! He could have been gentler is all!"

My heart clenches at the tears streaming down Riley's cheeks.

"Gentler?" V scoffs. "You mean like your father's been with us? She's just like him, and if we give her half a chance, she'll betray you too. She'll try to kill you."

"You don't know that—"

"She's right," Rebel interrupts him, not showing any signs of the devastation I expected her to feel. "We can't trust her. We don't know what she'll do." She turns to Dante. "Babe, go out to the garage and get some rope. We need to tie her up to make sure she doesn't do any more damage before we can get out of here."

"We don't have long," Draven says. "If she called your dad, he or his goons could show up any moment—"

"We've got to go!" Deacon heads to the nearest window and looks out at the front lawn. "We can't be here when they show up. We can't let Rex—"

His voice breaks and he stops talking. He's breathing heavily, his eyes darting around, and it hits home again just how messed up he is from being held captive. He's been better the last couple days, his body finally healing from the torture. But the emotional scars are a lot deeper than the physical wounds, and for a second I think he's going to fall apart.

Not that I would blame him. Not that any of us would blame him. He's been through hell, and the fact that he's doing so well shows just how strong he really is.

"We'll go," Draven tells him, stepping away from me to put a supportive hand on Deacon's shoulder. "Let's figure out what to do with Mrs. Malone, and then we'll get out of here. Regroup somewhere and try to figure out what to do next."

Deacon nods, but he doesn't stop staring out the window. I don't know if it's because he's watching for Rex's troops or if he's too ashamed to face us. I hope it's the former, because he has nothing to be ashamed of. I'm pretty sure I'd be in a lot worse shape if Rex had done to me half of what I know he did to Deacon.

Dante comes in with the rope, and he and Nitro set to work tying up Mrs. Malone. I rack my brain as they do, trying to figure a way out of this mess, which seems to get worse with every hour that passes. But before I can come up with anything, my phone buzzes in my back pocket.

As I pull it out, I realize that everyone else is doing the same. All of our phones are getting messages at the same time? That can only mean one thing: an SHN Alert.

Jeremy is the first to read the message. "Holy shitburgers."

The pop-up message on my home screen confirms my guess.

Hero League Offers Villain Amnesty

I click into the private SHN app and read the full article.

> In an unprecedented move, Rex Malone, president of the Superhero League, has announced a new truce initiative that, if successful, will end the longstanding battle between heroes and villains and quell the recent outbreaks of violence that threaten the secrecy essential to our world. According to the press release, the program will grant retroactive amnesty to all villains and villain sympathizers who voluntarily register their identities and powers with the League's Powers Protection Agency (PPA) within the next thirty-six hours. Full details of the program are available on our website. For up-to-the-minute coverage, tune in to SHN Live.

"What the hell?" Rebel whispers. "My dad's giving the villains amnesty?"

"No way," Draven says. "No way this deal is legit."

I shake my head. "Rex would never just forgive and forget. Not after everything that's happened."

Deacon nods. "He hates us way too much for that."

He's right. Rex Malone is not the type to wipe clean decades of hate and war. And he's definitely not the type to let go of the public humiliation he suffered at Draven's and my mom's trial. He'll want to make us suffer for that—make all villains suffer for it. The amnesty must be a trap so he can start exacting his revenge.

"We have to go," V orders. "We need to warn Anton—"

"He must have figured it out," Riley interrupts, his voice soft and sad.

"Figured out what?" Dante asks.

"How to break the resistance," Riley explains. "How to control villains too. Why else would he want them all to come in?"

Everyone falls silent as we consider his words.

I don't want to believe it. I mean, sure, Rex will stop at nothing in his quest for power. But this? Dangling the carrot of peace in front of the beleaguered villains, when instead of the carrot they'll get a baseball bat to the skull? It's beyond cruel.

"No one will fall for it," I say, my voice barely a whisper. "Right? No villain will be dumb enough to believe he would really—"

"Won't they?" Jeremy holds out his phone, showing me the SHN website.

The live feed from the SHN broadcast has a crawl across the bottom of the screen that reads, *Thousands of villains seek amnesty.*

A field reporter is on-site at a League district office in Colorado Springs, where a line of villains—the marks that define them as such clearly visible on their necks—is already waiting to register. Dozens of them. Maybe even hundreds.

Draven pounds his fist on a nearby table. "Damn it. How could they be so stupid?"

"Hope makes a desperate person let go of logic." Deacon's voice has that same haunted sound as when we first rescued him, and I know his mind is back in the hell that Rex and the Collective put him through.

And that fills me with even more rage. Because as awful as it is that Deacon has to live with those memories, it would be even worse for him not to have them. To have suffered and to never know because someone screwed with his mind.

Which is surely what Rex intends to do to every villain on the planet.

That is not okay.

"We have to stop this," I say.

Rebel's voice is shaky. "How?"

"I can break into the SHN live feed," Jeremy offers. "We can tell the world what Rex is doing so the villains won't trust him."

"They already don't trust him," Dante counters. "Still, they're lining up to turn themselves over to him."

Rebel wraps herself around his waist. "Not to mention many of them won't trust us because some of us are heroes."

"And all of us are wanted fugitives," Deacon adds.

"Besides," Nitro says, "that won't help the scores of villains who have already surrendered."

My stomach roils at the thought of just how many villains Rex might already control. We've seen, up close and dangerous, what happens when a hero is under the Collective's control. Add villains to his army of super drones, and we don't stand a chance.

Neither does the ordinary world. The idea that Rex's greed for power is limited to the super world is as naïve as the villains who think the amnesty offer is for real. Villains have been the only thing keeping him in check over the years. Take them out of the picture, and the rest of the world is next. He's not the kind of guy to rest on his laurels or be content with some power when he could have it all.

"We *have* to stop this." I can't take my eyes off the news feed, which has shifted to the loading dock behind the League office, where relieved and eager-looking villains are being loaded into unmarked white vans. "We have to end it. Once and for all."

"But how?" Dante asks. "We don't even know where Rex is taking them."

Riley makes a sour face. "The League owns property in every corner of the globe. We—" he begins, then quickly corrects himself. "*They* have hundreds of locations."

"They could be heading literally anywhere," Nitro adds.

"I could track them remotely," Jeremy suggests. "Between traffic cameras, cell phone towers, and surveillance drones, I could probably follow them anywhere."

"Probably?" Draven asks.

"There are physical limits to every technology. If they leave urban areas, tracking them gets harder. But I can do it. Hell, I can hijack an NSA satellite if I have enough time."

"We don't have that kind of time," I tell him. "We have no idea how fast Rex can implement the mind control. The villains might have only a few hours before their thoughts belong to him."

"Or less," Rebel says. "It only took seconds with me."

We all fall silent. It's one thing to think of this in the abstract, to imagine some nameless, faceless villain under Rex's control. It's another to know it happened to my best friend.

Seeing her turned from the heroes' most vocal critic into a lockstep mouthpiece for the bad guys tells me exactly how badly this can go. If they can do that to the girl who started the Zeroes, Not Heroes Facebook group, there are no limits to what they can do. To who they can control.

It could be any of us. Or all of us.

Suddenly, an idea occurs to me. Maybe the answer isn't to fight Rex's control, but give in to it. Or at least pretend to.

"What if I turn myself in?" I suggest.

"What?" Draven turns to stare at me, fury burning in his gaze. "No way."

"If I go in outfitted with a tracker, Jeremy won't have to task a satellite to follow me."

Draven crosses his arms over his chest, narrows his eyes. "Absolutely not."

"Just hear me out—"

"There's nothing to hear," Draven barks. "If you think for one second that I'm sending you gift-wrapped into that lunatic's clutches, then you don't know me nearly as well as I thought you do."

"Seriously, Kenna," Deacon says, and this time it's his turn to lay a calming hand on his cousin's shoulder. "That's a terrible idea. You know what Rex will do to you if he gets his hands on you."

"It's too dangerous," Rebel adds.

"Not if I take the immunity serum." Especially not with the version that lets me keep my power. Scratch that, power*s*.

Draven rolls his eyes at my argument. "Immunity to powers doesn't make you immortal."

I know he's only freaking out because he cares about me, but I'm tired of everyone telling me what I can and can't do. Of other people deciding what's too dangerous for little old me to take on.

I'm not powerless Kenna anymore. It's time people stopped treating me like I am.

Draven of all people knows how powerful I can be.

"If he thinks I'm having regrets," I argue, "that I want to rejoin the hero side, maybe he'll—"

"No." Riley says the word so forcefully that we all stop and stare at him.

His face is bright red. Not with embarrassment, but with anger. He is literally vibrating with rage.

Nitro wraps a supportive arm around his shoulders. Riley closes his eyes and leans into the touch. For several long seconds, he doesn't say anything—just seems to take strength from Nitro's support. But when I'm about to share more of my plan, he says, "Rex doesn't forgive. Rex doesn't believe in second chances. One strike with him and you're done."

This is a new Riley I haven't seen before. One who finally has his hero blinders off. And while I know it's important that he sees his father for what he is, I can't help mourning the guy who wore Superman pajamas and a coat that looked like a cape. The guy who believed that every decision really was black and white, that heroes were good, villains were bad, and there was no middle ground.

A tiny part of me misses being able to see the world that way. But once you start seeing things clearly, there's no going back.

"He will kill you, Kenna," Riley continues. "After what you did at the trial, after you embarrassed him like that, he won't rest until you're dead. And he'll make it as painful as possible."

Riley's certainty sends a sickening chill down my spine. It's no more than I said earlier, but it's awful to hear it laid out like that. Awful to truly understand how badly this plan can go wrong—and what will happen if it does.

"You were spot-on about the tracking though," Jeremy says. "I've been working on a new microscopic device that is totally organic and can be rendered undetectable. If we sent someone in, I'd be able to follow them directly to the source."

"We could recruit someone," Rebel suggests. "Ask some other villain to go in with the tracker."

Draven shakes his head. "Out of the question. We're not asking someone else to put their life on the line."

"We can't ask someone to risk suffering what I went through," Deacon says. "I won't do it."

He has a point. But I'm sure there are plenty of villains who would risk almost anything if they knew what the heroes were really up to. In the scheme of things, one life versus the perpetual mental prison of tens of thousands? Any villain with even an ounce of integrity would see that as a no-brainer.

That's not the only concern though.

"There's another problem," I argue. "How could we trust someone to be our mole even if they offered? We couldn't know for sure whether Rex has them under mind control already. We might be putting our faith in someone who is already lost."

Riley nods. "And that person could tell Rex everything about our plans."

"We use the immunity serum," Rebel says.

Deacon gestures at the room around us. "That worked out so well here. We can't guarantee it will work fast enough to keep us safe."

Draven covers my hand with his. "The only supers we can trust for certain are the ones in this room."

"Too bad we've all been burned," Nitro says.

Dante snorts. "Some of us literally."

Nitro glares at him. "I mean Rex knows our faces, arsehole."

"Guys, come on," Rebel says, trying to prevent another all-out war between them. "He didn't mean anything by it, Nitro."

"Then your boyfriend shouldn't have teased him about his control issues," Riley shoots back. "Especially since all he can do is blow a little hot air around."

"Wow, hero boy, don't hold back. Tell us how you really feel."

In an instant, everyone is yelling, tossing barbs, and hitting below the belt. The great thing about being friends is we know each other's vulnerabilities and can watch each other's backs. But in a fight, we know exactly where to hit to do the most damage.

And right now, it seems almost all of us are intent on causing damage of one type or another. Emotions are on edge; nerves are frazzled to the breaking point. And it's no wonder. We know what Rex is planning, what he's *implementing*, and we have no idea how to stop him. It's starting to feel like we'll never get ahead of this, like we'll be chasing Rex and his evil plans forever. The very thought is exhausting.

"He doesn't know my face." V's quiet words silence the chaos.

Dante turns to face her. "What did you say?"

"Malone doesn't know me," she tells him. "Which means I'm the perfect person to go in. You know I'm not compromised. You know you can trust me. Give me the immunity serum and I'll turn myself in."

Every last one of us stares at her as she finishes her mini speech. Not because we think it's a bad idea, but because V is actually volunteering. Over the few days she's been with us, she's had our backs. She's kept us safe and—with some coaxing—pretty much gone along with all of our wild plans.

But she's always seemed kind of...removed from it. Removed from us.

It's been us and her. As in two separate forces.

And by volunteering, she's saying she's part of us. She's part of the team. I don't know how to respond to that.

"What?" she asks, looking irritated that we aren't immediately either jumping up and down or telling her we can't let her do that. "You idiots are the only ones allowed to come up with suicidal plans?"

Draven breaks the stunned silence first. "No, you're right," he says. "You're the best option."

"Screw that," she snaps. "I'm the only option."

That's when I see the fear lurking beneath her bravado. She likes to keep up the tough-girl image, but underneath it all she is just as vulnerable—just as human—as the rest of us.

"You are," I tell her. "You are the only way we can keep Rex from getting total, unstoppable control."

She nods and takes a deep breath. "Now what?"

"First," I say, gesturing at where Mrs. Malone is tied up on the couch. She's awake now and staring at us with huge eyes. "We have to find someplace to leave her."

Because the last thing we need in our quest to stop Rex is his wife getting in the way or, worse, tipping him off. He has to know we'll be coming for him. Hell, he might have even set up this whole amnesty ruse to draw us out. But right now he doesn't know where or when or how we will come for him. Our only advantage is surprise. We need to keep it that way.

"I know where we can dump the old bag," Nitro says.

From the maniacal look on his face, I can tell this idea is either devious or delightful. Or maybe both.

CHAPTER 19

Quake lives in a quonset hut east of downtown Boulder, just a few blocks from the Lair, the nightclub he and Nitro own. From the outside, his place looks like an abandoned warehouse, covered in rust, surrounded by weeds, and with a huge hangar door on the end that looks like it hasn't been opened in decades. The driveway is cracked and jagged, broken concrete jutting up in all different directions. As if it's been in an earthquake.

And maybe it has.

Whatever's happened to it, everything about this place says *stay away*.

Which is why my heart is pounding as Nitro leads us to the side door and rings the bell.

"He's probably still asleep," Nitro says. "He's always the last one to leave the club at night."

Wow, that makes me feel so much better. By all means, let's wake up the exhausted supervillain.

I know my fear is unfair, that Quake is on our side. He teamed up with Draven and Nitro to bring down the hero bunker at Lima Whiskey, and—according to the guys—he's way more gentle giant than cold-blooded killer.

Still, it's hard to shake a decade of brainwashing. It's like facing down the bogeyman. As much as I tell myself Quake's reputation is an exaggeration, I can't stop my body from entering panic mode at the thought of him.

Nitro rings the bell again. There are still no signs of life inside. Hell, there are no signs of life *outside*. Anyone passing by would think this place is totally abandoned.

Maybe it is.

Jeremy points out a security camera well-hidden above the door. "Someone doesn't want surprise guests."

"Are you sure this is the right hut?" I ask Nitro.

Draven gestures at the other, similarly dilapidated buildings on this block. "They do all kind of look alike."

"I'm sure," Nitro says with a growl.

I have a feeling that one day Nitro is going to get fed up and blow all of us to smithereens. I probably wouldn't blame him. He does take the brunt of a lot of teasing.

Only Riley seems to always have his back. If that's not the irony of the century, I'm not sure what is.

Besides, who would have thought that Nitro, one of the most feared and dangerous of all the villains, would be such a...harmless goofball?

Remembering that gives my Quake fears a big punch in the gut. If all the fearmongering about Nitro was way off base, maybe the stories about Quake are too.

Hell, if the hero reports are to be believed, now *I'm* one of the most dangerous villains to ever live.

Then again, when it comes to Rex Malone, maybe I am.

As Nitro pounds his forearm against the door, I find myself relaxing with the promise that Quake is just a big, old teddy bear. Maybe he'll even invite us in for a cup of tea or hot co—

Suddenly, the door bursts open, sending Nitro stumbling into Riley with the force of the swing.

"Do you know what time it is?" a male voice roars as one of the largest men I've ever seen fills the open doorway.

Now, I've seen Quake before, but always from a distance. Seeing his imposing form up close and personal, coupled with the menacing scowl on his face, sends my heart rate right back to pre-self-reassurance levels. The guy is huge. And looks like he eats mountains for breakfast. Which, according to the reports, he does.

That thought, more than anything, straightens my spine. I will not succumb to the paranoia. I will not be the unwitting pawn of Rex's schemes and smear campaigns.

I will, however, keep at least one other villain between Quake and me. I inch closer to Draven's side.

"Time to make our play," Nitro tells his brother.

Quake squints at him. "Are you being funny?"

Somehow the British accent makes him less intimidating.

"No," Nitro says. "We're getting real."

"All right." Quake straightens up to his full height of six-foot-something. "I'll get me keys."

"Actually…" Now Nitro looks nervous.

I'd be nervous too if I were about to tell someone as huge as Quake that we don't need him to come along, we need him to babysit.

Nitro swallows hard.

I take pity on him.

"Actually," I say, stepping in, "we have an important job for you to do right here from home."

Quake spears me with a burning glare. It's kind of a miracle that I don't pass out on the spot.

"You're Kenna, right?" he asks, like he's not sure if he likes me or not.

That's fine. He doesn't have to like me. He just has to trust me—or at least trust his friends enough that his trust splashes over onto me.

"Yes. I'm Kenna Swift."

He looks me up and down, then runs his gaze over the rest of us gathered on his doorstep—well, not so much a step as a worn spot in the dirt. When he sees Mrs. Malone, unconscious and cradled in Riley's arms, Quake's frown deepens.

I notice Riley wince, but he doesn't say anything to defend his mom. I don't know if that's good or bad.

"That's the job we're talking about," Draven tells him. "We need someone we can trust to watch her—"

"Huh-uh," Quake says, shaking his head and starting to close the door. "No way. One run-in with her in a dark alley is enough. I'd rather keep my bollocks out of the freezer."

"She's harmless," I start to explain.

"Harmless?" Quake looms over me. "Tell that to Mickey Lee. Spent a week as an ice cube, thanks to her. Literally, one week in a massive block of ice. Lost half his toes to frostbite."

"What I mean is," I continue with a chiding tone, "that we can make it so her powers can't hurt you."

Assuming he's willing to take the immunity serum.

Quake stares at me. Still uncertain of me.

"Look, can we come inside?" I suggest. "We'll explain everything."

After several tense seconds in which I am totally prepared

for him to shake the world around me to the ground, Quake steps back and waves us inside.

The interior is nothing like I expected from the exterior. In fact, it's pristine. Like someone with hospital-quality cleaning standards scoured the entire building from top to bottom. The floor is a gleaming polished concrete; the furnishings are modern industrial, like something out of an old-school sci-fi movie; and the space is lit by warm overhead lighting.

It's all completely at odds with the worn-out look outside. But it's all so calming that I immediately feel my tension easing.

We follow Quake past the kitchen area to a massive farmer's table that could easily seat twenty. Quake takes the seat at the head of the table, and everyone else fills in around him.

I sink into the chair gratefully, my hand finding Draven's under the table. This feels like the first truly relaxed moment we've had since the cabin blew up. Or, more precisely, since Rex blew up the cabin. Since then we've been on the run, hiding, sneaking around, fearing for our lives and the lives of our loved ones. Always trying to stay one step ahead of the hero's kill squad.

We're still doing that obviously, but here at Quake's I feel… safe. Secure. Like nothing can hurt us here. And like we all can take a huge sigh of relief.

Even V seems more at ease than she has since I've met her. And she doesn't seem like the sort to *ever* relax. Especially considering what she's just volunteered to do.

I allow myself to sink into Draven. For the space of a couple breaths I allow myself to let it all go. To…be.

When I open my eyes, Quake is looking straight at me.

For some reason, my fear is gone. I have no worries.

"You like that, huh?" he asks.

I frown at him. "What?"

"The calming sensation." He braces his massive forearms on the table. "My girlfriend is a serenity inducer. She leaves a trail of it behind even when she isn't here."

"She the yoga instructor?" Nitro asks.

Quake nods.

"Wow." The scientist in me is unwittingly fascinated. "I've never experienced that power. Is it pheromone based?" I ask.

"Kenna," Dante says, his voice tinged with impatience as he recognizes my detour. "Can you turn off the science geek for a few minutes?"

"Oh, right!" I say. "Mrs. Malone. The reason we're here."

The serenity inducement is obviously working a little too well.

After considering several different approaches to bring Quake up to speed, I decide I should probably get straight to the point. "Rex is mind-controlling supers."

"What, like hypnotism?" he asks.

"No. As far as we can tell, it has to be a superpower. He has to be using someone to do it. We're just not sure who or what the exact power really is."

Draven leans forward, resting his elbows on his knees. "Until recently, he'd only been able to control heroes."

"Well, that explains a lot of what's wrong in heroland," Quake says.

"My thoughts exactly," Nitro agrees.

"But we think he's finally figured out how to control villains too," I add. "Which means he's implementing his endgame."

Quake runs a hand over his smooth-shaven head. "The amnesty."

I nod. "The amnesty," I confirm.

He spits out an epithet so nasty I think it's only legal in England. And then only when your favorite football club loses.

"My thoughts exactly," Nitro says again.

"So where does this one come in?" Quake nods at Riley. "Isn't he daddy's lapdog?"

"Not anymore," Riley says with an edge to his voice.

Nitro pats Riley's hand. "He's with us."

Quake's brows hit his hairline, and the two brothers exchange a long look. Then Quake smiles at Riley. "All right then."

"We need you to watch Mrs. Malone while we carry out the plan," Dante explains, wrapping his arm around Rebel's shoulders. "She's not safe. She could tell her husband we're coming, and we'd be dead before we got there."

Rebel reaches up to squeeze Dante's hand. "My dad won't hesitate to kill me and Riley. Apparently my mom doesn't care enough to stop him."

I glance at the armchair where Riley set his unconscious mother.

If she were awake, would Mrs. Malone say something to contradict Rebel? As insane as it seems, as much as I can't imagine that she actually believes in Rex's philosophies enough to be okay with him killing their children, I'm not so sure. I've stopped being surprised by that kind of loyalty. Clearly she's not the only one in the hero world who believes that Rex's ends justify his means, that the big picture is more important than a few—or a lot of—lives.

"You want me to play babysitter while you go off and save the super world?" Quake leans back in his chair. "Not bloody likely."

"It's the only way," Nitro says. "Your cover is as blown as the rest of ours—there's no way Rex will think you want to turn yourself in for amnesty. Better for you to stay here, out of the way, than risk…"

"What?" Quake snarls, looking totally unconvinced.

"I already lost Mum and Dad because of Rex Malone. I can't take a chance on losing you too."

Quake looks like he's going to throw up at the sweetness of Nitro's confession, but he doesn't protest anymore. Instead, he asks, "What am I supposed to do with her?"

"Just sit on her," Nitro says with a cocky grin.

"Literally, if necessary," Riley adds.

Quake nods. "All right. For a while anyway. You said something about making it so her powers won't work on me?"

I explain how the immunity serum works, leaving out the part where the version my mom made suppressed my own powers. He might be less likely to take it if he thinks it might leave him powerless. At this point I think his safety—and the overall safety of our mission—is worth the cost of a lie of omission.

"It really works?" he asks. "Seriously?"

"As a bloody heart attack," Nitro replies, then lobs a fireball at Jeremy's head.

"Hey!" Jeremy complains as the fireball dissolves in front of his face. "Was that necessary?"

Nitro smirks.

"All right," Quake says. "I'm convinced."

Without preamble, he pushes up his shirtsleeve, revealing

an upper arm that is roughly twice as thick as my thigh. Just like that, he's ready for the shot. I'm a little humbled by his trust. We never spoke before today, and now he's letting me dose him up with immunity serum. All because he trusts his brother and the Cole boys enough to trust me.

The loyalty that heroes show to Rex is nothing compared to the loyalty I've seen villains display. I hate that I was so wrong about them for so long.

My hands shake a little as I prepare the injection, but Quake doesn't even flinch as I send the serum into his bloodstream.

"I can't sit around here all day," he says when I'm done, pushing his sleeve back down. "What do I do with her when I head in to work tonight?"

"Put her in the walk-in," I suggest.

If it could keep Draven and Dante locked up the night Rebel and Jeremy and I broke into ESH Labs, it can keep Mrs. Malone under control for a while. Her power won't do her any favors through six-inch-thick walls designed to contain cold.

"I like the way you think, Swift," Quake tells me.

Jeremy gives me a thumbs-up.

"Now if you idiots don't mind, I need a shower." Quake pushes to his feet. "You staying long enough for me to do that? Or do I need to handcuff her to my toilet?"

"We'll be here," Nitro says at the same time Deacon asks, "You have handcuffs?"

"Actually," I venture, emboldened by my new not-fear of Quake and his apparent approval of me, "we'd like to stay for a little while. We need to get our tracking equipment up and running before we begin."

Quake nods. "Stay as long as you like. Just don't break

anything." As he walks toward the back of the space, toward a door that probably leads to a bedroom suite, he adds, "And know that the serenity will wear off in a bit."

Good to know. For now, tempers and tensions are at a minimum, but that won't last.

It never does when you've got nine different personalities trying to fit together like mismatched puzzle pieces.

"What's the plan, K?" Rebel asks.

I nod to Riley and Nitro. "You guys make sure Mrs. Malone doesn't wake up. Jeremy and I will get V set up for her infiltration."

"What about us?" Draven asks, gesturing to his cousins. "We aren't going to sit around doing nothing."

"No," I say. "You're going to get us more appropriate transportation."

"What's wrong with the van?" V asks.

"Nothing," I reply. "But we have no idea where they'll take you, no clue how far we might have to drive. I'd rather have a car with the best gas mileage around."

"So, hybrids?" Deacon guesses.

I smile. "Exactly."

"And while we're at it," Dante says, "we'll get provisions for the road. Food, water—"

"Orange soda," Jeremy pipes in.

Draven shakes his head. "We'll get what we can."

"Draven," I call out as they head for the door. When he turns back, I say, "Be careful."

He nods, winks at me, and then they're gone.

"And me?" Rebel asks.

I give her a sympathetic smile. "You've been through"—I

flick a glance at Mrs. Malone—"a lot in the last couple days. You should get some rest."

Soon, before the calming effects from Quake's girlfriend wear off. It might be Rebel's only chance of getting sleep for quite a while.

"I don't need rest," she says defiantly, even as she stifles a yawn.

"Sure you don't," I tell her. "But you'll be a lot more help if you get some."

She reluctantly agrees, letting me lead her over to a couch to lie down.

It's funny. Rebel and I have kind of gone through reflections of each other's experiences lately. I found out my mom was a better person than I ever imagined; she found out hers is way worse.

For once, I wouldn't trade places with her for anything.

Jeremy and I set up our station at Quake's kitchen counter.

"Imported marble." Jeremy smooths his hand over the countertop. "Very nice."

"Stop screwing around," V snaps. "Let's get this started."

Jeremy looks wounded, but I understand where V is coming from. She's scared—an emotion she's not used to dealing with—and rather than to succumb to it, she trying to muscle through.

"Yeah, let's not waste any time," I tell Jeremy. "The longer we take, the more villains Rex gets under his control."

Jeremy starts laying his equipment out on the counter. His laptop—which has miraculously survived every explosion and battle we've had to go through—plus an array of gadgets, a bunch of wires, some dime-size devices, and a soldering iron.

He looks like he's ready to build a robot. Or NASA's next spaceship.

"This is the tracking device," he explains, holding up a small silver disk. "I call it the Watchdog."

"I'm warning you, HB2," V says, but her voice has a hint of humor.

Jeremy clears his throat. "It looks like and acts like a basic watch battery, but it is so much more."

He pulls up a screen on his computer. It is a map display, like an old-school eighties-style interface—neon bright colors against black. It shows a satellite view of Colorado, the rectangular outline of the state glowing in blue.

A bright-purple dot blinks over Boulder's location within the state.

Jeremy taps his trackpad and the map zooms in. First to the amorphous shape of the city of Boulder, then to the gridded streets of downtown, and finally to the block where Quake's quonset hut sits between an auto parts warehouse and an appliance repair shop.

The purple dot glows in the center of the screen.

"This baby speaks to seven different satellites at once, giving me precision, down-to-the-inch, better-than-the-freaking-NSA location tracking anywhere on the globe."

V rolls her eyes. "Very impressive, geek boy. You can track me. Any cell phone can do that." She leans one elbow on the counter. "But can you keep Rex from finding it."

"Of course—"

"And any technopath he controls."

Jeremy grins. "Allow me to demonstrate."

He pulls an ordinary-looking analog watch out of his

backpack. He twists the back off, removes the existing battery, and replaces it with his tracking device.

When he flips the watch back over, the second hand is ticking away. "See, just an ordinary watch."

"Rex isn't going to pat me down," V argues. "He'll have technopaths scanning every inch of me."

"This is a technoscope." Jeremy picks up one of his gadgets. "It mimics, to ninety-nine-percent accuracy, the scanning powers of a technopath, such as myself."

He pushes a button on the side, and the gadget starts beeping.

"With the tracking device engaged," Jeremy says, waving the technoscope over the watch, "the signal is easily detected."

The gadget emits a high-pitched siren.

I slap my hands over my ears. V just glares at him.

"But," he says, leaning out of reach when she tries to punch him in the arm, "with the tracker turned off"—he presses against the winding dial on the side of the watch—"it becomes invisible."

This time, when he swipes the technoscope over the watch, it doesn't make a sound.

"You're sure?" I ask.

"Positive," Jeremy promises. "Just push the dial when you're being actively scanned. No one will ever know."

"How will I know when I'm being scanned?" V asks.

Jeremy grins. "I'm glad you asked. This"—he picks up what looks like a pack of chewing gum and pulls out a stick—"is my other masterpiece. Here, try a piece."

"You have got to be—"

"Trust me." Jeremy holds out the stick. "Just try."

V reluctantly opens the gum, tears off half, and pops it in her mouth. She hands me the other half.

"Now, chew."

Spearmint. Gross.

When we're busy chewing, Jeremy raises his hands and waves them over us.

"Feeling anything?" he asks.

I shake my head. "Nothing."

"Good." He winks. "Because I wasn't scanning."

V punches him in the arm.

Jeremy rubs his shoulder with one hand and keeps waving the other over us. "How about now?"

The instant he asks the question, the gum starts vibrating. Not enough to make a sound or probably even be noticeable, but enough to make the small blob feel totally weird.

V spits it out into her palm.

"What the hell?"

"Nanobots," Jeremy explains. "They react to the ultrasonic frequency of a technopath's scan."

"Are they safe?" I ask, dropping my gum in the trash can.

"Absolutely," Jeremy replies. "But I wouldn't swallow them. They might cause a variety of unpleasant side effects."

"Noted," V says, tossing out her gum.

Great, we've got the tracking part of the plan covered. We'll be able to follow her wherever Rex takes her, without him being any the wiser. Now we just need to dose V up with the immunity serum, and she'll be good to go.

CHAPTER 20

As we pull out of Quake's driveway, I'm driving the first car in a mini-procession of two identical hybrids. The atmosphere inside is eerily silent.

We've been on the edge of danger for weeks. We've broken into labs and bunkers, been hunted and chased and nearly blown up more than once. But this is the first time that we are willingly sending someone into Rex's grasp.

V is a true hero.

I steer the car through the streets, knowing the directions to Martin Price Elementary School by muscle memory. It's the same hero school where I met Rebel. Where I had my first crush on a hero boy who could change the weather. Where I realized what it really meant to be powerless.

When I went there, I wanted more than anything to be part of the hero world. I wanted a power. Wanted to be able to help them protect the world. And now…now everything is different. I'm more powerful than anyone but Draven knows. And, if things go according to plan, I'm about to bring the hero world to its knees—and, hopefully, save the villain world, my world, while I do it.

What a difference a few weeks makes.

"If you think your cover is blown," I explain, meeting V's gaze in the rearview mirror, "turn your tracker off and back on. Three times fast, three slow, and then three fast again."

I expect a scathing response, something about how she knows how to send an SOS in Morse code. But she just nods and says, "Got it."

In the backseat next to her, Jeremy is typing away on his laptop.

He's always a fast typist, but he sounds even more frenetic than usual.

His crush on V has been obvious since the moment he saw her—well, after she stopped shooting at him. He cares about her and he's worried about her. I totally get that.

As if reading my thoughts, Draven reaches over and takes my hand that's resting on the gearshift and laces our fingers together.

Yeah, I totally get that.

We drive the rest of the way to the school in silence.

There is something truly evil about using an elementary school for such nefarious purposes. It's like Rex is destroying the innocence of childhood too, along with all the villains.

Not that he hasn't been doing that all along. This time it's just more ironic.

I come to a stop around the corner from the school. Dante pulls the second car past me, giving us a little mock salute as they go by. They're going to meet us at the rendezvous point—the bagel shop parking lot where we're going to sit and watch V's tracker until it tells us where to go next.

We can't risk following the transport vehicle directly from the school. Who knows what kind of hero surveillance is active in this neighborhood right now? We could be surrounded and captured before V is off campus.

Once the other car is safely out of range, the four of us climb out onto the sidewalk. For several seconds, we stand in awkward silence. V looks over her shoulder to the corner she'll be disappearing around in moments.

It's, I don't know, kind of heartbreaking to see someone so tough look so worried.

"We've got you," I say, feeling the need to reassure her. "Jeremy is the absolute best. Wherever they take you, we'll follow."

When V turns back to face me, her lips are kicked up in a cocky grin that I'm starting to think all villains possess. I'll have to practice mine.

"I know," she says, all traces of her worry are gone.

I press a syringe of immunity serum into her hand. "If you get in a tight spot, use it on someone who's being controlled. Then at least you'll have an ally on the inside."

She nods and tucks the capped syringe into the inside pocket of her jacket.

"Take the full pack of gum," Jeremy says, his voice strained. "In case you lose the piece you're chewing. And as soon as you feel the vibrations, you punch that dial. Your tracker will cut out until you punch it back on. And if you can't punch it back on, I can activate it remotely. I won't do that unless I think something's wrong. I just want you to know that I can. That I will, if…if things look…"

He looks lost.

"I won't let them—"

V slides one hand behind his neck, yanks him close, and

kisses him. For several long, awkward, I-have-to-look-away seconds. Draven grins and nods in that male gesture of appreciation—he clearly approves.

When V finally releases Jeremy, he's panting, his mouth hanging open in shock, and she's grinning. She says simply, "I know."

Then, without another word, she turns and starts down the sidewalk.

I want to stand there watching, waiting until she's around the corner and out of sight. That's the natural instinct when you're sending a friend into danger.

But time is a luxury we can't afford to waste. Who knows how long it will be before V is on the move. Ten minutes? Twenty? Five? It could be as soon as she walks through the door or after a lengthy interview or examination. We have to be prepared for either scenario.

So, with V's life potentially hanging in the balance, we jump back into the car and I gun it for the bagel shop.

"I've got her," Jeremy says from the backseat.

He hunches down over his laptop, following the blinking purple dot on the screen. "She's inside the school. It looks like"—he punches some keys—"she's in the cafeteria. They must have a staging area set up in there. Too bad I don't have access to an infrared satellite. I would love to know just how many villains are in there right now."

Next to me, Draven growls. "Too many."

Agreed.

I steer the car through the narrow residential streets, heading for the bagel shop that's popular with the college students. It shouldn't look too conspicuous for us to be hanging out in the parking lot, crowding around a laptop to watch a livestream.

As long as no one knows what we're livestreaming, we're good.

"Oh!" Jeremy yelps. "Her tracker just went dark."

His voice is higher than usual.

"They must be scanning her," I tell him. "She'll turn it back on as soon as she can."

Even if he knows I'm right, I can still feel the tension radiating from the backseat. And from the passenger seat next to me. My own tension ratchets up a notch.

My brain knows we expected V to be scanned.

My heart isn't so confident. My heart seems determined to beat a rapidly increasing rhythm of runaway fear for what might be going on in that cafeteria.

Not knowing really sucks.

I pull into the bagel shop parking lot, guiding the little hybrid into the spot that Riley and Nitro are holding for us. As soon as we're stopped, Deacon yanks open the back door.

"Any news?"

I swivel in my seat. Jeremy is focused on his computer, oblivious to everything except whatever is—or isn't—blinking on his screen.

"She turned off her tracker," I tell Deacon.

"But that's—?"

I nod. "Totally expected."

No one looks reassured by that reminder.

Seconds tick on into minutes. We are all in suspended animation. All of us have our full attention on Jeremy, waiting for something to change. Waiting for news.

"How long until you remote activate?" Dante asks. When Jeremy ignores him, he turns to me. "Kenna? How long?"

"I—" I what? I don't know? I don't want to make that decision? I wish there was some way to know what was going on inside that school.

"Yes!" Jeremy shouts, saving me from having to come up with answers. He squirms in the backseat, a space-confined version of his victory dance. "She's back on!"

He pushes Deacon out of the open door, climbs out, and circles to the front of the car. He sets the computer down on the hood, where we can all gather around to watch.

"There," he says, pointing to the purple dot. "She's right there."

I watch as the purple dot moves slowly through halls marked by lemon-yellow lines. Familiar halls. She moves out of the cafeteria, making the turn toward the first-grade hall. I had Mr. Carvelle for first grade. His classroom was the first door on the left-hand side.

V's purple dot moves past Mr. Carvelle's room. Past the bathrooms in the middle of the hall. Past the art room and the computer lab.

The dot stops, then enters the last classroom on the right. The music room.

I can picture it as clearly as if I were sitting there. All the little chairs lined up in rows, cabinets full of musical instruments and sheet music and so many wonders to a little six-year-old mind. The dot doesn't move again for a long time. That must be the interview room.

We go through three rounds of coffee, a dozen bagels for breakfast, and a run to the sub shop up the block for lunch.

Dante and Rebel are just getting back with the sandwiches when the dot finally moves.

"We're up!" Jeremy shouts. "She's on the move."

It's the signal we've been waiting for. No one says a word as we split up into the two cars. This time Deacon rides with us, so they don't have to cram three into the backseat of the other hybrid.

We have no idea how long this is going to take, but we have full tanks of gas, enough food and water to last at least as long as the gas, and we have a direction. With Jeremy guiding me from the backseat, I follow V out of town to the south.

CHAPTER 21

I'm careful to keep us at least two miles behind the vehicle we're tailing. Far enough to be out of sight for even a super with vision powers. The last thing we want is to be spotted and captured—or worse—before we can stop Rex's mind-control scheme.

As impatient as I am to lay eyes on them, I force myself not to get overly anxious.

The purple dot keeps moving on Jeremy's map until we reach Pueblo. We drive past the gas station where they've stopped and then circle back around to the drive-through taco place next door.

They're in a white van with blackout windows, just like the one in the SHN newscast. The driver gets out to fill the tank, while another guard sits in the front passenger seat, presumably to keep an eye on the passengers.

I can't help but imagine scenarios to break V free. My power could disable the gas pump, sending the driver inside to pay, while Draven's knocks out the guard. Rebel and Dante could send the van soaring away from the gas station while Riley flies up to grab our girl. Nitro could blow the whole thing up while Deacon keeps the van safe with a downpour.

Strategizing has become as natural as breathing to me. But for once, I have to put all of the possible chess moves aside. Getting V back isn't the endgame. Following her to the source is.

"Want me to drive?" Draven asks.

I let my head flop back against the headrest with a groan. "God, yes."

If I have to stare out on the monotonous stretch of highway for one minute longer, I am going to lose my mind.

When the van pulls away, we take its place at the gas station and fill our tanks. Just in case. Then we're following again, farther south with every passing minute.

If I thought driving was bad, I had no idea. At least driving gave me something to think about. But when I'm sitting in the passenger seat with Draven behind the wheel, my mind is free to wander, to imagine what's happening with V. To wonder what we're going to find when her purple dot stops for good.

To think about my mom.

I push those thoughts aside as soon as they surface. I can't afford to let my emotions take over right now—not when so many lives are depending on the success of this plan.

Four hours into our tailing assignment, we cross the border into New Mexico.

There isn't an obvious change, no bright-red stripe on the road to indicate we've crossed a state line. Just a yellow sign dotted with red and green chili peppers and yet another long stretch of nothing. A few mountains peek up above the horizon in the distance, but for the most part, the Rockies have dipped out of sight.

I lose track of time as the miles roll by.

"They're turning," Jeremy says, his voice excited and breaking up the monotony of the highway.

"Where?" I twist in my seat.

Deacon is looking over Jeremy's shoulder at the display.

"There's a road off to the right about two miles ahead." He squints at his computer screen. "It leads to what looks like... This can't be right."

"What?" Draven and I ask at the same time.

"The satellite image..." Jeremy says, his voice trailing off.

"What?" Draven asks more emphatically.

Deacon looks at me. "The image is blank."

"What does that mean?" I ask.

"I don't understand," Jeremy says, his fingers flying over the keyboard. "I'm using U.S. government satellites on the highest clearance levels. Nothing should be redacted."

"Maybe it's protected," I suggest.

"Maybe..." Jeremy says. "But that would entail huge amounts of constant power use. No single super could sustain it for long."

Draven makes a disgusted sound. "Well, we know Rex has countless hero drones available to him. Maybe he's using all of them..."

"He could literally use them up completely, until they die," Deacon says with a dark tone, "then toss them aside and get new ones."

I shudder at the thought. Imagining being under Rex's control is bad enough, but I hadn't really considered the extent of the physical control he could have. He could make a mind-controlled super do literally anything...even kill themselves.

If that's not horrifying, I don't know what is.

But I can't be overwhelmed by that right now. We have a plan. We have a mission. We have to get this right. If we don't, the future we're all afraid of is going to become the present.

"So we have no idea what we're driving into," I say, bringing the conversation back to the plan.

"Not a clue," Jeremy agrees.

"And we're okay with that?"

Draven stares grimly at the road ahead. "We'll find out when we get there."

I face forward, anxiously awaiting what the next turn will bring. "I guess we will."

Jeremy traces the path of the purple dot off the main road and onto a winding one. His tracker is apparently outfitted with an altimeter, because he tells us that the road seems to be winding up a hill or the face of a mountain.

None of us answer him. We're all too busy worrying about V and our messed-up situation. At least until Jeremy gasps a few minutes later. "Her tracker is off."

My heart stutters in my chest.

"That's okay," I force myself to say calmly, though a part of me wants to completely freak out. "We expected that. We expected Rex to scan her again at the destination."

"I know," Jeremy says.

I don't like hearing the anxiety that's tightening his voice. Jeremy is usually the cheerful, joking, optimistic one. The one who always believes we're going to succeed in taking down the heroes. I wish I could soothe his fears away.

I reach between the seats to give him my hand and am relieved when he takes it and gives it a quick squeeze.

But then he's back to speed-typing on his laptop, and the reassuring contact is gone. For both of us.

When we reach the turnoff, we slow down to a snail's pace and follow the route. I focus my power on keeping any electronic surveillance from spotting us. Unfortunately, I can't do anything about powers-based surveillance. If Rex has a super scanning for power signatures, we're sitting ducks.

But we've got enough trouble to deal with right now. No use borrowing more until we find out if it's warranted.

"The van stopped over that next rise," Jeremy tells us, leaning forward between the seats. He points to a spot where the road we're on disappears. "Wherever they're taking them is right over that hill."

Draven steers the little hybrid off the road to the left. The car isn't really made for this kind of terrain, so it takes every bump hard.

I don't think any of us feel it. We're too wrapped up in all the things that can go wrong—or right—with my plan.

My heart is pounding so hard I think it's going to thump right out of my chest. I'm eager and anxious to see what this mystery facility is.

"Shouldn't her tracker be back on by now?" Jeremy asks.

"Not necessarily," I say, trying to be reassuring. "They could be performing an extended scan."

Draven guides the car farther into the brush. "Or something could be blocking the signal."

"Yeah," Deacon says optimistically. "Like the same thing that's blocking the satellite images."

"No way," Jeremy insists. "My tracker is completely unblockable."

"Then I'm sure she's just being scanned again." I make myself sound more certain than I feel, for Jeremy's sake.

We park both cars in a spot that's hidden from the road. Dante wind-sweeps our tire tracks so no one will see where we've driven, and then we start for the rise on foot. Up the hill, toward the spot where V's tracker turned off. Over to where the white van stopped. Down to where Rex is mind-controlling villains.

I'm not sure what I expect—something like the shiny facade of the ESH Lab building or an underground bunker like the one at Lima Whiskey. But what sits on the land before us looks more like an abandoned mining operation, all weird metal shapes painted with dust and dotted with lights and wires.

Nitro says, "That's so…"

"Unimpressive?" Riley finishes.

"Maybe there's more below the surface," Rebel says.

I turn to Jeremy. "Can you techno-scan the building, see if you can tell us anything about it?"

Jeremy doesn't look up from his computer screen. "No."

It's not the answer any of us are expecting, and for a second, we just stare at him, nonplussed, until Draven asks, "Can you at least try?"

"No," Jeremy says, sounding distracted. "I mean, I already tried. I couldn't scan it. That place is a total black hole for technology. Nothing seems to be working on it at all."

Deacon shakes his head. "Which must mean technopath protections, right?"

"It's the only explanation that makes sense," Dante says. "Rex is serious about protecting this dump."

"V's tracker should be back on by now," Jeremy says, his voice tense and more serious than I've ever heard it. "Something's wrong."

My stomach lurches at the suggestion. Still, I try to keep calm. "We don't know that."

"I can feel it in my gut." Jeremy shakes his head. "I'm going to remote activate."

"Give her time," Dante says. He places a hand over the laptop keyboard.

"Dante's right," Riley agrees. "We don't want to compromise her if she's still being scanned."

It's the right decision, I know it is. But still, my hands are shaking.

The seconds tick by. Then minutes.

Then, just when I'm about to turn to Jeremy and suggest that we've waited long enough, his computer beeps.

"Is that her?" I ask, hopeful.

The ghostly look on his face is all the answer I need.

"No," Jeremy says, and something about his tone sends chills down my spine. "Someone just hijacked my screen."

"Is that even possible?" I demand. "You've got the best technology defenses."

He grimaces as he twists his laptop toward me so I can see the screen.

Rex Malone's smiling face stares back at me.

CHAPTER 22

C an he see us?" I whisper.

My heart is trying to beat its way out through my throat.

Jeremy shakes his head. "I removed the mic and the webcam. He's deaf and blind."

Rex looks picture-perfect as usual. Not a hair out of order, the collar of his powder-blue button-down without a wrinkle, eyes the same icy blue as Draven's sparkling. Pleasant smile in place.

I'm embarrassed to say I spent most of my life thinking that smile was genuine. Now I know it's the placating grin of a sociopath. Of an egomaniacal, power-hungry sociopath at that.

If only I had believed Rebel sooner.

"You know," Rex says in a patronizing tone, "I used to think you were smarter than this, Kenna."

My breath catches when he says my name. My hands shake with a mixture of rage and fear. Despite Jeremy's assurance that Rex can't see or hear us, it's as if he's looking right at me. Like he's talking only to me.

But that's not possible. He can't even know for certain that we're watching.

"You had so much potential," he continues, "until you strayed from the path. You aligned yourself with the wrong crowd."

No, he's got that backward. I spent the first seventeen years of my life aligned with the wrong crowd. I'm finally on the right path. One that ends with him out of power for good.

"Then again, considering who your mother was—" His eyes squint, and I can't tell if he's wincing or hiding a smile. "I am sorry about that. I always liked Jeanine. She couldn't help the circumstance of her birth, of course, but I couldn't suffer a mole to live—even if she was a brilliant scientist. The trial wasn't personal, you understand."

Nitro spits on the ground.

If I could reach through this computer, through the wireless connection that is allowing him to transmit to Jeremy's laptop, I would strangle him with my bare hands.

"Anyway, considering what we now know about your mother, it's no surprise that you're supporting the wrong team." He shakes his head. "Still, I thought you were smarter than to believe that sending a villain girl to do your bidding would turn out well for anyone."

He moves to the side of the screen, and V appears next to him, kicking and struggling against whatever—or whoever—is holding her. Her head is encased in a powers-neutralizing helmet, and through the shiny surface I can see a trickle of dried blood under her nose and a dark-purple bruise appearing around her left eye.

"It's a trap!" V shouts, her voice muffled by the helmet. "Whatever he threatens, don't—"

Suddenly, her entire body stiffens and shudders. I recognize that physical reaction. It's the same one I saw when Rex was torturing Deacon, when he was sending God-knows-how-many volts of electricity through him.

He's frying her.

She slumps, unconscious. Rex shoves her off screen.

"That bastard," Jeremy says, his voice barely controlled. "Can we kill him now?"

"You didn't already want to kill him?" Dante asks.

Jeremy scowls at the screen. "Yes. But now I want to kill him more."

Nitro pats him on the back.

"As you can see," Rex says, "your infiltrator has failed. And as for this—" He holds up the syringe of immunity serum that I sent in with V. "My loyal scientists are already hard at work analyzing the contents."

"Shit," Draven mutters.

There goes that plan. And now Rex has a sample of the immunity serum in his possession. It won't take much for his team to figure out what it does. Then it will only be a matter of time before they reverse engineer it and start churning out batches of it.

The only bright side is that Rex won't know that it breaks the mind control. But it's kind of hard to look on the bright side right now, when everything is going straight to hell.

Plus, the last thing I wanted to do was put another weapon in Rex's hands. Why had I thought that was a good idea?

"Now, I didn't reach out to you just to have a little chat. I have some requests. First," he says, holding up one finger, "I want every last one of you off my property in the Land of Enchantment."

He knows we're here, on-site in New Mexico. I twist away

from the camera, checking over my shoulder for the hero squad that could take us out at any moment.

"Does he know where we are?" Riley asks.

Jeremy shakes his head. "No way. Between my cloaking and Kenna's electromagnetic power, Rex can't have a clue."

"He's guessing," Deacon says.

I turn my attention back to the screen. "It's a good guess."

"Second," Rex continues, "I want my children returned to me for…extensive deprogramming."

An image fills my mind of Rebel returned to her Stepford daughter personality, to Riley backsliding into the hero-supremacist he once was. Once their immunity wears off, Rex can control them and turn them into whatever he wants.

He could turn them against us in an instant.

Next to me, Riley starts shaking. Nitro rubs a hand down Riley's spine as Dante hugs Rebel to his side.

None of us will let that happen.

"And last, but most definitely not least"—Rex's smile could make me throw up on the spot—"I want you to surrender, Kenna. I want you to turn yourself in."

I shake my head. "Why?" I ask, as if he could hear me. "What makes me so special?"

"I told you," Riley says. "You publicly humiliated him. He wants to punish you."

Draven steps up behind him, wraps his arms around my waist. "No way he gets that chance."

"I think you understand the seriousness of what I'm trying to accomplish here. And just in case you're inclined to turn down my polite invitation," Rex stares intently into the camera, "I think you've figured out the special tool I have at my disposal."

Mind control. I know he's talking about the mind control.

"You might not fully comprehend the ramifications yet. But you soon will."

My stomach twists.

"If you don't knock on my door within the next fifteen minutes, Miss Swift, I will kill a super. Thanks to my current… capabilities, I can do so from the safety of a great distance. I might start with your friend Victoria here." He nods offscreen toward where he shoved V. "Or maybe your blundering ex-boyfriend. What was his name? Oh yes, Abernathy."

I flick a glance at Jeremy who is, literally, white as a sheet.

"He can't," I remind Jeremy. "You're on the immunity serum. He can't control you."

"I know," Jeremy says. "It's not…I'm not scared for me. But…" He turns to look at me, his eyes wide and more serious than I have ever seen him look. "He can do it, Kenna. He can really kill a super—any super in the world who's under mind control—from anywhere."

I place my hand over Jeremy's, and Draven reaches around me to pat him on the shoulder.

"That's why we're going to stop him," I say. "That's why we're going to make sure he can never hurt anyone again."

"And I'm going to keep on killing supers," Rex says, "every fifteen minutes until you turn yourself in. I might start with one. I might start with fifty. Their blood"—he leans in closer to the lens—"will be on your head. The clock starts now."

The video feed cuts out, and we all sit there staring at a black screen.

Jeremy fiddles with his smartwatch and a countdown timer appears on the face. Ticking down from fifteen minutes.

Fifteen minutes until a super dies. Until *another* super dies at Rex's command.

My mind is racing, trying to process everything he said, everything he is capable of doing and, apparently, prepared to do. It's overwhelming.

"What do we do?" Riley asks.

Nitro's hands fist at his sides. "I say we blow the whole place, soup to nuts."

"We can't," Draven says, sounding unhappy to be the voice of reason. "There could be hundreds of innocent villains inside. Innocent heroes."

"Well, we're not doing what he wants," Dante argues. "We're not turning Rebel and Riley over to him."

Rebel clings to his side. "And we're not sending Kenna in there alone."

The cumulative gravity of our situation steamrolls over me. All the horrors I've seen flash through my mind like an old-timey movie.

Deacon being tortured in the secret sublevel at my mom's lab.

Guards at the lab tossing villain-filled body bags into an incinerator.

My mom's lifeless body.

The devastation at Dr. Harwood's lab.

The death toll keeps rising, the tragedy becoming more and more unbearable. But I have to bear it, and I have to do something about it.

My mom had a favorite quote by Ella Wheeler Wilcox. I never truly understood the meaning—and what it meant to my mom—until now.

To sin by silence, when we should protest,
makes cowards out of men.

My mom couldn't sit by and do nothing when she knew what Rex and the heroes were doing, and neither can I. Even if I have to pay the same price.

All the fear washes out of my body, and I'm left with a calm. I'm at peace with what needs to be done. What *I* need to do.

My voice steady and my spine stiff, I say, "We are going to do exactly what he's asking."

There is a moment of stunned silence, and then everyone speaks at once.

"Are you crazy?"

"Kenna, no."

"That's suicide."

"Bloody batshit."

"You can't."

"I won't let you."

Everyone, that is, except Draven. While our team is loudly proclaiming me completely insane, he watches me with those icy blue eyes, hooded by dark lashes and even darker shadows. For just a moment, a fleeting look crosses his face—agony and panic and more worry than anyone should have to endure. But it's gone almost as soon as it comes, and then he's nodding.

"So what's the plan?" he asks quietly.

Though it's little more than a whisper, his voice carries through the pandemonium and the rest of the team falls silent, stunned that he is actually going along with my suicidal idea.

"That depends," I say, my confidence growing with Draven's support. "How attached are you to your powers?"

✦ ✦ ✦

Once the others are safely off the grounds of Rex's secret compound, Rebel, Riley, and I walk the long dirt road up to the front door of the facility.

"Are you sure this is going to work?" Riley whispers.

Rebel snaps, "As long as you do your part."

"Well, forgive me for being scared out of my mind, Rebel," he throws back. "It's not like Dad tried to kill us both or anything… Oh wait, he did!"

"It's not like we have another choice," Rebel argues. "We can't just let him kill an innocent—"

"I'm not saying we should."

"No, you're just saying it shouldn't be us."

"I'm not saying that either. I just think—"

"Shut. Up." I grit my teeth as we approach the door.

They stop bickering.

Rebel reaches over and squeezes my hand.

We've been over the plan a million times. Or at least as many times as possible, given that Rex's countdown was underway.

There are so many things that could go wrong, but this is our best shot. Our only shot.

I stand there patiently—okay, impatiently—waiting for the door to open. It doesn't. I glance up at the security camera staring down at us. I wave, if you can call flipping Rex off waving. Nitro would be proud.

Still, nothing.

"You have got to be joking," I mutter to myself.

Riley asks, "What?"

I ignore him as I step up to the door. Lifting my fist, I give the security camera an angry glare as I rap my knuckles against the rusty metal door.

Only Rex would be egomaniacal enough to make me actually knock.

Almost immediately, the door swings open on creaking hinges.

"Here goes nothing," Rebel whispers.

Together, we step across the threshold.

The inside is just as run-down and dilapidated-looking as the exterior, but it is spotlessly clean. Not a speck of dirt or a dust mite on-site. I always knew Rex was a bit of a clean freak. Rebel's disaster of a room was one of the many things she and her father clashed over.

Obviously it was not the last.

"I guess we go down?" Riley doesn't sound thrilled at the suggestion as he peers over the edge of a metal railing covered in chipped paint and even more rust.

His voice echoes around the metal space.

We join him at the edge, and I find myself staring down into a never-ending spiral. Like something out of a postapocalyptic movie, a staircase winds its way around and down, deeper than my eyes can focus.

We start for the stairs, but before we take four steps, Rex's voice booms into the chamber.

"Only Miss Swift, if you please," he instructs. "I will send someone for my children shortly."

The three of us exchange nervous—but determined—looks.

Then, even though I know Rex is watching, I wrap my best friend in the tightest hug I've ever given—tighter even than one of her patented oxygen-deprivation hugs. I'm confident in our plan, or at least as confident as I can be when facing down a genocidal megalomaniac in person, but that doesn't mean I'm not scared.

That doesn't mean I'm not realistic about what could go wrong.

"I'll get you back," I promise softly in her ear.

"No matter what it takes," she whispers back. "You stop Rex, no matter what it takes."

My gut twists at the implication of her words, but I won't let myself think that is a possibility, even for a second. Because it's not.

"I will get you back," I repeat.

And then I release her, turning away before I can see the look in her eyes. Because this won't be the last time I see my best friend. I won't let it be.

✦ ✦ ✦

The climb down the spiral staircase feels never-ending. Around and around, down and down. When I am half a spiral from the bottom, a light floods the space below me and the floor finally comes into view. I keep descending until I reach the source of the light: an open door.

I fight the urge to turn around and look back up the shaft.

Knowing how far down I've come will only freak me out, and when I'm about to stand toe-to-toe with Rex, that's the last thing I can afford.

But when I walk through the door, Rex isn't there. A pair of tall guys, in matching gray suits and shiny aviator sunglasses—seriously, who wears sunglasses in a freaking mine shaft?—greet me with matching grim expressions. The only difference between them is one is wearing a stainless-steel dive watch and the other has a black rubber watchband.

"Well, well," I say, trying for as casual a tone as possible, "if it isn't the Ray-Ban brigade. I've missed you guys. What've you been up to? Hitting the semiannual sale at the Shade Shack—oof!"

I buckle over as one of them punches me in the stomach.

"Touchy, huh?" I gasp. "Maybe you should think about shaking up the uniform. Try some tortoiseshell or maybe even—oof!"

Oh, that one's gonna hurt.

Or it would, if I didn't know Draven's power could heal it in an instant.

I'm not normally one to bait people with words. Maybe I've brought a little too much Nitro in with me.

The guy on the left pulls back for another punch, but Rex's voice booms into the room from a speaker somewhere in the ceiling. "Enough. This one is mine."

As the two guys reach for me, I hold up my hands in mock surrender. Or, I suppose, actual surrender, since that's what I'm supposed to be doing. I don't put up a fight as the guys pat me down for weapons and then cuff my hands behind my back. And then, for the final touch, the one with the stainless watchband grabs a powers-neutralizing helmet from a cabinet in the corner and heads my way.

Right before he slides it over my head, I send out a tiny

pulse of my electro-power, frying its circuitry. Take that, powers-zapping helmet.

Nothing like giving Rex a false sense of security.

CHAPTER 23

"So nice to see you again, Kenna. It's been too long," Rex says, walking into the room as the two members of the Ray-Ban Brigade shackle my legs.

My immediate reaction is to panic.

This is exactly what I wanted, what we counted on happening—Rex wanting to confront me, to destroy me face-to-face. That doesn't mean I'm not absolutely terrified of him. My heart is stuttering like a machine gun, and it takes every single ounce of my strength to keep my legs from shaking.

I refuse to show him my fear. The more confident I act, the more immune I seem to his position of power, the more likely he will let his emotions take over.

"You know that it's ridiculous to be this afraid of one teen girl," I taunt, glancing down at my bound ankles. This wasn't part of the plan—the shackles or the mouthing off— but if I've learned nothing else in the last few weeks, it's how to improvise.

"You mistake caution for fear. It's not the same. Besides, how am I going to put you on display if you look like you're out for a stroll in the park?"

His voice is gentle and so are his eyes, but when he grabs

me, his grip is too tight, his fingers digging into my arms hard enough to leave bruises. Clearly my jabs are getting to him. Score one for Nitro's tactic for keeping Rex off balance.

"The powers-signature scanners confirmed that the rest of your little band of misfits are long gone," he tells me. "You're all alone down here."

It's almost funny how he can be so right and so very wrong at the same time.

Rex pulls me back into the hallway and then we're walking, his two goons behind us. I don't want to blow my advantage by attacking him directly. But that doesn't mean I can't mess with his attack dogs.

Closing my eyes, I breathe deeply. Try to focus, at least as much as I can while shackled and being dragged to God only knows where by a madman. I try to activate the powers inside me. I'm still new to this game, so it's harder for me than the others, and even harder now that a half dozen powers are wrapped up inside me.

But I have to do this. The whole plan hinges on me controlling these powers, so I focus like I've never focused before. Try to find the strengths I'm looking for in the spiraling mess inside me. I practiced a little—a very little—before I got here, but it's not like I had time to master them all.

It's easier to find the powers I'm looking for than I expect. Then again, how can it not be when I carry so much of Draven inside me? Both of his powers are blue, like his eyes. I reach for those two threads and call them up. Try to tell them apart. I can't make eye contact right now, so messing with the Ray-Ban Brigade's memories won't work. No, it's the biomanipulation I'm after.

I finally get it sorted out, can feel Draven's ability welling up in me. I try to focus, but it's hard. How does Draven manage to hold all this power inside himself? The control it requires is unbelievable, and I'm terrified that I'm going to make a mistake, let it loose, and do way more damage than I intend.

But I can't think like that now. Not when there's so much at stake. Certainly not when I'm prepared to level this place and everyone inside—including me—if that's what it takes to bring Rex to his knees.

I send a little jab of Draven's power behind me, focusing in on the two agents as tightly as I can. I don't hear them react, but that doesn't mean much. It's hard to hear much of anything inside this ridiculous helmet—well, except Rex's voice. That seems to come through loud and clear. Besides, it's not like Draven's power is a loud one. It's not like I lobbed one of Nitro's fireballs at them or something. Now that would be unmistakable.

I send another small jolt of power. I know that's not how Draven usually does this—his is a steadier stream—but I'm new to this ability. I don't want to kill them by mistake. Rex may have no problem murdering with impunity, but I do. No matter how awful the Ray-Ban Brigade is. Unless the plan goes to hell and I'm facing the worst-case scenario, no one dies.

I still haven't decided if that no one includes Rex.

One more small flash of power directed at the guys behind me finally gets a measurable result. Something hits the wall next to me, and I glance over in time to see one of Rex's goons kind of listing against it, arm braced against the cool rock in an attempt to hold himself up. A look in the other direction and Rex's second lapdog is rubbing his temple, his eyes shut and a grimace on his face.

I take another deep breath and feel the power flow down to my fingers. Then I let out another small blast straight at each of them.

The first one stumbles and falls to his knees, and the second raises a hand to his nose, which is suddenly gushing blood. Rex turns around with a scowl, ready to growl at them. But when he sees the state they're in, he immediately turns to me.

"What are you doing to them?" he demands.

"I'm not doing anything," I tell him, chin raised defiantly. "I'm in a powers-neutralizing helmet. And handcuffs." I lift my wrists. "What could I possibly be doing?"

Rex's eyes narrow suspiciously, but he doesn't say anything else. At least not until I send one more tiny blast of power at the two goons and they hit the ground, totally unconscious.

Rex reaches for me, and for a second, I think he's going to break my neck. Our plan is totally going to fail—because of me.

Instead, he rips the powers-neutralizing helmet off my head and examines it. When he sees that the indicator light is out, he throws it to the ground in a fit of rage. Then he grabs me by my upper arms and pulls me up to my tiptoes. "Let me guess. Electromagnetism?"

I shrug as casually as possible.

"Then what did you do to them?" He nods at the unconscious goons.

"I told you," I say, "I didn't do—"

He shakes me. Hard. "You don't want to screw with me, Kenna. I will kill you right now."

"No, don't think you will," I answer, my scowl at least as fierce as his. "Not down here in the depths of this place where no one can watch. You don't just want me dead. You want to enjoy it. You want me humiliated in front of as many people as possible. You want me powerless and disgraced. There's no way you're going to kill me when the cameras aren't rolling."

I'm pushing him too far, I know. Poking at the beast. It could backfire. But at this point, I don't have a lot of other options. I need to buy enough time for the others to execute their parts of the plan. This is a risk I have to take.

Besides, I can tell by the rage in Rex's eyes—a mix of hate and arrogance—that it's working.

For long seconds he doesn't say anything, but then he lets me go, his hands dropping from my shoulders as he reaches for the communicator on his belt loop.

"You're right. I'm going to enjoy watching you die," he sneers, right before he hits the transmit button and calls for backup in the south tunnel. Which I'm guessing is where we currently are.

It's not what I was expecting. I figured Rex was arrogant enough to think he could handle escorting me by himself. But I guess I underestimated just how much he hates me—or how much he wants me to die. He's willing to admit a weakness if it means he gets to see me burn in the end.

I probably have only seconds before his backup arrives, so I try to concentrate and roll with the punches as the first steps of my plan go right out the window. I can only hope the rest will go more smoothly.

I've got the powers untangled now—green for Dante's wind, red for Nitro's fireballs, yellow for Deacon's water, along with the blues from Draven. Not for the first time I wish I could have taken the hero powers too, but the immunity serum makes them immune to all powers—including mine. If that's the price of making sure their minds are never under Rex's control, then that's a price I'm willing to pay.

Deciding to go big or go home, I draw on the red thread and lob a small, orange fireball straight at Rex. It dissolves inches from his shoulder.

Shit.

Rex's evil smile fills his entire face. "I had my suspicions about the contents of the syringe," he tells me, shaking his head ever so slowly. "Your mother kept your power hidden your entire life, and knowing Jeanine, she would want to protect you from other powers as well."

It's hard not to back away as he approaches.

"I didn't want to wait for the test results, so I injected half of the dose in myself." He spreads his arms wide in triumph. "I was pleasantly surprised to discover that powers no longer affected me."

Great. A powers-immune Rex. That is not something I want to face.

Not that I have a choice.

The door at the end of the hallway flies open and six hero soldiers come pouring in. I grab hold of the yellow and green threads of power. The first hero fires a bolt of electricity at me so fast I don't have time to dodge it. I brace myself for impact…but it never comes. The bright-white streak flows around me like the filaments in a plasma ball.

I've gotten so used to *not* being immune to powers anymore that I'd forgotten how it felt. How powerful it made me.

The hero stares at his fingers, as if he misfired.

Rex laughs. "Now why am I not surprised?"

Before any of the rest of them have time to figure out that their powers don't work on me, I throw every ounce of concentration I have into accessing all the powers at my disposal. A high-powered jet of water shoots straight down the hallway, knocking my attackers back through the open doorway.

I could get used to that combo.

Weapons go flying—and so do people—until no heroes are left standing. Except Rex. My powers don't touch him.

Before his troops can recover, I send another gust of wind to shut the door and follow it with a fireball that I hope is hot enough to melt metal.

With a roar, Rex lunges toward me. In this fight, we are both equally powerless. No force he or his goons can summon will touch me, and none of the half dozen powers coursing through my system will harm a hair on his perfectly gelled head.

And since Rex has at least six inches on me and a whole lot more muscle, I'm not about to win in a fair fight.

Pulling on the red thread of power within me, I lay down a line of fireballs on the cement floor between us. Nitro's flames won't hurt him, but I'm betting he won't entirely trust that. It would take a lot more courage to walk through fire than a man like Rex Malone possesses.

"You're going to pay for this, Kenna." He inches back from the wall of flames. "No one does what you're doing—"

"No, Rex, that's where you're wrong. No one does what *you're* doing. And I'm prepared to do everything I can to stop you."

There is a huge crash at the end of the hall, and I turn just in time to see the door fall flat to the floor. Four of the heroes rush through the opening. I guess my water jet wasn't as much of a deterrent as I thought.

I send a huge blast of wind, knocking them back out of the room. As the wind rushes through, the flames lick higher. Rex jerks back. Then I watch as the reality registers with him. He stretches his hand out, through the fire. He looks at me and smiles.

Fine. He might be immune to my powers, but his backup goons aren't.

Digging deep for the glacial blue of Draven's biomanipulation power, I focus on the four conscious heroes in the hall. The power is becoming a little bit more familiar, and as I reach out, it's like I can feel them. Almost like I'm pulling up the mental image of a full body scan.

Two of them are already on their feet and the other two are struggling to stand. Before they can make it back to the door, I lower their blood pressure, dropping it just enough to knock them out cold, but not out for good.

"Stop right there, Kenna!" Rex shouts, stepping through the flames.

As I turn back to face him, the light from the flames I created glints off the barrel of a gun.

"Cameras or not," he tells me, "I *am* prepared to kill you."

And just when I thought my heart rate couldn't get any faster.

One of two things is going to happen. Either Rex is going to shoot me, in which case the plan will be an abysmal failure, I'll be dead, and everyone will be doomed. Or I can surrender to save my own life, which will give Rex all the power and everyone will still be doomed.

Those are lose-lose options, and I'm just naïve enough to believe there is a third.

I lower my head in pretend surrender. Then, as Rex relaxes and starts to lower the gun, I reach for the red thread of power and send a volley of Nitro's fireballs over his head. The floor beneath us may be concrete, and the walls may be covered in paint and plaster, but the ceiling is covered with good, old—extremely flammable—acoustical tiles.

At first nothing happens.

Rex actually starts laughing.

And then it starts. Just a trickle of smoke at first. But soon, almost before I can blink, the entire hall is filling with thick, gray fog. I can barely see my still-cuffed hands in front of my face.

I drop to my hands and knees—keeping below the blooming smoke and, hopefully, Rex's aim.

"You can't kill me," I taunt him, "if you can't see me."

A bullet whizzes two feet above my head. If I'd still been on my feet, I'd be bleeding from the gut right now. Good to know Rex is playing for keeps.

His coughing breaks up the eerie silence. I use Dante's wind to keep a small bubble of clean air around me. If I stay low, hiding in the smoke, and keep moving, there's a chance I can sneak out of here. A chance I can buy enough time for at least one part of this plan to work.

But I can't leave the two Ray-Ban goons to die of smoke inhalation.

I'm not sure what I'm going to do with them. The only thing I can do, I guess. Drag them out of this hall.

Rebel's telekinesis would be really handy right now. Or even Riley's flight.

Or V's echolocation. My racing heart would feel a lot better if I could pinpoint Rex's exact location.

As I'm dragging the first guard out the far door, I hear Rex's footsteps an instant before a bullet sails through the open doorway. I dive back inside, rolling out of the way as another bullet slams into the doorjamb. For the first time since this nightmare began, I wish I'd cooked up some of my mom's version of the immunity serum. This would be a lot easier if Rex didn't have his super-hearing right now.

I send another fireball crashing halfway across the room, and Rex whirls, shooting in that general direction. If I knew anything about guns, I'd count the bullets he's expending. But since that's just about as useful to me as the hero powers I *don't* have, I go about my plan of getting the other guard out of the hall.

As I dump him next to his buddy, the chains of my leg shackles clank against the concrete.

Another round of bullets.

I fire back with a different kind of fireball—I'm not sure what the purple ones do, but it sure feels destructive. The smoke in the hall turns a darker gray.

I lean over the second goon, the one who'd cuffed me in the first place, and pat down his jacket until I find his keys. I start trying them in my handcuffs and am thrilled when the third key slides in and the catch releases. I yank off the cuffs and stuff them in my back pocket. Then I crouch and take off the shackles, even as I use Dante's wind and Deacon's water to churn the smoke into a mini-tornado, with Rex trapped inside.

He could walk right out of it if he wanted, but I'm hoping it takes him a few seconds to remember he's immune.

The smoke is getting kind of out of control. I'm really not interested in killing myself, V, and who knows how many innocent people with this ceiling fire. Since fire can't exist in a vacuum, I suck in a deep lungful of air and then use Dante's power to suck the rest of the oxygen out of the hall.

Gee, I hope Rex has been practicing his free-dive breathing. When I'm sure the fire has been starved, I let the air back in.

"Enough, Kenna!" Rex shouts. "Enough!"

Damn immunity serum.

I draw on the red thread of power and conjure up a small pink fireball in my palm. It may look innocent enough, but I can feel its lethal energy tickling across my skin. And, like a dead man's switch, if Rex shoots me, it will unleash a devastating explosion.

"Give me one reason," I yell above the sound of my mini-tornado, "why I shouldn't blow this entire place up, and you along with it."

"Because," he gasps, still hacking a little from smoke inhalation, "if you destroy this facility, it won't only be me and a few heroes you're killing."

"I know. You've been luring innocent villains into your evil clutches." I shake my head, even though he can't see me. "I'm sure most of them would gladly sacrifice themselves if it meant ending you."

If the other parts of this plan are going according to design, *no one* will be sacrificed. Hopefully it's only my end of the mission that's going sideways.

"Not just villains," he says, and the way he says it makes the hair on the back of my neck stand up. "Your father is here. Blow up this place, and he'll die right along with the rest of us."

CHAPTER 24

My father? My *father*? The words echo in my head and chase themselves around in there as shock rips through me. *Rex* has my father? And he's *here*?

How is that even possible?

Mom's final words echo in my mind. *Rex is holding him somewhere. Using him...*

Now I know where.

I blink at him, for a moment not able to think or speak or even breathe. The mini-tornado fades, the smoky water falling to the floor with a splash. It takes all my energy to keep the pink fireball alive.

"Did you hear me, Kenna? I have your father."

Think, Kenna. Think. How can you sell this to Rex?

I should be shocked. As far as Rex knows, I think my father is dead. But I've already gone through the shock of learning that he's still alive. Now I'm just shocked to learn that he's here, right now. That somehow he's tangled up in all of this.

I use the shock I feel to project the shock Rex expects from me.

"My father is dead." I say the words very carefully, making sure they come out right.

"That's what everyone thinks," Rex says just as carefully. "But he's not. If you put that fireball away, I'll take you to him."

He's manipulating me. I know he is. I can hear it in his voice. That's the same tone he always used with Rebel when he wanted to bend her to his will, tried to get her to do what he wanted when she was acting out. She never fell for it. I'm not going to either.

"You're lying."

He takes a step toward me, his gun pointed at my chest. With shaking hands, I hold the pink fireball in front of me. Rex gets the message. He doesn't lower his gun, but he takes a step back.

"Why would I lie?" he asks me.

"Oh, I don't know," I retort, "to screw with me? To throw me off balance? Or maybe just for fun? When have you ever needed a reason to lie, Rex?"

"There is always a reason."

"Okay," I say, pretending to play along, "then tell me why he's here. Why would my dad, who loved me and my mom more than anything, be hanging out in your…" I wave my free hand above me in an all-encompassing gesture. "Whatever this place is?"

"Well, it's not like he has a choice," Rex replies with his trademark good-guy grin.

His words go through me like lightning, and my fireball turns a bright lime-green before shooting out of my palm. It glances harmlessly off Rex's shoulder.

He smirks and holds his gun steady. I rush to get another pink fireball going.

Even though I had been warned, even though Mom told

me Rex was holding my dad, hearing the words was like a punch in the stomach. Some reactions you can't fake. I finally understand why Nitro has so much trouble controlling his power. When you're playing with fire—literally—it's hard to keep your emotions out of the mix.

But I've got them under control again, and Rex and I are back to our standoff.

And I'm back to my clueless act.

"You were friends," I yell at him. "Everyone says so. Why would you keep him prisoner?"

"Because he had something I wanted." He shrugs, like his answer is no big deal. "His power is the key to everything. Sometimes the good of the one has to be sacrificed for the good of the many."

"What good?" I demand. "Torturing innocent villains? Brainwashing innocent heroes? Perpetuating this war between the two sides?"

"Everything I've done, I've done to keep heroes safe."

Liar. Everything he's done, he's done to feed his own thirst for power. And, if his mind-control program is allowed to succeed, *unchecked* power.

Everything inside me screams for me to run, to get as far from this psychopath as I can as quickly as possible. But self-preservation has to take a backseat to the plan to stop Rex. And right now, my part of the plan is to buy the others more time.

Besides, just because Rex knows my dad is still alive doesn't mean he's telling me the truth. It doesn't mean my dad is actually *here*. He could just as easily be a prisoner at any of a dozen different secret hero facilities around the globe—and those are just the ones Riley's told us about.

"I don't believe you."

"Fine," he says casually. "Don't believe me. It's your loss."

I freeze, not because of his words—they're what I would expect—but because of his inflection. There's something in his voice that tells me it's a trap. A ploy to get me back in handcuffs and under control.

And I have to play along. "I want proof."

"My proof is that he's here. All you have to do is come with me."

"That's not proof," I throw back. "That's a trap."

He stares at me with a blank expression. "I guess that's a risk you'll have to take."

I weigh my options. I could choose not to believe him and keep this standoff going, hoping I can keep Rex from killing me long enough for the others to get in place. Or I can find out if he's telling the truth by taking his bait on the unlikely chance that my father really is here.

Both options probably end with me being dead, but at least the latter buys me some more time.

And I'm not going to lie, even the tiniest possibility that my dad is in here is worth the added risk.

"Put down the gun," I tell him.

He laughs. "I don't think so."

I launch a small blue fireball with my left hand. My aim is dead on, and it hits the gun square in the barrel. It recoils but remains secure in Rex's hand.

"Nice try," he says. "I'll hold on to my insurance policy."

I allow the pink ball in my right hand to grow until it's the size of a basketball. As it turns orange, I shout, "I will melt this entire room around us."

"That won't change anything. The scarlet phoenix protocol will continue unfettered. Another member of the Collective will step into my shoes. The only difference is, we'll both be dead." He gestures toward the door behind him. "*Or*, you could come with me. See that I'm telling the truth. See that your father is still alive."

He's playing me. I know that without a shadow of a doubt. But still…it's my father. The man I've thought dead for more than a dozen years. The man I believed until recently I would never see again.

Trap or not, I know I don't have another choice.

"If you're lying, I *will* kill you," I tell him, my voice shaking with conviction.

"I'm not lying," he tells me, taking a step toward the open hallway door. "Put your fireball away and I'll take you to him."

I lift a brow at him. "Me putting away this fireball isn't going to happen, Rex."

"Your powers won't work on me anyway," he says. "Thanks to that little injection you sent in with your friend."

"True," I reply, "but they still work on everyone else. And they still work on the objects around us."

He tips his head at me, as if acknowledging my point.

The truth is, I think I could whip the gun out of his hand in a number of ways—with Dante's wind, Deacon's water, or a good old-fashioned fireball. But if the gun makes Rex feel safer, makes him relax his guard, that can only be a good thing.

I just have to make sure he doesn't use it.

"Okay," I say, trying to sound reasonable, "you keep your weapon, and I'll keep mine."

"Fair enough," he says with a smirk that tells me he doesn't think it's fair at all. He thinks he has the upper hand. But he's going along with it, and for now that's all that matters. "I'll lead the way, shall I?"

I give him a fake smile. "Please."

He turns and starts for the door, and I focus on keeping the pink fireball alive while using Draven's glacial-blue thread to sense for any conscious heroes who might be lying in wait.

"It's another serum, right?" Rex asks as we step out of the hall and into another stairwell. "You've managed to make some kind of serum that gives you multiple powers. Is that another one of your mother's secret projects?"

I snort—quietly, so he doesn't hear.

No, it's not a serum; it's my second power. But the last thing I want is Rex knowing that I can absorb additional powers simply by reaching out with my mind and taking them. I have a feeling that would change whatever he has planned, and not in a good way.

So I ignore his questions, let him assume what he wants. I'll let my little revelation be a surprise for later.

If I thought that first staircase descended into forever, I had no idea. We go down so many levels, pass so many landings with doors that lead to who knows what, that I'm beginning to feel like we're actually journeying to the center of the earth. We finally reach the bottom, which opens onto a short hall that leads to a steel vault door. It's guarded by two very large heroes with very large guns. Most supers would rather rely on their powers than a traditional weapon. That Rex thinks they need the added security of automatic rifles tells me that whatever is inside is really valuable to him.

There is an access panel with a retinal scanner and a hand-print reader in the center of the door.

The hero guards don't even blink at the fireball I'm holding on Rex, which makes me wonder just what they see down here on a regular basis. And whether or not an ambush is waiting for me inside that room.

Though I try to keep my cool, my stomach clenches and my heart starts beating double time. This is an awful lot of security in a place that is already more secure than the president's underground bunker.

As Rex gets his palm and his eye scanned, I scoot closer to one of the guards. I can feel his power—super strength, big surprise. I reach out with my mind, grab onto the silver power pulsing through his body, and then draw it into mine. I might not be able to use any powers against Rex, but that kind of strength might come in really handy down here.

I start to scan the other guard, but I can't get a read on his power, and before I can try harder, Rex yanks the giant lever and the door glides open. He gestures for me to precede him into the room.

I almost don't do it. I'm not stupid. Walking in front of him is a terrible idea. But at the same time, I can't *not* go. Not when he says my father is in that room. Not when the others haven't signaled that they've succeeded. Not when they still need more time.

And so I do as he indicates, sliding into the room sideways so that I can keep my fireball trained on him the whole time. No way am I letting Rex out of my sight.

Once we're inside, with the door sealed behind us, I take a chance and look around. Disappointment burns in my stomach. I knew it was a trap, I *knew* it. And yet…I still wanted to believe. I wanted so much for it to be true, that I convinced myself Rex might actually be telling the truth.

Bracing myself for whatever attack is coming, I press my back into the nearest corner with my fireball in front of me like a shield.

"Nice trick," I say.

He just raises a brow. "Your lack of faith in me is devastating."

"Your lack of humanity is repulsive," I throw back. "So I guess we're even."

"You never did answer my question." He flashes me that hero-perfect grin. "How did you create all these powers for yourself?"

I ignore him, focusing my attention instead on studying the room. It appears to be the interior of a large vault. The walls are the same two-foot-thick steel as the door. So thick that Draven's power can't sense anything beyond.

So thick they would probably contain all but the most destructive of Nitro's fireballs. Unless I'm willing to conjure a nuclear bomb—which would not only kill me and Rex, but everyone in a two-mile radius. Including my friends and the innocent heroes and villains of Rex's drone army.

"You'll tell me eventually," Rex says.

I pull my attention back to him. "They say hope springs eternal."

"Now, now," he chides. "Is that any way to treat the person who reunites you with your long lost father?"

I keep my fireball aimed at him as he turns to face the door, then punches a code into what looks like a standard alarm panel. The floor in front of me starts to rise, and I brace myself, expecting the worst. Expecting an army of mind-controlled superheroes to come running out, determined to kill me at any cost.

But as the floor slides up, what I find is so much worse. Because it turns out Rex was telling the truth. Lying in what looks like a coffin-size aquarium, suspended in a thick, clear liquid, with a web of wires hooked up to his head, is a pale, fragile, sick-looking imitation of my *father*.

CHAPTER 25

For long seconds, I don't know what to do. What to say. I just stand there looking at this man whose absence has haunted me for so long and wonder what the hell is going on.

Why is he here?

Why does he look so frail?

Why has Rex kept him prisoner for so many years?

And why, after all this time, is Rex letting me know of my father's existence? He must know that there is no way I'm going to leave him here for Rex to continue torturing him.

"What are you doing to him?" I demand, whirling around, fireball raised and itching to ignite the air around me.

"It's not what I'm doing to him," Rex says. "It's what he's doing *for* me."

I gesture to my father. "Get him out. Now."

Rex holds his hand out, palms up, and shrugs. He doesn't move away from the door.

I reach out with Draven's power, push through the Plexiglas that is holding my father prisoner, and let myself sense his body. What I feel almost knocks me to my knees. He is completely wrung out. A mere shell, connected to machines that are barely keeping him alive, and others that are probing his mind. Hijacking his power.

"Why did you bring me here? Why are you showing me this?"

"Because I want you to understand," he tells me.

My veneer of pretending to play along with his game shatters. "Oh, I understand, all right. I understand you are a sick freak."

"All this time in the superhero world and you don't get it. You think all of those powers churning inside you give you power? Those aren't true power any more than this weapon is." He gestures vaguely with the gun. "*Control* is power. Let me show you."

He pulls back his shirtsleeve, and I see something shiny on his forearm. It looks like an interface panel, a touch screen on a flexible smartphone, has been implanted in his flesh.

What the hell?

He reaches over and opens the door. An instant later, the big, beefy guard steps inside. His eyes are glazed over, like he's not seeing anything.

The door closes behind him.

"What are you doing?"

Rex doesn't look up from the screen implant.

I watch in horror as the guard draws his gun.

I let the fireball grow bigger, preparing to defend myself. "Please, Rex, don't do this."

"What?" Rex replies with an innocent tone. "I'm not doing anything."

The guard slides his finger over the trigger.

Oh God, I have to stop him. I struggle to find Draven's glacier-blue thread as panic tears through me. It hovers out of reach, tangled with the new power I grabbed from the other guard. If I can't find it, I'll have to—

Before I can even complete the thought, the guard presses the barrel to his own temple and pulls the trigger.

I'm still screaming when Rex walks over to me.

"You see, Kenna. Control is power. And he"—he nods toward my father—"gives me control."

Oh my God. In a flash, all the pieces of the puzzle fall into place. My dad. My dad is the super whose power is being used to control the minds of heroes and villains everywhere. My dad's power is mind control.

I never knew.

The earbud hidden deep in my ear crackles for a second, and I jerk away from the painful sound.

"Kenna?" Jeremy's voice comes in softly. "Kenna, are you there?"

Finally! This is the signal I've been waiting for.

If Jeremy has gotten the earbuds working again, that means he's inside the facility's system and he's figured out how to bypass whatever anti-technopath protections were in place. This cat-and-mouse game I've been playing with Rex has paid off. I've bought us—I've bought the *team*—enough time.

Relief floods through me, even though I know the game is far from over.

"Yes," I tell Jeremy, not taking my eyes off Rex.

He still has a gun and he's still immune to my powers. Right about now I'm wishing the serum had a shorter shelf life. But since that's not exactly going to happen, I'll have to do this the hard way.

Rex's eyes narrow as he tries to figure out what I'm doing.

I smile blandly.

"We've got them out," Jeremy tells me. "We've got every-one out."

"Rebel and Riley too?" I ask. "And V?"

"What about them?" Rex demands.

My heart pounds as I await Jeremy's answer.

"All of them," Jeremy says. "I repeat, everyone is out. The building is clear."

"Good job. I'm just finishing up here."

Rex lurches across the room, grabs my shoulder with his free hand, and shakes me. Hard. "Who are you talking to?"

"It's over, Rex. All your hero drones are out of the build-ing." I do my best to ignore the gun he's waving around. "They're being dosed with immunity serum as we speak, which means they're no longer under your control."

His eyes grow wide, wild with rage. I duck just before he pulls the trigger, sending a bullet buzzing across the chamber. Not waiting for him to recover and fire off a second shot, I use a jet of Deacon's water to knock the gun out of his hand. Then follow it with a swirl of Dante's wind to bring the gun back around to me.

But before I can grab onto it, Rex is on me. He knocks me to the ground and lands on top of me with a thud as he too reaches for the gun. There's no way I'm going to let him get it—no way he's going to win.

I don't know much about hand-to-hand combat, but every day I've spent with the villains has been a learning experience. And so I think about slamming my hand into his nose, think about throwing an elbow. But in the end I go with the tried-and-true. I jam my knee up and into his groin as hard as I can.

At the same time, I lash out with Dante's wind and send the gun spinning across the room, far out of Rex's reach.

He's cursing now, gasping—one hand cupping his groin even as he curls his other hand into a fist. He pulls it back, prepares to slam it into my face. But I've got both hands free now and gravity is on my side.

With a carefully placed, two-handed shove, I send Rex rolling off me—in the opposite direction from where I sent the gun. I may not be as strong as him, but I'm faster. In a flash, I'm on my feet and putting as much distance between us as possible.

I throw a hand out, using Dante's wind to send the gun swirling across the room to me. This time I do grab onto it and hold it tight. It feels weird in my palm. Too heavy—and too treacherous. Too easy to just squeeze the trigger and end this all right here, right now.

For a moment, I consider it. Consider destroying him the way he's destroyed so many others. My mother, Draven's mother, my father. So many people whose lives have been taken or ruined because of Rex's desperate thirst for power. His maniacal belief that he could do whatever he wanted without consequences.

Death is the ultimate consequence, and if anyone deserves to die, it's him.

I lift the gun, point it at his head as I walk closer to him. He scuttles backward across the floor until he is pressed up against the wall. I'm no crack shot, but at this point I'm close enough to him that that doesn't matter. I wouldn't miss at this range.

My finger trembles on the trigger. It would be so easy to

just pull. So, so easy. I take another step closer, do my best to aim right between Rex's eyes. He's terrified now—I can see it in the way his eyes widen with alarm. In the way he holds his hands out in front of him like he's trying to protect himself. Or like he's begging for mercy, something he's never, ever shown anyone else.

The bastard.

Jeremy's in my ear, demanding to know what's going on and if I'm okay. I ignore him. The temptation to end this right here, right now is that great.

And still I hesitate. If I do it, I'll be a killer, just like Rex. I'd like to think I'm better than that.

"Kenna, please," he begs. "Just listen—"

"No, Rex," I tell him. "I'm done listening to you."

Then I grab the gun by the barrel and slam the hilt into his temple, hard. His eyes roll back in his head and he's out cold.

I step over him, step around the lifeless body of the security guard, and head for the door, but when I try the handle, it doesn't budge. I mutter a soft curse.

"Kenna?" Jeremy's voice asks in my ear. "What's going on? I'm blind here. Is everything okay? Did Draven make it down to you? Are you—"

"I'm fine, Jeremy," I reassure him. "I'm in a vault at the lowest level. The door is locked. Can you get me—"

The door beeps three times and swings open before I can finish the question. Draven is standing in the hall, the second security guard unconscious at his feet.

"Thanks," I tell Jeremy.

He replies, "Any time."

"Can you do me one more favor?"

"Of course," Jeremy says.

"Come down to the vault room," I say. "I need your help."

"Really?" he says with a whine. "Do you know how many steps that is?"

"It's important."

There is only a heartbeat of hesitation before he says, "I'll be right down."

Draven pulls me close and wraps his arms around me, and I sink into him. Until this moment, I didn't realize just how scared I was. How much I was operating on adrenaline and sheer determination to beat Rex, once and for all.

Now that the imminent threat is over, it all rushes out of me.

"Your handiwork?" Draven asks, nodding at his father's unconscious body.

I smile, leaning back. "Yeah. Impressed?"

"Very." Then his gaze drifts to the dead guard on the floor. "And that one?"

My whole body starts shaking.

I bite my lips and shake my head. "Rex. Made him do it to himself." Draven squeezes me close again, and I burrow into him for one second, two. Just long enough for the protection of his arms to provide a buffer between the safety of the present and the terror of the last few horrific minutes. There's a part of me that wishes I could stay right here, head on his chest and arms wrapped around his waist forever. But we're not done here and we need to be.

When I have myself back under control, I step out of Draven's embrace. I cross to the apparatus in the center of the room and stare down into the ghostly pale face inside.

"What is this?" Draven asks as he stops beside me.

"This," I say, placing my palm on the Plexiglas as if he'll somehow be able to sense my presence, "is my father."

And with Draven and Jeremy's help, I'm going to get him out of this half-living hell.

✦ ✦ ✦

An hour later, the team has reunited on the overlook above the secret mind-control facility. From this distance, the building still looks like nothing more than a mining operation. No one could have guessed what evil was going on below the surface.

"Are you sure you want to do this?" I turn first to Rebel, who nods sharply, and then to Riley.

His gaze is focused on the building below us. "It has to be done."

"Nitro, would you like to do the honors?"

He grins like a maniac. "It would be my pleasure."

He holds his palms out in front of him, but nothing happens.

"Oh right," I tell him. I close my eyes and return his power to him. "I was just getting used to that."

"That's more like it, love," he says. A moment later, the biggest, blackest fireball I've ever seen goes sailing toward the building, followed by a deafening explosion.

The entire structure collapses into the ground. Quake would be proud of his little brother's capability for destruction.

To anyone passing by or a satellite flying overhead, the explosion would look like the result of an ordinary mining accident, an underground detonation gone wrong.

Only we know the truth. We know that the facility had been evacuated of all personnel...except one. Somewhere beneath the rubble, two endless staircases below the surface, in the vault room that held my father prisoner for more than a dozen years, Rex Malone lies in suspended animation. Kept alive by the very barely life-sustaining system he helped design, with one slight tweak. He is still conscious.

Killing him would have been the easy way out. I kind of like the dramatic irony of him being destined to spent the rest of eternity—or until some court somewhere chooses a more fitting punishment—trapped with his own thoughts. Trapped with the knowledge that the powerless little girl who used to practically revere him turned out to be powerful enough to defeat him, and that a group of heroes and villains working together brought about the destruction of everything he spent his life building.

I can't imagine a more fitting punishment.

I turn away from the site and start back for the cars. One by one, the others do the same.

Rebel, Riley, and Draven are the last to return. Saying a not-so-fond farewell to their shared father.

As we pile into the vehicles, our little band of hero and villain misfits—Team Hillain and Team Vero, as Jeremy likes to call us—I can't help but marvel at what we've accomplished by working together. And I wonder if the super world will ever know how close it came to being totally controlled.

It's only a matter of time before another power-hungry hero decides to seek control of our world, to seek control of *us*. Rex's disappearance will leave a power vacuum that all too many unscrupulous heroes will want to fill. But for now, we take pride in the fact that we made a difference. We made our world a better place. And we'll be stronger and more prepared if—*when*—we have to do it again.

CHAPTER 26

TWO DAYS LATER

Kenna, you're live in five, four, three—" Jeremy holds up two fingers, then one, and then points at me.

I look into the camera he has set up as the red light comes on.

For a moment, I freeze. After what I've been through, it seems more than a little ridiculous to be afraid of a camera, but the entire super world is going to see this broadcast. Tens of thousands of heroes and villains around the globe will be watching as I tell them about Rex and the Hero Collective's agenda. I'll be breaking the news to them about Rex's mind control and explaining the immunity serum cure. This broadcast will turn their entire worlds upside down.

That's a lot of pressure.

But then a movement off to the left catches my eye. Draven steps into my line of sight, and immediately I feel at ease. He gives me a smile that promises a whole lot of that forgetting-the-world-in-his-arms time as soon as I'm done.

I smile back and pan my gaze over the others gathered behind the camera.

Rebel, with her hair bleached back to her normal,

near-platinum color, is grinning despite the sadness I know must be lurking in her heart, and Dante's arms are wrapped around her from behind.

Riley holds Nitro's hand tightly in his.

V has her arms crossed over her chest, but there is an uncharacteristic smile on her face.

Deacon's hands are braced on the back of the chair where my dad—my *dad*—is sitting. He's barely more than a shell of his former self, having suffered far worse than an ordinary could have survived. Or an ordinary hero, for that matter. He has a long way to go for recovery, but I will be with him every step of the way.

It doesn't make losing Mom any easier. It just means I'm not going through it alone.

None of us are.

Finally, my attention shifts back to Draven. To the villain who started me down this rabbit hole in the first place. The bad guy who showed me that you are defined not by your powers but by how you use them.

And today, we're proving that bad guys—and bad girls— can use their powers for epic good.

"My fellow supers," I say to the camera, "my name is Kenna Swift. I am the daughter of James and Jeanine Swift. I am a villain. And I have something important to tell you."

ACKNOWLEDGMENTS

An unrelenting thank-you to…

…our agents, Emily Sylvan Kim and Jenny Bent, for their unflagging and enthusiastic support for this project from the very beginning. It's been a wild ride and they've been there every step of the way. We love you and are so, so thrilled that we get to work with you!

…the entire team at Sourcebooks Fire for giving us the chance to tell Kenna and Draven's stories, and for giving us such beautiful, beautiful books.

…our friends Alesha Claveria, Shana Galen, Chris Marie Green, Sophie Jordan, Emily McKay, Crystal Perkins, Shellee Roberts, Daria Snadowsky, Sherry Thomas, and Katrina Tinnon—you guys are one of the best parts of this writing thing and we're so thankful to have you in our lives!

ABOUT THE AUTHORS

One fateful summer, Tera Lynn Childs and Tracy Deebs embarked on a nine-hour (each way!) road trip to Santa Fe that ended with a flaming samurai, an enduring friendship, and the kernel of an idea that would eventually become *Powerless*. On their own, they have written YA tales about mermaids (*Forgive My Fins, Tempest Rising*), mythology (*Doomed, Oh. My. Gods., Sweet Venom*), smooching (*International Kissing Club*), and fae princes (*When Magic Sleeps*). Between them, they have three boys (all Tracy), three dogs (mostly TLC), and almost fifty published books. Find TLC and the #TeamHillian headquarters at teralynnchilds.com. Check out Tracy and the #TeamVero lair at tracydeebs.com. Hang out with all the heroes, villains, ordinaries, and none-of-the-aboves at heroagenda.com.